TAMING THE BODYGUARD

MAURA TROY

Autumn Spring Enterprises LLC

Sign up to join The Troy Inner Circle for a special Taming The Bodyguard bonus scene (just be sure to read the book before you read the bonus scene).

Join The Troy Inner Circle Today.

DEDICATION

To Mary Evans, for always making me smile.
Your enthusiasm and support has meant more than you know.
Thank you.

CHAPTER ONE

It was just sex, for pity's sake.

Ignoring the nervousness flickering in her eyes, Erienne Stuart flipped up the vanity mirror and exited her champagne-colored Mercedes Benz SL, thankful the warmth of autumn's second summer meant she didn't need a jacket. The raucous tune of an old George Thorogood song drifted through the open door of the Steel Horse Tavern in Candlewood, CT. With the flock of hummingbirds flitting about in her stomach, she doubted even George's recommendation of a bourbon, a scotch, and a beer would be enough to quell her nerves. It wasn't every day — hell, there wasn't *any* day — she was about to walk into a bar where the police were known to come in to break up a fistfight at least once or twice a month.

She could turn around right now and forget the whole thing, but in all her thirty years, Erienne had never been one to back down from an unpleasant task, and she wasn't about to start now. Besides, there was every possibility this undertaking could turn out to be an enjoyable experience. She'd never know unless she tried.

Decision made, she took a deep breath before remembering she shouldn't do that, not if she wanted to keep her body-hugging, coral-colored silk sheath from splitting its seams. Maybe buying it two sizes too small hadn't been such a good idea after all. Releasing her breath, she walked inside.

A few couples gyrated on the large dance floor, but most of the patrons were either at the bar, which took up most of the wall to her right, or clustered around the high, square tables scattered about the perimeter of the dance floor. Beer was the prevailing scent of the room, although from the large array of bottles perched on the shelf behind the bar, she figured just about any preferred drink could be accommodated.

Several young men at one table looked her over, and she willed herself not to blush. The nearest one got up and approached her. The sway in his step indicated he and his companions had been here a while. His belly flopped a little over the top of his worn jeans, further cementing the idea that drinking large quantities of beer was a frequent pastime. She wasn't exactly sure who she was looking for, but she was fairly certain drunkenness on her partner's behalf wouldn't help her.

She turned and strode toward the bar, ignoring the howls and good-natured jeers the drunk's buddies tossed at him. A glance in the large mirror behind the bar showed him scowling at her before turning back to his laughing friends with a shrug.

The seats at the bar were all taken, but there was space to stand between some of them. Several men were looking at her, either directly or through the reflection of the mirror. Fingers of doubt poked her resolve. Her plan had seemed simple enough, but now she wondered...

After a quick scan up and down the bar, she chose to slip in next to the one guy who wasn't paying any attention to her. His dark-blond head tilted down a little as he tapped the screen of his phone, and a nearly empty beer glass stood before him. A short-sleeved, black tee shirt accentuated firmly toned arms, the right bicep sporting some sort of a military emblem with the phrase "The Only Easy Day Was Yesterday" written under it, the sleek muscle flexing a little as he worked the phone. Bringing her gaze up, she noted the shirt did wonders for his broad chest, too.

She stood quietly next to him, uncertain what to do next and thankful the seats on her other side were occupied by a young couple who had eyes only for each other. The bartender, a thirtyish-looking woman with short, spiky black hair and an armful of brightly colored tattoos, worked her way down the bar. Erienne eyed the bottles on the shelves. What should she order? A beer, maybe. Tonight was about breaking taboos, and she'd never tried a beer before. Somehow, her usual white wine spritzer just didn't seem right.

Damn! The man next to her lowered his phone and drained his beer, his eyes looking over the rim of his glass and landing on her reflection in the mirror. His attention caught, and his arm froze for a second before he lowered the glass back to the bar, openly staring at her. Oh well, she was going to have to talk to someone here sooner or later, so she might as well get started. Ignoring the second flock of hummingbirds joining the first in her stomach, she faced him as he turned in his seat. Her smile faltered as his honey-colored eyes practically pinned her in place.

"What brings you in here, sweetheart?" he asked. "Slumming?"

The birds started doing double time, but she made herself speak. "Would it bother you if I was?"

He slowly raked his gaze up and down, and she strove to maintain a somewhat bored expression on her face. It wasn't easy. As he looked her over so deliberately, she now knew what it felt like to be undressed by someone's eyes. A man's eyes. *This* man's eyes. Heat pooled between her thighs as he continued his calculating assessment. The warmth of a blush swept across her cheeks, and she could only hope the dim lighting of the bar concealed it.

Because, if truth be told, she *was* slumming. The men she'd known throughout her life would never dream of looking at her like this, not in public, not with a crowd of people surrounding them. But this man didn't seem to care. The bar was busy enough, but not super crowded, and plenty of people could see what he was doing, see that he was sizing her up with what she could only describe as naked lust.

A sexy smile emerged from between his short, slightly scruffy beard and mustache. "Nuh-uh, sugar," he said, returning his gaze to hers, his eyes crackling with amber fire. "I wouldn't have a problem with that at all. Slum away."

Her mouth went dry. He was dead serious. She had no idea it could happen so fast, so easily. She'd come here tonight to lose her virginity, but now that the moment was quite possibly at hand, she wasn't so sure she could go through with it.

***

"BUY YOU A DRINK?" Fitz saw the fear in the blonde's eyes. She hid it well otherwise, but the truth was crystal clear in those sweet baby blues of hers. Others might not have noticed, but in his line of work if he hadn't honed the ability to tell whether people were lying or putting on an act, he might have been dead a long time ago. She wasn't dangerous, though. No doubt about that. She came from money, her carriage and demeanor dead giveaways no matter how hard she tried to hide it.

He wondered what brought her here. The Steel Horse had a reputation as a biker bar and thus held a certain appeal to the students from the Ivy League college one town over, so she wasn't the first rich girl to wander into the place. Every now and then a group of them would show up wearing tight leather skirts and even tighter cut-off shirts. After ordering a pitcher of something silly and fruity, they usually just sat at a table, looking around with wide eyes and keeping to themselves as they whispered and sniggered their way through their drinks. They went to the bathroom in packs and rarely strayed far from one another.

Occasionally, one or two of the more brazen of them would play a flirty game of pool with one of the tattooed regulars, but they always left with their friends. Fortunately for them, the Steel Horse was frequented mostly by blue-collar laborers who were also bike enthusiasts rather than real hard-core bikers, the kind that lived by their own set of rules as far as women were concerned. The guys here — himself included — were all on the make, sure, but there were more than enough willing women in the bar. Fitz never had trouble finding one to spend his energies on.

But the long-legged, stacked, stunning — albeit timid — blonde package of sex standing next to him was a few years past college age, which made her that much more appealing. Unlike the college girls, this one was old enough to know what she was doing, and he certainly wasn't above giving her a nudge in the direction she was dressed to go.

The skin-tight, orangey-pink dress she wore left nothing to the imagination, and it had been a long time since he'd been with a woman. His last job had been long and difficult, leaving no time for any kind of a social life. Now that it had wrapped up, he was more than ready for a little R & R of the horizontal kind.

He slipped his phone into his back pocket, careful to keep the gun tucked into the back of his pants out of sight. "Terri!" he called to the bartender, "I'm running dry, darlin'."

"Sounds like a personal problem," Terri laughed as she walked over.

"I'll take a boilermaker." He turned back to his new companion. "What would you like?"

The question appeared to catch her off guard. She scanned the bottles behind the bar for a second, her brow wrinkled in confusion. Terri folded her arms and looked at Fitz with a smirk. The blonde turned back to him with a dainty shrug. "The same," she said.

Inwardly, he smiled. He hadn't pegged her for a "let's do a shot" kind of gal, but he was glad to see she had some spunk. That could bode well for what he had in mind for later on. She'd come alone, too, so she wasn't entirely afraid to take some chances. His night was looking better and better.

Terri delivered their drinks, and Fitz picked up his shot glass, catching the eye of several other male patrons in the mirror behind the bar. It occurred to him that the blonde was damned lucky she'd met him before anyone else. He knew she didn't have the street smarts she'd need to effectively dismiss some of the pushier guys here, the kind that often needed something more blunt than a simple "no thanks, not interested" before they got the message. Fitz could recall two occasions where he'd had to step in and tell an obtuse yet persistent guy to back off a woman when her own objections weren't being understood.

One by one, he faced down each man's stare long enough to let them know he'd staked full claim to the golden goddess beside him. A tall guy with dark hair and a large tattoo of a hornet on his neck stared back a little longer than most before he, too, dropped his gaze. Good. Fitz had no qualms about fighting somebody for her, but he had a feeling she'd be long gone before any scuffle got settled.

"Cheers." Her soft voice reclaimed his attention. Biting back a grin at her delicate toast, he clinked his glass with hers. He tossed the Jack Daniels back, watching her as she studied his movements and then quickly followed suit. Her eyes flew wide open and she fought down a sputter as she groped for her beer. Her cheeks turned rosy but she hung on to her composure, watery eyes the only evidence of her discomfort when she set the mug back down on the bar.

Oh yeah. He'd lucked out when she came to stand by him. She'd need a little wooing. A game or two of pool, a couple of slow dances when the band started, but she would be worth every effort. He had no doubt about that. "What's your name, princess?"

"Erienne."

"Erienne what?"

"I'd rather not say, if you don't mind." She smiled at him, but nervousness crept back into her eyes.

An ugly thought struck him. "You're not married, are you?" He hoped to hell she wasn't, because no way was he getting in the middle of anyone's marriage, no matter how much he wanted her. That was trouble he didn't need right now. Ever.

She lifted her left hand, and waggled her bare fingers at him. "Nope."

"Rings come off easily enough."

Her smile disappeared. "I'm not married, and I don't appreciate being called a liar." She yanked open the sparkly silver purse dangling from her shoulder. "I'll buy my own drink."

"Whoa, slow down, I didn't mean to hurt your feelings. Just want to be sure I'm not poaching another man's territory." He'd have to remember she was pretty skittish, whatever her reason for being there might be. If he wanted to see her naked later, he'd have to handle her carefully now. "I'm sorry."

Her eyes softened and she gave him a slight nod.

The band took to the stage. It was retro night at the Steel Horse, and they opened with a raucous version of "Twist and Shout." Fast dancing wasn't Fitz's favorite thing, but he'd do it if it would put her at ease. "Wanna dance?"

She looked at the couples cavorting around the dance floor and shook her head. "I've never played pool. Can you show me how?"

"Sure. Let's go." He picked up their beers and stood. "Lead the way, princess."

She gave him another one of those nervous smiles before heading around the perimeter of the dance floor to the pool tables. Two of them were already in use, but the third one was available. She walked toward it, ignoring the drunken frat boys near the door who were openly staring at her. Not that Fitz could blame them. The silky material of her dress skimmed over her hips and ass in a sinful invitation no man's eyes could decline. He could just picture his hands sliding the dress down over her curves and revealing her creamy skin, inch by delectable inch.

"I saw her first," one of the frat boys muttered as Fitz passed.

Tightening his face into a well-practiced scowl, he stopped and faced the little dweeb. "And? What's your point?"

The wannabe Romeo's eyes narrowed as he and two of his buddies got to their feet. Fitz would have laughed if it weren't so important to make sure the lamebrains knew the foolishness of trying to interfere now. He would have no trouble laying them all flat. Hell, drunk as they appeared to be, it wouldn't even take him two minutes to do it. But he just wasn't in the mood, and it was two minutes he would rather spend with the mystery blonde. The sooner he could put Erienne at ease, the sooner he could entice her to a more intimate locale.

Fitz stared hard at the kid who spoke first. He supposed it might be more expedient to flash his gun at him, but that could potentially lead to police attention, and Fitz's boss wouldn't appreciate that. Fortunately, the frat boys weren't drunk enough to be stupidly brave, and the one who'd complained turned back to the table and sat. A quick glance at his *compadres* showed none of them were willing to pick up the gauntlet, and Fitz moved on.

Unaware of the silent duel that had taken place over her, Erienne carefully studied the rack of pool cues hanging on the wall, as if there would be some sort of marker on them to indicate which one would be best for a beginner. Fitz placed their beers on the small shelf surrounding a square post between the tables and joined her. He picked up a cue and hefted it for weight. After years of abuse by drunken players, they all pretty much sucked, not that she would know the difference. Still, he hated to do things half-assed, so he'd make the best of the materials at hand. "Since you're a beginner, you'll probably do better with a heavier cue. It will give you a little more control."

"And control is important?"

He met her gaze dead on. "Always."

A faint blush tinged her skin, but she gamely picked up two cues and tested them for weight. "I think this one's heavier," she said, putting the other one back.

"Maybe, but it's not long enough for you. You'll do better with a bigger shaft."

She blushed deeply this time. Damn, she was easy to tease. But he'd better knock it off before he spooked her away completely. He helped her find a better cue and then set up the balls on the table.

"I'll go first this time," he said. "After you've played a little and gotten used to the feel of the stick, then you can break the balls." Oops. He really had meant for that to be instructional, not raunchy.

She arched a golden eyebrow at him. "If you're going to talk to me like that, don't you think you should at least tell me your name?"

He chuckled, relieved to learn she had a sense of humor. "Mordecai Fitzjames."

"Mordecai?"

"It's an old family name. Most people call me Fitz."

"Is that what you prefer I call you?"

He gave her another quick glance up and down before he could help himself. "Sweetheart, you can call me any damn thing you want."

Blushing furiously, she straightened up a bit. "Well, how about I call you 'coach' and you get on with teaching me how to play?"

"Fair enough." He leaned over and gave the cue ball a solid whack. The balls scattered across the table and two of them went in the pockets just as the band wrapped up their song.

"You got two balls!" Erienne cheered in the ensuing quiet. "Is that good?" Several people snickered, but she paid no attention as she looked up at him.

"Um, yeah, that's good." Fitz bit back his own laugh. "Normally, that would mean I keep shooting, but I want to make sure you get a turn."

"No, I want to learn how to do it right."

"You will. I'm a good teacher, but I'm also a good player. You won't learn anything if I clear the table and you don't get a chance to shoot. We'll play for real after you get the hang of it." Although if he had his way, they'd be out of here long before she became any kind of a pool hall wizard.

He showed her how to chalk her cue and then how to hold it. "Now, get down low over the table and look at how the cue ball lines up with the blue ball." He bit the inside of his cheek for a second before continuing. "See how it's lined up with the corner pocket?"

"Yes."

"Okay, now pull the stick back, then give the cue ball a fast hit and pull the stick back to the original position quickly."

She closed one eye and concentrated a moment more. Fitz took the opportunity to let his eyes wander over her lush figure, from her silky hair drifting over her shoulder, down her graceful back, to her rounded butt as she bent over the edge of the table. She took her shot, giving her ass a little wiggle. His mouth actually watered.

"Fudge!" Erienne straightened up and whirled around. "I missed."

Fitz swallowed. "That's okay. You can try again. I'll help

you." He looked at the table and found another easy shot. "Try the red one."

"Okay." She bent over the table again. "Like this?"

"Exactly." He stepped to her side and bent over her, placing his hands on hers and bringing his head next to hers. A scent, soft and sweet, cut through the smell of spilled beer and stuffy air, her perfume far more intoxicating than the shot he'd had earlier.

"Now what?" she asked.

"Now we hit it. Dead center of the cue ball." He guided her hand back, his fingers brushing the outside of her thigh as he did. He snapped the cue, and the red ball dropped into the pocket they'd been aiming for.

Erienne pushed up in excitement and Fitz reluctantly dropped his arms as he stood back. She'd fit so nicely underneath him it seemed a shame to let go.

"It went in the hole!" Her eyes sparkled like pale blue ice.

"Yeah," he laughed, "it did." One more innuendo and they would officially be behaving like junior high students. But she didn't seem to be as aware of them as most women he knew, and he found that refreshing.

"I'm going to try again." She scanned the table. "The purple one." It was another easy shot, and she let out a small shriek of satisfaction when she sank it on her own.

The next shot was harder and she missed. Fitz took a turn, dropping two of the more difficult shots, leaving her a few more easy ones to try. She missed her second attempt and asked him to help her with a third. It was a tricky angle, and she was lying flat across the table with one foot on the floor. He leaned over her, stretching his arms around her to help her line up the shot. As her perfume invaded his nose again, a hazy vision of tangled sheets and golden hair spread on a pillow flooded his mind. She jerked the cue and the shot went wide. No surprise there. He'd been too busy fantasizing to actually line it up.

"I thought you were an expert at this," she said impishly from beneath him. She turned her head, and their lips were millimeters apart. The laughter in her eyes drifted away, replaced by desire tinged with a little nervousness.

The band launched into an old rock ballad. "Let's dance," he whispered, feeling a strong need to make that nervousness go away.

She nodded slightly, and they straightened up. He took her hand, leading her to the dance floor. She looked around at the other couples, and then looped her arms around his neck as the other women were doing with their partners. He slid his arms around her waist and pulled her a little closer, but not too close. This was all about making her comfortable, so he'd let her set the tone.

She tilted her head back a little and smiled at him. Encouraged, he slid his hands a little farther around her waist. Heat shimmered through him as she slowly slid one of her hands up the back of his neck and slipped her fingers into his hair, just barely touching his scalp with captivating circular motions. Her eyelids drifted shut, and she leaned her head against his chest. With a barely contained growl of pleasure, he wrapped his arms around her and dispensed with the notion of keeping any space between them. Her firm breasts were heaven against his chest, and he smiled in anticipation of seeing them in all their glory in another hour or so.

Maybe less.

CHAPTER TWO

Fitz turned her around in that slow, shuffley way that couldn't really be considered anything other than foreplay done upright and set to music, silently praising whoever it was that invented the barroom rock ballad slow dance. Just as he closed his eyes, he noticed a man staring at them. That shouldn't have been surprising. Most of the men in the place had taken a good look at Erienne at one point or another this evening. The frat boys and those men at the bar hadn't been the only ones he'd warned off with a glare.

But this guy was different.

First, he was doing a piss-poor job of pretending *not* to stare. Second, just before the guy had jerked his gaze away, Fitz was certain the man had been staring at *him*, not Erienne. As they danced their slow, lazy circle, he periodically opened his eyes and scanned the crowd, spotting the guy a few more times, once in deep conversation with another guy at the bar, and twice more staring at him. Maybe the guy was gay and had wandered into the wrong bar. Whatever. It had to be pretty obvious to the man by now that Fitz's sexual preference placed him squarely on the boy-girl team.

The song ended and the band switched back to an upbeat tempo. Fitz reluctantly loosened his hold, and Erienne stepped back a millimeter and looked up at him, her eyes darkened to a smoky blue. "Can we...can we go somewhere else?" Her voice was a raspy whisper.

Although his libido was doing a rather lewd happy dance, Fitz managed to suppress the mile-wide grin threatening to surface. "Whatever you want, princess."

"I'll need the ladies' first."

He guided her back toward the bar and pointed to a little hallway at the end of it. "In there. I'll wait for you here." She nodded and headed off. His eyes feasted on her butt as she walked away until she disappeared into the ladies' room. He called to Terri and quickly settled his bar tab.

"Have fun, Casanova," Terri smirked as she returned his credit card and sauntered away.

As Fitz put the card back in his wallet and double-checked he had a few condoms tucked in there, his phone rang. He dug it out of his pocket, his heart sinking when he saw Tobie Armstrong's name on the screen. His boss calling him now could only mean bad news. With the morose feeling he was about to kiss goodbye any quality time with Erienne, he moved into the hallway for the bathrooms where it was quieter. "Hi, Tobie."

She got right to the point. "I just got word that Tommy Pruitt was shanked in lock-up last night. He's dead."

"Dammit!" Fitz's last undercover operation for October Armstrong Security and Investigation Services — aka OASIS — had helped get the nasty little bastard arrested. But it was Tommy's brother, Dave Pruitt, the authorities really wanted to get their hands on. "I don't suppose you're calling me to say that before he died, Tommy told every-thing he knew about his brother's operations, and even as we speak Dave is being processed and fingerprinted by New York's Finest."

"Fat chance. Getting Tommy to flip was always a long shot. He adored Dave."

And, Fitz knew, Dave adored Tommy. It was common knowledge among New York's underworld that messing with Tommy was risking the legendary wrath of Dave. "I wouldn't have believed there was anyone stupid enough to shank Tommy. Not unless they had a death wish."

"Word is that Dave has already put out contracts on those responsible for Tommy's murder," Tobie said.

"Contracts? More than one? How many guys shanked him?"

"I don't know, but all this went down during a small inmate riot. It's all still being sorted out. The Department of Corrections isn't sharing a lot of information about the attack. But Dave is blaming a whole host of people for putting Tommy inside in the first place. The arresting offi-cers, the assistant district attorney, and the judge who denied Tommy's bail have all been placed in protective custody."

"Sounds like everything's under control." If all the prin-cipals were already being protected, maybe his evening wasn't ruined after all. Tobie's company was exclusive. She charged exorbitant fees from wealthy clients and delivered exemplary results. The City of New York couldn't afford her rates, so it wasn't likely she was calling him to come in for a bodyguard detail. "Well, thanks for letting me know. I'll call you tomorrow. Right now I've got a hot—"

"Forget it. There's a contract out on you, too."

"What?"

"My sources tell me that Dave doesn't believe you escaped the arrest scene on your own. He's saying you set Tommy up. Which means there may have been a leak somewhere."

Fitz's pulse began to throb in his temple. "Who the hell would have told him?"

"I don't know yet. I'm not even sure there was a leak. Pruitt could just be flying off the handle. But we cooperated with a lot of official departments on this one – the police, the FBI, ATF. If there *was* a leak, that's where it came from. Not from us."

"I know that." Fitz trusted his fellow OASIS agents with his life. He knew some of them from as far back as boot camp and had served with all of them at one time or another during his tours with the Navy SEALs.

"Maybe someone in the DA's office was bought off," Tobie went on. "And let's not forget we've pissed off some very important people when we had them arrested for participating in the Iceman's auctions."

Fitz's blood boiled as he thought of the now deceased Iceman and those men to whom he'd auctioned his victims. Men, many in public office, who had bought and sadistically tortured young women. The only good thing the Iceman ever did was record those men in action. "Those scumbags deserve everything they get."

"And then some. But until they are tried and sentenced, any one of them can still be dangerous. Many of them still have the power to compromise police investigations and leak sensitive information. We're already looking into it. If there was a leak, we'll find it. But right now, we know that Dave's threat is real, and we need to keep you safe. Ian and Jake are going to look after you. Where are you?"

"I don't need babysitters. Give Jake and Ian something

more useful to do. I'll come to the office as soon as I can get there."

Two women passed him on their way to the ladies' room, reminding him Erienne would be along soon, not that it was going to do him any good now. Damn Pruitt and his stupid contract anyway. But Fitz knew better than to ignore the threat. Pruitt was a lethal bastard and had more than enough money to hire a top-notch hit man.

Or hit*men*. What if some of Pruitt's goons had found him already?

Fitz moved to the hallway entry and quickly scanned the room. There was no sign of that guy who'd been looking at him or the other guy he'd been talking to at the bar. Just where the hell had they gone? They hadn't passed him to go to the men's room.

"Fitz? Are you still there? Where the hell are you?"

"Sorry. Yeah, I'm here. I'm at a bar called the Steel Horse. It's just outside Candlewood. But tell the guys to meet me at my place. I've got a date, and I need to get her out of here safely. There's a couple of guys here that might be a problem."

"A Pruitt problem or a poaching on your woman problem?"

"I'm not sure. Either way, I can't leave her. If it is a Pruitt problem, they've seen her with me. She's not safe." Not to mention Erienne had caught the attention of way too many guys here. Even without the threat of Pruitt, she was in over her head in a place like this.

Tobie swore. "Stay there. Wait for backup."

"No. If these guys are Pruitt's men, they won't have any qualms about opening fire in a public place like this. It will be easier for me to give them the slip if they think I don't suspect anything."

"All right. I'll have Jake and Ian meet you at your place. But until you get there I want you to call or text me every five minutes. And do not turn your phone off for any reason."

"Okay. I'm on my way."

Fitz disconnected and scanned the bar again, annoyed with himself for having let his guard down. No matter how gorgeous and pliant Erienne was, he'd been careless not to pay more attention to his surroundings. That's what he got for thinking with the wrong head.

Mentally urging Erienne to hurry up, he kept a constant vigil of the bar area, dance floor, and pool tables. The guy with the hornet tattoo still sat at the bar, but his attention was riveted to a dark-haired young woman as she read his palm. Still no sign of the other two guys. He wanted to believe they hadn't been from Pruitt, but the hairs standing up on the back of his neck told him he probably wasn't that lucky. Fate was screwing with him. He could feel it. Why else would a blonde and horny goddess fall into his arms, only for him to discover he had to take a pass?

Yeah, fate was a cruel bastard.

***

ERIENNE WASHED her hands and then looked through her purse, making sure she had everything she would need. Condoms? Check. Personal lubricant? Check. Her research indicated her nerves might prevent her from getting sufficiently aroused. But thinking of Fitz waiting for her outside, remembering the way her body responded when he'd stretched himself on top of her on the pool table, had her believing the lubricant would remain unopened. Her panties were still damp.

After touching up her lipstick and combing her hair, she reached into her purse and pulled out her perfume atomizer only to discover it wasn't her perfume. With a chuckle, she tucked the small canister of mace back into her bag. She certainly wouldn't keep Fitz in the mood if she sprayed *that* on her neck.

Not that she was worried about keeping his attention. Although inexperienced, she wasn't stupid. Fitz definitely wanted to be with her.

Her hands shook a little as she rooted around for the perfume, but she wasn't anywhere near as nervous as she'd thought she would be. Initially, she'd owed her lessening nerves to the shot and the beer, but that wasn't entirely it.

Her attraction to Fitz was real. At least on a physical level. His whiskey-brown eyes were warm and full of good humor. The silky texture of his blond hair had been paradise to her fingers. *And that body!* Six feet of tight muscle and broad shoulders. Every time he'd touched her, it was as if he enhanced her own femininity. She couldn't remember the last time she'd felt that way.

All too often, Erienne's devotion to her career left her little time to relax and have fun. She didn't regret her decision to continue her late mother's biofuel research, but sometimes she missed having the time to do the things other women her age did.

Like date and have sex.

Well, she wasn't expecting — or looking for — any kind of dating relationship with Fitz, but she thought he was an excellent prospect to help her with the sex part. Something primal inside her told her he would be a good lover. Her plan was working out much better than she'd hoped. She was still a bit nervous about the whole thing, but that was only natural. The good news was since she'd met Fitz her excitement level had risen, and she no longer worried she wouldn't have the courage to go through with it.

She returned her perfume to her purse, and her fingers brushed against the mace. In her gut she knew she wouldn't need it, not with Fitz, but what was the point of carrying it if she couldn't find it? With a shrug, she moved it to an easily accessible pocket of her purse.

The door to the ladies' room opened, and two giggling girls came in. "Did you see that guy on the phone?" said one. "Damn, he was hot!"

"Hell yes!" said the other. "Makes me wish I wasn't here with Frankie."

Erienne caught sight of Fitz talking on his phone before the door swung shut and smiled, feeling a little smug that she had the attention of the hottest guy in the room. Knowing he'd be occupied for another few minutes, she pulled out her own phone and dialed her cousin, Kylie. The call went straight to voicemail. Good. Kylie had been very clear on what she thought of Erienne's scheme.

The two girls were still laughing and talking with each other, paying absolutely no attention to Erienne, but she kept her voice low anyway. "Hi, its me. Don't be mad. I decided to go through with that plan I told you about yesterday. I'm at the Steel Horse, but I'm leaving in a minute with a guy named Mordecai Fitzjames. He seems all right. I'm not sure where we're going yet, but I'll call and leave you another message when we get there. Please try not to worry. I've got a really good feeling about this. I think it's going to be a very good experience for me. Talk to you soon." She tossed her phone back in her purse. With a last quick glance in the mirror, she smoothed a wayward strand of hair into place and exited the ladies' room.

Fitz was no longer on the phone, and she approached

him with a smile. He barely looked at her as he took her hand. "Stay close to me."

Fine by her. Close to him was exactly what she wanted.

He led her to the exit and stopped just outside the door, turning his head left and right as if he were looking for someone. "Is something wrong?"

"No, but I'm afraid something's come up, so we're going to have to take a rain check. Where's your car? I'll walk you to it."

What? He was sending her home? Ten minutes ago, he'd been all over her. "Did you get some bad news?"

He whipped his gaze back to her. "What do you mean?"

"I saw you on the phone. Was it bad news?"

"Something like that."

He scanned the parking lot again, definitely looking for someone, and not appearing too pleased about it, either. Her mind tripped back to when they'd first spoken at the bar. He'd asked if she was married. Maybe that was the problem. Maybe *he* was married and his wife had called. Maybe she was on her way here to collect her gorgeous, wayward husband.

Erienne pulled her hand from his. "Don't worry about me. If you have to leave, you go right ahead."

A determined glint entered his eyes. "Where's your car?"

"Is your wife on her way? Is that why you're trying to get rid of me?" Her petulant tone grated her own ears, but she couldn't help it. She wasn't sure if she were more angry or disappointed.

"My wife? What are you talking about? I'm not married."

"You couldn't wait to leave with me until that phone call. Now you can't ditch me fast enough. No wonder you were quick to think I was concealing a marriage earlier. I bet you're the one with a spouse to hide."

He took her hand again and pressed her palm to his lips. "I swear I'm not married," he whispered, his beard tickling her hand as he kissed it again. "Believe me, there is nothing I would rather do than take you to bed this minute." Heat tingled up her arm from where his lips and fingers touched her. "But I can't right now. If you give me your number, I promise I'll call you in a few days."

A few days! Absolutely not. She was ready to do this now. As ready as she was ever going to be, anyway. She'd come too far to have her hopes dashed like this.

He kissed her palm again, the warm light in his eyes a sensual promise. "That's not a line. I will definitely call you. Give me your phone number."

She believed him. He would call her and they could go out and then, hopefully, pick up where they left off. Only that sounded too much like a date, and after the pain of her last boyfriend's betrayal, that's not what she wanted. Her goal was to lose her virginity with no strings attached. Besides, despite his devilish appeal, Fitz was not the kind of man she dated. It was his killer body she wanted, and she wanted it now.

Eager to regain the warm, sticky, dreamy feeling she'd had as they danced, she rubbed her thumb over his full lips. Encouraged by the flare of heat in his eyes, she moved in closer and slipped her hand up his neck, tangling her fingers in his sumptuous hair. A growl purred in his throat as he closed the distance. She parted her lips and he accepted her invitation, his tongue caressing every part of her mouth. The warmth at the pit of her belly turned to lava as he wrapped his arms around her and pulled her flush up against his granite chest.

Oh yes, he's the one. Her world dissolved to a sensual haze as she held on tight. Perhaps it had been a sheer stroke of luck, but Erienne knew he would be an expert lover, and after having this heady taste of what was in store she didn't want to settle for anything less. She doubted she'd be so lucky a second time if she had to go back inside and start all over.

He broke away from her lips and trailed succulent little kisses along her jaw and down her neck. "Erienne... princess," he muttered, "I really can't right now. I have to—"

"Yes, you can. I know you want me," she whispered.

"You bet your sweet ass I do."

"It's all right, I want you, too."

"That's not the problem. I really have to go."

Determination fueled her brain, reminding her of the stack of old romance novels she and Kylie had found as children playing hide-and-seek in the attic of their grand-mother's house. Once discovered, those novels proved to be an irresistible temptation. She and Kylie had always snuck up there to read them whenever they visited their grand-mother. The men in those books seemed to crave virgins. She knew the mores of the times were different now, but not so much that a man wouldn't appreciate being a woman's first lover. That's the sort of stuff they bragged about to their friends, wasn't it? Visions of Kevin's angry face tried to creep across her mind, but she slammed the lid on that line of thinking. She'd been wrong about him on so many levels.

"Shhh." Erienne kissed Fitz's neck like he was kissing hers. "You don't want to pass this up. Trust me."

He chuckled against her skin. "I'm sure it will be fabu-lous, darlin', but—"

"No, you don't understand." She smiled inwardly as she played her ace in the hole. "I'm a virgin."

He jumped back from her so fast she could have

believed he'd been poked with a cattle prod. "You're what?" he croaked.

"A virgin. Well, sort of. But I don't want to be one anymore." She reached for him, missing the warmth of his body, but he grabbed her wrists and halted her progress.

"So, what, you were planning to jump into bed with the first guy you met at a bar?"

"Well, technically, you weren't the first guy I met." She smiled up at him, hoping her stab at levity would remove the scorn that twisted his mouth into a scowl.

No such luck. "Are you crazy? Do you have any idea how dangerous that is?"

"Oh, come on, Fitz. Strangers hook up at bars all the time. You're not dangerous, are you?" Doing her best to be flirty, she tilted her head to one side. "You said you were a good teacher. I know I'm a good student, and I'm guessing someone like you has lots of experience."

"Not with virgins."

"Well then, now's your chance to get some." She straightened up and gave her hips a little wiggle. "Some real hands-on experience, if you know what I mean."

He shook his head and rolled his eyes. "C'mon," he said, dropping one of her wrists and stepping into the parking lot. "Where's your car? You have to go home."

Disappointment warred with disbelief within her. He meant it. He really wasn't going to spend the night with her. She should have known it was all going too smoothly.

"That's your car, isn't it? The Mercedes?" He towed her along toward it without waiting for an answer. "Get your keys out."

Erienne stopped, almost toppling out of her shoes as he kept striding along. She grabbed the door handle of the nearest car and yanked her other arm free. He whirled and reached for her, but she backed up. "Thanks for the escort, but I'm not leaving yet."

"Erienne, please, you've got to go. It's not safe here."

"What do you mean?"

"I don't have time to explain. Please trust me."

"Why should I trust you? You're nothing but a tease!"

She spun and took one step before he managed to grab her arm. "Erienne, I can't let you do this. It'll be a big mistake."

"Well, it's my mistake to make."

"I can't let you stay here."

"What are you? The morality police? If you're not interested, then I'm going to go find someone who is. It really isn't any of your business." She jerked away and headed back toward the bar, wrath fueling her steps. How dare he? He didn't want to sleep with her? Fine, that was certainly his prerogative. But trying to dictate her actions as if she were a child? No way.

"Erienne, wait." He caught up with her and stepped in front of her.

"Leave me alone!" She tried to get around him.

"Erienne—"

"Hey! I believe the lady said she ishn't interested."

GREAT, *just what he needed.*

Fitz faced the frat boys as they approached, obviously drunk yet seeking to come to a lady's aid. He moved in front of Erienne, blocking their path. "Stay out of this, guys. It's not your concern."

One of them, the same one he'd warned off inside the

bar, stepped forward. "We're not gonna just shtand here and let you force her," he slurred. "That'sh rape, buddy."

His friends muttered their agreement. The five of them squared off their shoulders and stood up a little straighter, scowling at Fitz all the while. The effect might have been intimidating if they weren't also weaving a bit like a pack of alcohol-infused bobblehead dolls. Physically dealing with them wouldn't pose much of a problem in and of itself, except he would have to let Erienne walk away to do it. And if he let her go, she'd march right back into the bar to implement her ridiculous plan.

A plan that, as she'd correctly pointed out, wasn't any of his business. He shouldn't really care, and heaven knew a foolish virgin was a distraction he didn't need right now. Those other guys he saw earlier were gone, and they probably had nothing to do with his last case anyway. He should let her go on her merry way while he met with his teammates and figured out a plan to deal with Pruitt.

That's what he *should* do, but he still couldn't help being concerned about her well-being anyway. He eyed the frat boys. While their intentions were honorable and heroic enough at the moment, they *were* pretty drunk. Alcohol could do strange things to people, and they outnumbered her. Despite their high intoxication level, she wouldn't be any match for them if things happened to turn ugly.

He faced her again. "Erienne, please let me walk you to your car. I can't stay here much longer, and it's not a good idea for you to stay here alone."

"Why not?" Anger crackled in her eyes, and something told him the word "docile" wasn't in her vocabulary. She arched a golden eyebrow at him. "Well? Surely you're not suggesting that a man can stay here by himself but a woman can't?"

"That's right, man," one of the frat boys chimed in. "Haven't you heard of women's lib? Bucking the patriarchy?" He and his buddies laughed uproariously.

Fitz threw them a glare. "Excuse us." He pulled Erienne a few feet away. The boys stopped laughing and watched them with the intensity of a hungry dog waiting for its master to drop a scrap of food. They were one step away from hanging their tongues out of their mouths. Between them and the nagging feeling he had about those men in the bar belonging to Pruitt, he grew more certain Erienne was not safe here.

"Look, Fitz, I've only known you for a little while. I thought we could have some fun, but you obviously don't want to. That's your business. But how I spend the rest of my evening is *my* business. Got it?" She moved to step past him and he blocked her way.

"Erienne!" he hissed, frustrated he didn't have time to explain the situation more clearly. "It's not gonna happen. You are not staying here."

She practically snarled at him as she planted her hands on his chest and shoved. Her effort barely moved him, but it galvanized her drunken knights into action.

"Leave her alone, you bastard!"

Fitz turned to face them as they fell on him en masse. Erienne broke away, a flurrying flash of pink as she skirted the lot of them and headed back toward the bar.

His attackers brought him to the ground, but fortunately one of the drunken fools hit the pavement first, thus softening the impact. Fitz managed to deliver a sharp elbow jab to the guy's temple. Judging from the yowl that elicited, he had only four of them left to deal with. With a mighty heave, he rolled over and managed to pin two of his combatants underneath him, one on top of the other as he straddled them with his knees.

The remaining two got unsteadily to their feet. One grabbed Fitz's right arm, so he belted the kid with his left fist, connecting with the kid's nose, which began gushing immediately. The fight fizzled out of him as he dropped Fitz's arm and brought his hands to his face. "Shit! I think you broke my node!" he said, his words somewhat strangled.

"I'll get him, Bob!" The second topside assailant swung at Fitz's head, but he easily deflected the blow with his forearm. He was pitched to the side as the ones beneath him bucked and struggled to stand up.

Fitz rolled away and regained his feet. One of the boys launched himself off the ground directly toward Fitz and was greeted with a solid fist to the stomach. The boy doubled over with an *oof* before he staggered away a few steps, vomiting up a fair portion of all the beer he'd recently consumed. Fitz whirled to face the rest of them.

The boy who'd first gone down was still down, eyes shut. Fitz panicked for a second that the kid was really hurt until he heard him give a loud snore. Bob of the broken nose was leaning against a car with his head tilted back and moaning. One of his friends was trying to pull him away as he kept a nervous watch on Fitz.

That left only one knight-errant ready to do battle. The one who earlier muttered something about seeing Erienne first. Arms spread wide, he charged with a wordless roar. Fitz jumped out of the way and kicked the would-be champion right in the ass as he staggered by. The kid went sprawling, and Fitz dropped down and put his knee in the kid's back. He grabbed an arm and twisted it up high between the kid's shoulder blades.

"Listen, jerk-off," Fitz said, ignoring the kid's yelps of

pain, "you're damn lucky I don't have the time to really kick your ass. Now mind your own busin—"

"Hey!" one of the other guys yelled. "Hey, they're taking her!"

Fitz looked up as a feminine scream pealed across the lot. The two goons he'd seen earlier had Erienne by the arms and were dragging her away from the bar entrance. A large black van screeched into the parking lot, and the side door slid open. Erienne struggled and screamed as her captors pulled her toward it.

Dropping the kid's arm, Fitz lunged to his feet and raced across the lot. "No! Let her go!"

CHAPTER THREE

Erienne heard a yell, and momentary relief flooded her veins as Fitz charged across the parking lot. One of the men, both of whom had appeared out of nowhere and accosted her at the bar entrance, dropped her arm and reached into the back of his pants as he turned to face Fitz. She saw a flash of metal in his waistband, but Fitz tackled him before the man could pull out whatever weapon he'd been trying for.

The other man was still dragging her toward the van that had come roaring up beside them. She kicked him as hard as she could. He grunted but didn't let go. With her free hand, she dug into her purse, groping for the side pocket.

The man almost had her to the gaping side door of the van where several other men waited to grab her when her fingers finally brushed up against something cool and metal. She clutched the tube of mace with a fear-driven grip of iron and yanked it out. Flipping up the safety guard with her thumb, she sprayed her captor directly in the face. He howled in agony and dropped to his knees.

"You bitch!"

Erienne whirled away, determined to get to the safety of the bar, but one of the men in the van grabbed her by the hair. She screamed again as he dragged her back. Other hands grabbed her and hauled her kicking and screaming into the van. She raised the mace, but the man nearest her slapped the tube from her hand.

A couple of the frat boys were stumbling toward them, one of them talking wildly into his cell phone. Fitz had knocked out the man who'd first grabbed her and was now tearing toward the van, reaching out to her. "Erienne! Jump!"

She lunged forward, but one of the other men in the van wrapped an arm around her from behind. She scratched at him but stilled when she saw the gun in his other hand — a gun pointed squarely at Fitz's chest.

"Get in, Fitzpatrick."

Fitz stopped short and glared at the man holding her. "Let her go first. She's got nothing to do with this."

"Maybe not. But I think Mr. Pruitt would like to meet her anyway. She's a pretty little piece. He might want to add her to his collection."

A shudder of revulsion raced down her spine. She had no idea who Mr. Pruitt was, but she knew she had no desire to meet him. "Please, let me go."

"Quiet, sugar-tits," the man said, tightening his hold on her waist. "C'mon, Fitzpatrick. Get in. We haven't got all night."

"Listen, Maddox, if you insist on taking her, I'll fight you with everything I've got. Let her go and I'll come quietly."

Maddox chuckled. "This is not up for negotiation. You think I'm kidding around? Think again." He shifted the gun to the right and shot one of the frat boys.

The poor boy fell to the ground as his friend dove

behind a parked car. Blood pooled on the pavement, and Erienne fought off the sudden urge to vomit.

"Not so fast, Fitzpatrick," Maddox said as Fitz took a step toward the boy. "Do as I tell you, or say goodbye to your girlfriend." He pressed the barrel of his gun against her temple. A sharp, acrid smell, like exploded firecrackers, increased her nausea. Only the paralyzing terror of the gun at her head kept her from lunging out of the van to throw up.

"Get in here right now or she dies. Either way, she's not getting out of this van," Maddox said calmly, as if he shot people every day. Maybe he did. He hadn't hesitated to pull the trigger just a few seconds ago.

Fitz glared hatred at the man behind her. "You prick."

"Shut up and get in, Fitzpatrick. That's the last time I'll say it."

With a curse, Fitz vaulted into the van.

The guy she'd maced was struggling to his feet, coughing and cursing.

"Get in here, Cooney!" Maddox roared. One of the other men jumped out and shoved Cooney toward the van door before heading toward the man Fitz had left sprawled unconscious several feet away.

"Leave him!" Maddox barked. "We don't have time."

The goon made no protest and hurried back, jumping into the van. Maddox took the gun from Erienne's temple and pointed it at the man on the ground.

"No, no, no," she moaned, but it was drowned out by the gunshot. A black hole appeared in the supine man's forehead, followed by a gush of blood from the back of his skull.

The last man into the van slammed the door shut.

"Go!" yelled Maddox. He shoved Erienne onto the bench seat beside him as the driver hit the gas.

Two of the men had forced Fitz into the bench seat in

front of Maddox and Erienne. They searched him, relieving him of a gun before they took a seat either side of him. Why did Fitz have a gun?

Cooney and the other man scrambled into the third bench seat, behind Maddox and Erienne. "Where is she?" Cooney bawled. "I'll rip her fucking head off!"

"Please," Erienne whimpered. "Don't hurt me. My father will pay you anything you want!"

Cooney yanked her hair from behind. "Do you think I give a shit who your daddy is? You fucking maced me, you stupid bitch!"

Through the tears of pain flooding her eyes, Erienne saw Fitz twist around and rise from his seat. Maddox raised his gun and pointed it at Fitz. "Sit down and behave, Fitzpatrick. You too, Cooney."

"Hell no!" Cooney rasped between coughs. "She's gonna pay for—"

With his free arm, Maddox elbowed Cooney in the face. "I said knock it off!"

Cooney released her hair and sat back with a muffled curse.

"Now," said Maddox calmly. "Just who is your father?"

For the first time, Erienne got a good look at Maddox. He was huge. The top of his head nearly brushed the roof of the van. His head was bald and there was a long, jagged scar that started at the top of his left ear and climbed up over the top of his skull. She couldn't see where it ended. His eyes were dark, but she couldn't make out the color in the dim light of the van. Another wicked-looking scar began at the center of his nose and jutted out to his left cheek before it hooked down through both his lips and ended at the tip of his large, square chin. She didn't want to know what could have caused such a horrific injury. "Wh-what?"

"Your father? You were saying he would pay anything to get you back. Who is he?" He cocked his head to one side. "Answer me. I'm tired of asking."

"Leave her alone." Fitz's voice was low, but it silenced everyone in the van.

Except Maddox. "If I were you, Fitzpatrick, I'd worry about my own skin. Mr. Pruitt is really pissed at you. And you know how he gets when he's pissed off."

"She's got nothing to do with it, and you know it. Just pull over and let her go."

Maddox nodded at one of the guys next to Fitz. The guy pushed Fitz's shoulder, forcing him around back into his seat. Fitz made to turn back around, and the guy elbowed him in the stomach.

Erienne wanted to wake from this nightmare, safe in her own bed. But it was real. Maddox reached toward her, and she pressed herself as far away as she could. He chuckled softly and simply took her purse and pulled it from her arm.

"Relax," he said, patting her knee, ignoring her uncontrollable shudders. "I just want to get to know you a little better."

He opened her purse and meticulously rifled through the contents. He examined each item, placing them one by one on the seat beside him, away from her. Her lipstick and perfume were ignored, but then he pulled out the new box of condoms. "Ribbed Trojans? Excellent choice."

The rest of the goons laughed. "It's better bareback!" one of them chortled.

Heat crept up Erienne's face as Maddox continued pawing through her belongings. "Oh man, look at these!" he laughed, holding up the clean pair of panties she'd tucked in at the last minute before she'd left the house. Maddox stuck a beefy finger into the waistband and spun them around. "Damn, Fitzpatrick, she was hoping you were going to get her good and wet. Sorry we screwed up those plans for you." He flung the panties over Fitz's head and they landed in his lap.

Erienne was beyond mortification now, and a lump the size of Kansas grew in her throat. If she got out of this mess in one piece, she would happily listen to Kylie say *I told you so* for the rest of her life.

"Ah, here we are," Maddox said as he pulled out Erienne's wallet and cell phone. He turned her phone off before adding it to the pile on the seat. He flipped open the wallet. "Erienne Stuart, Greenwich, CT." He glanced askance at her. "Nice address. I guess you're not a high-class hooker after all." He looked back at her license. "And may I say you are one of the few people I've ever met who manages to look damn good in a driver's license photo."

He closed the wallet and put it back in her purse, along with the rest of the contents — with the exception of the phone, which he put in his pocket.

"So, Erienne Stuart, who is your father? Tell me the truth now," he warned.

Erienne's terror prohibited any kind of clear thought, let alone making up some kind of a lie. Besides, what she'd said earlier was true. Her father would pay any price to get her back unharmed. "His name is Marcus Stuart."

"Marcus Stuart? Never heard of him. What does he do that he can afford a Greenwich address and to pay untold sums to get his beautiful, slutty daughter back?"

"He's a—"

"Shut up, Erienne!" Fitz barked.

"Fitzpatrick, I won't remind you again what kind of deep shit you're in. And as long as we bring you to Mr. Pruitt alive, he really won't care if we break a few bones along the way."

"And I know something about her that Pruitt will be very interested in knowing."

"What's that?"

"Are you kidding? I'm not giving you that information."

Erienne's mind raced. Fitz sounded so smug. What did he know about her? He couldn't possibly be talking about her virginity, could he? She'd heard there really was such a thing as white slavery, where men would pay an especially high price for virgins. She hadn't seriously believed it was true.

But Fitz was obviously no stranger to these men, and the one named Maddox kept calling him Fitz*patrick*. He'd told her his name was Fitz*james*. What was that about? He was probably one of those con men like she'd seen on television, the ones with a dozen aliases who preyed on rich widows and lonely heiresses.

She was neither. Her father had a vast fortune, true, plenty of which she would inherit, but she wasn't lonely. And she'd long ago learned to be on the lookout for fortune hunters. Kevin's face flashed in her mind, but she pushed it away.

"I am really curious now." Maddox wrapped his fingers around her hand, which disappeared inside his giant fist. He squeezed slowly but consistently, grinding her knuckles together.

"Ow! Stop it. Please!" The pain intensified as Maddox stared at her with a bemused, patient expression. Tears leaked from her eyes as she tried in vain to pry his fingers from her hand.

"Maddox, dammit, leave her alone! You'll ruin everything!"

The pain eased slightly. "Ruin what?"

"I'm talking to Pruitt first. But don't worry, there'll be

enough for everybody. Her old man's got enough money to make all of us happy for the rest of our lives. But we won't see a penny of it if she's not in perfect condition."

Maddox stared at the back of Fitz's head and then looked back at Erienne, eyeing her curiously. He dropped her hand and reached up to wipe a tear away from her face with a thumb. She did her best to repress a shudder.

"Don't cry, Barbie Doll. We're practically there. I know Mr. Pruitt will be happy to meet you and make you feel right at home." He turned back and backhanded Fitz across the back of his head. "Which is more than I can say for you. No matter what kind of information you have, he's still going to make you pay for the death of his brother. You've bought yourself a short breather at best."

The skyline of Manhattan came into view, the van drawing Erienne closer to some unknown yet terrifying fate. The hummingbirds had long since left her stomach, replaced by woodpeckers that hammered away at her insides, sending reverberating tremors through her whole body. Though her hopes faded under that onslaught, she battled her rising panic, refusing to believe the situation was hopeless. She'd always fought for what she wanted, and what she wanted more than anything right now was to be going in the opposite direction.

She just wanted to go home.

Tobie Armstrong paced the floor of her Manhattan office. It had been twenty minutes since she'd last talked to Fitz. So much for his promise to call or text every five minutes. If he was pulling some kind of macho lone wolf act, she'd bust his thick SEAL skull.

Her phone rang. *Finally*. "Dammit, Fitz, where the hell have you been?"

"Sorry, boss, it's me. Jake."

"Are you at his house? Why hasn't he called me?"

"He's not here. We haven't heard from him either."

Her heart plummeted. This wasn't good. "He said he had a date, so maybe he's still dropping her off. Do either of you know who he's been seeing lately?"

"Not me. Hang on a sec." She heard him relay the question to his partner. "No, Ian doesn't know either. He's never mentioned anyone serious as long as I've know him."

"We need to find him. Fast." Pruitt was a threat none of them could take lightly. His track record was too full of bodies. "Get on the computer and trace his phone. See if he even left that bar yet." A consummate hacker, Jake could find anyone he set his mind to find.

"You got it. I'll call you back in a few minutes."

Tobie disconnected and tried calling Fitz's again. No answer.

"Dammit, Fitz. Where are you?"

CHAPTER FOUR

JAKE OPENED FITZ'S LAPTOP, bypassed the password security, and logged into the OASIS employee database. Bringing up Fitz's profile, Jake clicked on the tab marked "cell phone" and then clicked on "Trace" from the drop-down menu. A map appeared on the screen, a red dot flashing in the center. He clicked on the dot.

"You got him?" Ian looked up from the drawer he was searching, looking for anything that might tell them about Fitz's mystery girl.

"Maybe. The last call on his phone was the one from Tobie, when he was still at that bar. According to the tracker, he hasn't left there yet, even though he told Tobie he would meet us here. I don't like it."

Ian shut the drawer. "Me either. The Steel Horse is about ten minutes from here. We should check it out."

Jake called Tobie from the car and brought her up to date. "We're on our way now. We'll call you as soon as we find anything."

A few minutes later they rounded a curve and were greeted with a barrage of throbbing emergency lights. The parking lot of the Steel Horse was packed with police cars and ambulances.

"This doesn't look too good, but it's got Fitz's signature all over it. He wouldn't go down without a fight." Ian's grim statement echoed Jake's own thoughts. As they drew closer, an ambulance suddenly roared out of the parking lot, sirens screaming. "I guess that means whoever is in there is still alive."

"Think it's Fitz?"

"Could be. Let's see what we can find out here before going to the hospital. If it's not him in that ambulance, we need to find him and get him out of sight."

There was a police officer directing traffic, waving drivers past the entrance to parking lot. Jake lowered his window as he approached the officer. "What happened?"

"Sir, this is an active crime scene. You need to move along."

"Officer, I was supposed to meet my brother here. I saw that ambulance. I need to know if my brother is okay."

"There's been a shooting, but I can't let you in while they're investigating. If you want to pull over to the side of the road and remain in your vehicle, you can wait until the detective is free to speak to you. Otherwise you will have to move along."

Jake pulled away and over to the side of the road. "What do you want to do?"

Ian was already unfastening his seatbelt. "We can't wait for the detective. He'll be tied up for hours. Let's slip around the back and see if we can get in that way. If the person in the ambulance is Fitz, I want to start talking to witnesses right away. If it's not, maybe we can find him."

They made their way quickly to the back of the Steel Horse, and then slid along the side of the building toward the front. Another uniformed police officer came around the corner with a roll of yellow crime scene tape in her hand. "What are you doing back here?" she asked. "The detective wants everyone to stay up front or inside the bar."

Keeping their heads down as inconspicuously as possible, they kept walking. "Sorry. Nature called," Ian muttered as they passed her, adding a little slur to his voice.

"Next time go inside!" she snapped after them. "This is a crime scene!"

They came around the front of the building. A few knots of people were scattered about in front of the bar, talking nervously among themselves, some of them craning their necks trying to get a better look at the action and film it with their phones. Others were just looking a little green around the gills. One girl clung to her boyfriend and sobbed.

Detectives stood near one of the ambulances, interviewing a cluster of young guys who were all talking at once, with the exception of one of them who was sitting on the ledge of the ambulance door being treated for what looked like a nose injury.

Jake and Ian skirted the knots of people, getting as close as they could to the officers interviewing the kids. They could see a body on the ground now that had not yet been covered.

"It's not Fitz." Jake said, the tension brewing in his neck easing a little.

Ian blew out a breathy sigh of relief as he scanned the parking lot. "I don't see him anywhere. Do you?"

"No. Let's go inside. Maybe he's being detained in there." But a quick search inside the bar turned up no Fitz. They went back outside.

"I'd sure like to talk to those witnesses," Ian said,

nodding toward the three young men who were talking to the detectives, swaying on their feet and gesturing wildly.

"They look pretty drunk. I'm not sure how much help they'd be." Jake's gaze fell on the ambulance. The guy getting fixed up there was about the same age as the other boys and wore the same retro-looking fraternity jacket. He'd probably seen whatever the others had, but none of the police were talking to him yet. In fact, the door of the ambulance blocked him from the detectives' line of sight. As an added bonus, it looked as though the EMT had finished patching him up for the moment. She was just talking to him now, and gave him a quick rub on his shoulder before she started gathering up her supplies.

"Ian, take care of that EMT. I want to talk to that kid before the detectives get to him."

"You got it."

Ian wandered over to the ambulance just as the EMT was packing up her kit. He gave her a smile and started talking. In less than a minute, he'd drawn her away from the kid and toward the front of the ambulance.

With a last glance to make sure the detectives were still deeply involved with the others, Jake headed to the back of the ambulance. The kid looked up at him, his eyes glassy from booze or pain. Probably both.

"How's the nose?" Jake asked.

"How do you think? Hurts like a son of a bitch." The kid gave him a sullen glare. "Who are you?"

Jake flashed a generic badge. "I need you to tell me what happened."

"Well, there was this blonde, see? She was smoking hot, and Brian thought he had a chance with her, which just goes to show you how much he'd been drinking. Anyway, she hooked up with this other guy at the bar, and they looked like they were getting along just fine. But Brian didn't want to let it go. And I can't blame really blame Brian, either. I mean she was..." His eyes sort of drifted out of focus a little and Jake wondered if the EMT had given the kid a sedative or if he was just that drunk. Either way, it wouldn't be long before he passed out.

"She was hot?" Jake prompted.

The kid started and blinked, his eyes swimming back into focus. "Um yeah. *Real* hot. I mean, she was so hot she...she..."

"What about the guy she hooked up with? Was he from your school, too?"

"That guy? No way. He's too old. Thirty, maybe. He's the one who broke my nose, the fucker!" He glared up at Jake again. "I want to press charges."

"We'll get to that at the station. What happened next?"

"They were all cozy on the dance floor and then they were leaving. We told Brian to forget about it, but he wouldn't so we followed them outside. And it was a good thing, too, because she was trying to get away from the guy after all. But he wouldn't let her go. So she pushed him and that's when we jumped in to help her."

"You jumped the guy? How many of you?"

"Five. But he got away. And he broke my nose. He fought dirty!"

"You outnumbered the guy five to one but *he* was the one who fought dirty?"

"Hunh?"

"Never mind. What did he look like?"

"He was tall with blond hair. And he had a military tattoo on his arm."

Jake nodded. Getting the best of five attackers, the tattoo *and* picking up the hottest woman in the room? Yeah, that all added up to Fitz. "What happened after he broke your nose?"

"Brian and the rest of them kept fighting with him. And they would have won, too, but the lady needed us. Two other guys grabbed her and were dragging her to a van. We all ran to help her."

"Including the guy who punched you?"

"Yeah, him, too. He might be a dirty fighter, but he did try to help her get away from those guys."

Jake had no doubt that was true. Fitz would never stand idly by when a woman was in trouble.

"Besides, that guy wasn't anywhere near as scary as that big mutant fuck in the van. That ugly bastard shot Kenny!" The kid shook his head back and forth as if that would undo the awful action. "And then he shot one of his own guys! I'm telling you, man, that scarred-up dude was evil!"

"Scarred?" A chill ran down Jake's spine. Pruitt's right-hand man, Damon Maddox, had an unforgettably scarred face. And an unforgettably chilling criminal history. "What happened after he shot the two men?"

"I couldn't hear what they were all saying, but they talked and then they all got into the van."

The kid started groping around in his pockets. He pulled out a phone and tapped a few buttons. "Here," he said, thrusting the phone at Jake. I got picture of them getting into the van. Only the lady didn't actually *get* in. She was *dragged* in."

Jake took the phone and looked at the picture. It was skewed at an odd angle, so it didn't show very much of the interior of the van. It did show a guy in a black tee shirt and camo pants bracing his arms on the floor at the opening of the van as if he were about to vault into it. Fitz's head was in profile but it was enough for Jake to confirm his identity.

The blonde's face was contorted into a mask of horror, so Jake was going to have to take the kid's word on her level of hotness. A meaty arm held her around the waist while a beefy hand pointed a gun to her temple. The man's head was cut off in the picture, but judging by the breadth of his chest behind the woman, Jake was certain it was Maddox. "You didn't by any chance get the lady's name, did you?"

"Nah. She never even gave us the time of day. But if that horror-movie mutant hadn't shown up, she would have because we saved her from the other guy. He broke my nose! I'm glad I stole his fucking phone when it fell out of his pocket."

"*You've* got his phone? I'll take that, please. It's evidence." Jake held out his hand expectantly. The kid looked like he wanted to argue, but his eyes swam out of focus again. Jake started searching the kid's pockets.

"Hey!" he protested slowly. "You can't do that...you can't —" His chin hit his chest, and Jake gently guided the kid's torso toward the side of the ambulance. He found Fitz's phone and slid it into his own pocket. He quickly forwarded the abduction picture to his own phone before deleting the picture and the text from the kid's phone, which he then put back in the kid's pocket.

Jake glided away just as the EMT returned, followed by the detectives. He found Ian back over by the bar entrance. "Let's go."

They slipped back out the way they'd come and got back into their SUV. Jake relayed what he'd found out. "So it's pretty definite. Pruitt's got Fitz. The question is, who's the woman and what does she have to do with it?"

"I don't know. But I snapped a bunch of pictures of license plates to see if we can find out anything about who was here. One car really stood out, a Mercedes SL 550. It struck me as odd because it was the only car in that price range in the lot."

"Call it in to Tobie. She can look it up while we head back to the office." Jake started the ignition and then checked his mirrors as he reached to put the car in gear. "What the…"

"What?" Ian looked up from his phone.

"There's another Mercedes SL parked right behind us." The car was half in shadow and half in the faint arc of the street light. "There's a woman at the wheel."

"That blonde you were talking about?"

"I don't know. Let's go find out."

Ian hung back by the rear bumper of the SUV while Jake proceeded to the Mercedes. He quickly memorized the license plate before moving on to the driver's-side door. Sounds of the woman's quiet sobs drifted through the open window. Though blonde, her hair was platinum-colored and its buzz-cut style rivaled the work of any military barber. Her tears made a mess of her heavily made-up eyes and streaked black, blotchy lines down her thin face.

"Miss? Are you all right?"

"No! I can't find my cousin and that policeman won't let me in there to look for her. Something awful happened to her. I just know it!" She smacked the steering wheel. She looked back over her shoulder and glared at the officer directing traffic and blocking the entrance to the Steel Horse parking lot. She swiped the tears on her face, further smearing her mascara. "I don't want to, but I'm going to have to call my uncle."

"Do you have a picture of your cousin?"

Her head whipped back. "Are you a cop?" Hope glimmered in her gorgeous green eyes. She reached to the passenger seat and grabbed her purse. Yanking out a top-of-the-line cell phone, she quickly scrolled through some pictures. "Here." She thrust the phone up at him. "That's Erienne. Is she in there? She's not answering her phone."

The smiling woman in the picture showed a strong resemblance to the terrified woman in the van. Jake looked back into the woman's tear-streaked face, and his heart contracted a little. Dammit. Why did he have to be the one to deliver the bad news? "What's your name, ma'am?" he asked as he returned her phone.

"Kylie Stuart." She got out of the car and latched her fingers into his arm. "Please, where is Erienne? Is she all right?"

Jake took a deep breath. "I want you to look at a picture to confirm if it's your cousin. The woman in the picture is alive, but it still may be a bit difficult for you to see."

Her eyes widened, and her lips trembled. "Okay. Show me."

Her voice was steady when she spoke, and something about it jiggled a sense of familiarity in his brain. Exactly why, he couldn't say. He handed her his phone. The blood drained out of her face, eliminating the need for verbal confirmation.

"She's been kidnapped? Who's that man holding her? Is that Mordecai Fitzjames?"

Ian left his position by their SUV and strode over. "How do you know Fitz?" he growled.

"I don't. I've never met him. Erienne called me a little while ago and told me she was here with someone by that name."

"How long have they been dating?" Jake asked. Fitz was fairly open about hobbies and interests but played it very close to the vest whenever topics like families or girlfriends came up.

"They're not dating. She just met him tonight."

"How do you know that? Were you here when they met?"

"No," Kylie said. "Erienne left me a voicemail saying she was going through with her ridiculous plan and this Mordecai Fitzjames was the one she was going to use. I came here to stop her."

Jake raised an eyebrow. "What ridiculous plan?"

Kylie flushed pink. "I'm not at liberty to say."

"Are you kidding me? Your cousin's been kidnapped and you're going to keep your mouth shut?"

"No! It's just that…"

"Just that what? We don't have time for this crap. Tell me about the plan. Now."

She pulled herself up to her full height, which was about five feet four inches, and planted her hands on her hips. "You know, I don't think I like your tone. I want to talk to your boss. Who's in charge here?"

Jake and Ian exchanged a glance. Her eyes narrowed, then opened wide as her mouth formed a silent O. "My god!" she hissed. "You're not with the police, are you? Who the hell are you? What have you done with Erienne?" She backed up a step, pulling out her phone. "Stay away from me!"

Jake stepped forward and snatched the phone from her hand. She opened her mouth to scream, but he quickly snaked an arm around her waist and covered her mouth with his other hand. "Please don't do that. I'm sorry to frighten you like this. I'm not going to hurt you."

He nodded to Ian, who stepped forward and pulled out his wallet. Flipping it open, he showed her his Private Investigator's License as well as his OASIS Employee Identification Card. She examined each of them closely, and Jake took his hand from her mouth. "October Armstrong Security and Investigation Services? Never heard of them."

"We don't exactly advertise," Jake said.

"You can print anything off the internet these days. I'm going to need more than just a couple of ID cards."

"Like what?"

"Give me back my phone." Jake hesitated, and she twisted in his arms to roll her eyes at him. "I'm just going to call and verify you are who you say you are."

He wanted to ignore the request, but the fierce light of determination in her eyes told him he'd just lose more time. Precious time that Fitz, and most likely her cousin, too, didn't have. He handed her the phone. "Make it fast."

She glared at him but quickly punched in a number. "You really can let go of me now," she said as she waited for an answer.

"Oh, right." Jake dropped his arm, then immediately wanted to put it back. She was a pleasant armful. Plus the almond and vanilla scent wafting from her hair was really, really nice.

"Tanner? It's Kylie. Erienne is in trouble...She's been kidnapped...No, I'm safe. I'm with two men who claim they can help. Their names are Jake Hooper and..." She raised an eyebrow at Ian. "Your name?"

"Ian Westlake." He pulled out a business card, but she waved him off.

"And Ian Westlake. They claim to be with an organization called October Armstrong Security and Investigation Services...You have? Okay, I'll hold." She looked at both of them. "Tanner's heard of your company. He's checking with your boss to verify you work there and you're where you're supposed to be right now."

"Peachy." Jake was brutally aware of minutes ticking by.

"Who's Tanner?" Ian asked.

"Just a guy who gets things done."

Jake's phone beeped, and Tobie's name flashed on the readout. "Tanner Montgomery is calling, wanting info on the two of you. What's this about a kidnapping? Why am I hearing about it from Tanner instead of you?"

"You know this Tanner guy?"

"Answer the question."

"There hasn't been time to call you. We just found out about it ourselves. We're talking to someone who may have important information. She's the one who contacted Tanner. Go ahead and tell him what he needs so she'll talk."

"All right. But put me on speaker."

"Okay." He pressed the appropriate button.

Kylie listened for a minute and then nodded. She lowered her phone and pressed the speaker button. "I'm putting Tanner on speaker, too."

"*Now* will you tell us about your cousin's mysterious plan and what it has to do with Fitz?"

She chewed her delicate lower lip a little. "I can't. It's private. But I can tell you it wasn't illegal and it wasn't going to hurt him or anyone else."

"Kylie, time is important," a deep voice said from her phone.

"I'm not going to tell you the plan, either, Tanner, so you can just forget it."

"Jake, we've got to move," Ian said.

"I know. Miss Stuart, please—"

"I said forget it and I meant it." She sighed. "Look, other than putting Erienne in the wrong place at the wrong time, I'm absolutely sure her plan had nothing to do with what's happened."

Jake recognized the determined glint in her eye. He'd

seen it countless times in any one of his sisters' eyes when they refused to break the sacred silence of sisterhood. He knew from experience there would be no changing her mind. Which meant she was probably right about the secret plan not being relevant to the situation. Kylie had seen the picture; she knew her cousin was in trouble. He had no doubt her desire to help Erienne was genuine.

"Who's Mordecai Fitzjames?" she asked.

"He works for me," Tobie said.

"Well, I'm sure he's the one that got Erienne into this mess. Tanner, we have to call Uncle Marcus."

"I'm taking care of that."

"Jake, I want you and Ian to get back to the office immediately," Tobie said.

"I'm coming, too," Kylie said.

Jake shook his head. "You should go home."

"But I want to help. I can't just sit by the phone."

"Kylie, I'm sending one of my guys to meet you," Tanner said. "He should be there shortly. He'll follow you to the estate, and I want you to stay there. Marcus will be worried sick. He needs you."

"But Erienne needs me, too." Her voice cracked.

Jake met her tear-filled gaze, not at all sure why it was tearing him apart inside. She wasn't the first woman he'd ever seen cry. But something in that sense of familiarity he had about her voice made her tears heart-rending to him. "I promise we will do everything we can. We will get her back." He'd move heaven and earth to keep that promise.

Kylie bit her lip but nodded.

"Tobie, we'll wait here until Tanner's man arrives. Then we'll head back."

"Okay."

"I'll be at your office soon, too," Tanner said.

"That won't be necessary," Tobie responded. "We've got it under control. We'll keep you informed."

"I'm not asking. I'll see you all there." Tanner disconnected.

Tobie muttered something unintelligible as she, too, hung up.

"What's that about?" Ian asked.

Jake shrugged. "Beats me."

"I don't care," Kylie said. "Just bring Erienne home safe."

CHAPTER FIVE

THE VAN PULLED into the underground garage of the Beau Monde, one of Manhattan's most prestigious apartment buildings, where Dave Pruitt owned the penthouse. Fitz had been here as Tommy's guest for a few of the private parties Dave liked to throw for some of his most loyal cronies and henchmen. The guest list was very select, with trust and an acute sense of discretion being the strongest prerequisites for attendance. While drugs were allowed at these events, abuse of them was not. Reckless behavior was a surefire way to preclude any future invitations, and could very likely provoke worse and far more painful sanctions.

Tommy had once told Fitz that the penthouse was one of his brother's most prized possessions. The Pruitts had grown up in a roach- and rat-infested building in one of the city's worst neighborhoods. "Someday we'll live like kings" had been Dave's favorite mantra. Now that he had his palatial home, he never wanted to give the authorities the slightest provocation to invade his sanctuary with warrants blazing.

"Don't bother trying anything," Maddox said as they

pulled into a parking space. "Mr. Pruitt pays the guards here a good deal of money to look the other way whenever any of his friends and associates arrive."

Dammit! Fitz squelched his idea of provoking a struggle in front of the security cameras, prompting the staff to investigate and, hopefully, call the police. Maddox might look like a simple Neanderthal, but Fitz knew better. The man was as sharp as he was ruthless. Obvious plans would not get by him. Most subtle ones wouldn't either.

They got out of the van, and Fitz looked to see how Erienne was coping with the situation. Not good. Her normally pale blue eyes, wide with terror, appeared almost sapphire against her bone-white complexion, and her whole body shook as silent tears streamed down her cheeks. Maddox held her upper arm while Cooney stood on her other side, glaring at her with swollen, leaking red eyes.

Fitz longed to comfort her, but he couldn't. During the drive into the city he'd formulated a plan, and in order for it to work he couldn't let Maddox and the other goons know he had her best interests at heart. Maddox might not have recognized her father's name, but Fitz had, and he was pretty sure Dave Pruitt would know it, too.

They piled into the penthouse private elevator, its opulent appointments doing nothing to alleviate the grimness of the situation. The doors opened to an even more sumptuous foyer. It rankled Fitz to see the kind of luxury Pruitt surrounded himself with when the man's every action either bankrupted others or committed them to a life of drug-addicted squalor.

The door to the penthouse opened, revealing an extraordinarily voluptuous young woman wearing a Frederick's of Hollywood version of a French maid's outfit, complete with a feather duster in her hand. She scooted back on her six-inch heels and waved them inside, not batting an eye at Erienne's disheveled appearance and terrified expression. Fitz didn't recognize the maid from his previous visits, but obviously she'd been trained not to ask questions or show any kind of emotion.

Maddox led them through a hallway into a sunken living room with a spectacular view of the Manhattan skyline across Central Park, the kind of view that only the mega-rich could afford. Dark wood moldings, a high ceiling, and perfectly placed elegant furniture further emphasized that no expense had been spared in the effort to convey wealth, stature, and respect, all things Dave Pruitt craved like a drug.

The effect was ruined, though, by the presence of another French maid-bedecked young woman fluffing the pillows of the large sofa. Fitz did recognize this one. Her name was Anita, and with Dave's approval, she'd paid special attention to Fitz the last time he was here. That was another of the perks of Dave's parties — plenty of women to go around.

Anita ignored their arrival as she finished with the pillows and picked up her own feather duster. As she bent at the waist to dust the coffee table, her skirt hiked up enough to reveal she wore only garters and a thong beneath it. The tackiness of her barely-there attire combined with her overly ripe assets instantly reduced the exquisitely appointed room to nothing more than a cheap bordello.

"Fitzpatrick! How nice to see you!"

Dave Pruitt stood at a side entrance to the room, looking like every cliché from an old drug lord movie. Not very tall, he wore crimson silk pajama bottoms beneath a gold silk robe, trimmed in black and sashed loosely about his waist. The top of the robe gaped open, revealing an absurdly hairy chest. This forestation of man-fur was broken by several large gold medallions hanging from thick gold chains around his neck. He held a half-smoked cigar between two fingers. All that was missing from the picture was Dave whining, "Say hello to my little friend."

With a cheery smile on his face, as if he were having the best day of his life rather than grieving the loss of a beloved brother, Pruitt skipped down the two steps into the room and approached them, slapping Anita's ass as he passed her. She started but quickly recovered with a coquettish little laugh. He ignored her and continued his trek across the large room. Stopping directly in front of Fitz, Pruitt clamped the cigar between his teeth and delivered a savage punch to Fitz's stomach.

"That's for Tommy. Consider it a down payment. You can bet your ass that debt will be paid off in full before the sun comes up."

Fitz doubled over from the force of the blow. For all that Dave Pruitt barely topped out at five foot eight, he was a wiry collection of muscles. Erienne let out a keening little moan, reminding Fitz it wasn't just his own skin at risk here. He needed to talk fast if he was going to get them both out of this penthouse alive. "Mr. Pruitt, listen, it wasn't me who turned Tommy in," he wheezed.

"Bullshit."

"No, it's true. It was Branson." Keith Branson, an agent with the ATF, had been posing as an arms buyer and setting up a sting operation. When the gun bust that should have seen both of the Pruitt brothers behind bars went bad, Branson had been killed in the line of duty. But Branson's cover story was still intact. It sucked that he couldn't be recognized for his service, but it had made sense to keep his real identity under wraps until the Pruitts had been prosecuted.

"Very convenient to blame the dead guy, Fitzpatrick." Dave snapped his fingers. Anita abandoned her dusting and went over to the elegant bar in the corner of the room. "Why the hell should I believe you? You got away scot-free and now my baby brother is dead."

Dave went to the sofa and sat down. "C'mon, Fitzpatrick, dazzle me with some more bullshit. I could use a few laughs before we get down to the business of making your last few hours on earth the most miserable, excruciating hours you've ever experienced."

Anita brought him a drink in a heavy crystal tumbler. She set it on the coffee table, but before she could move away, Dave snaked a hand around one of her legs and gave her a firm squeeze on the inside of her thigh.

"Branson must have talked to the cops," Fitz said. "He was the only one who knew we were all going to be at the meeting."

Dave released Anita's thigh and sipped his drink. "You knew."

"But I didn't know where the meet was going to be. Tommy kept that information to himself right up until the very last minute. He said you taught him that."

For a moment it looked as if Pruitt would break down in tears, but he recovered quickly. "Tommy always was a smart kid. At least as far as following instructions went." He stared at Fitz over the rim of his glass. "But none of that explains why the cops didn't arrest you. They got everyone else."

"I thought something was off as soon as I walked in, so I stayed near the door. When things went bad, I slipped out and hid behind a dumpster. Once the gunfire started, it was easy to sneak away."

"You shouldn't have left my brother. You should have taken Tommy with you."

"I tried to warn him, but there wasn't enough time. He pulled his gun and started firing right away." This much was true, at least. Both Pruitt brothers seemed to thrive on violence. Tommy was dead, but Fitz couldn't wait to see a law library's worth of books thrown at Dave for Branson's murder.

"That's all very interesting, but I'm not buying it. You promised that gun deal would go smoothly, and it was anything but. You were the one who introduced Tommy to Branson. And, like I said earlier, you were the only one to walk away. If it happened like you say, why did you disappear? Why didn't you come to me?"

"I panicked. I didn't want to get blamed. I knew how it was going to look to you."

Dave didn't respond. He sat back, sipping his drink and looking out at the magnificent view of Central Park, the glow of the streetlamps twinkling among the trees like holiday lights. "Who's the blonde?" he asked finally.

Maddox pulled Erienne forward. "Her name's Erienne Stuart. She has an address in Greenwich and she says her daddy will pay anything to get her back. His name is Marcus Stuart."

Pruitt's attention perked up, just as Fitz suspected it would.

"Did you say *Marcus* Stuart?" Pruitt walked to Erienne and grabbed her face by the chin, examining her closely as if searching for a family resemblance.

Erienne's eyes were practically bugging out of her head. "Please," she whined. "It's true. My father will pay anything. Just don't hurt me."

"Shut up," Pruitt said, dropping his hand from her face. "What's she doing here?" he asked Maddox.

"She and Fitzpatrick here were pretty cozy at the bar.

And he sure as hell was anxious for us to leave her behind. Couldn't do that, though. She'd seen too much. Not to mention I thought you might like to add her to the fun and games you have planned. He seems mighty fond of her. Bet it would break his heart to see you slice a few pieces off her before you went to work on him."

Fitz wouldn't have thought it possible, but Erienne blanched even whiter. "That's a bad idea, Mr. Pruitt," he said.

Pruitt glared at him. "Really? I don't think so. Sounds like it could be fun."

"You know why. You know who her father is. He's a powerful man."

"Yeah, I know who he is. But I'm not afraid of him. And I don't need his money." Dave folded his arms and tilted his head, but Fitz wasn't buying the casual, confident stance. Pruitt had clawed his way out of the gutter, landing himself here in one of the city's most exclusive buildings, but it wasn't enough. Fitz knew Pruitt still wanted the respect of men like Marcus Stuart, far more than he would ever admit to anyone.

Aside from all of his illegal enterprises — drugs, guns, prostitution — Pruitt went out of his way to establish several legitimate business ventures. Not only were they a cover to throw law enforcement off his trail, they were an attempt to prove to himself he was just as good as anyone else living at this posh address. What a bitter way to live, wanting their respect and hating them for their disdain at the same time, because Pruitt had to know the old-money set would always think of him as a street hood.

It was a hatred that made the man unstable, and Fitz would have to play to it very carefully.

"Yeah, I don't need her father's money," Pruitt continued.

"So maybe I get a bonus tonight. I get to beat you to death, and when I want to rest my fists for a minute, I can slice a little bit out of your rich-girl squeeze here." He pulled a switchblade from the pocket of his robe as Maddox grabbed Erienne and held both of her arms behind her back. "It'll drive you fucking insane as I cut her up a little, make her scream—"

"You don't want to do that." Fitz spoke quickly. Pruitt was warming up to his terrifying ideas of torture.

Pruitt whirled to face him, his face contorting into a mask of rage. "Why the hell not? My little brother is dead because of you! All kinds of payback are coming your way. Starting with making sure your sweet little girlfriend here isn't so pretty anymore." He turned back to Erienne.

"She's not my girlfriend!"

Maddox laughed. "Who are you trying to kid? Cooney saw you in the bar. Said you two were all over each other."

"I've been conning her to get to her father. I swear, she's not my girlfriend. She's nothing more to me than a means to an end." A flash of relief blasted through him as Pruitt lowered his knife.

"A means to what end?"

"I wanted her to introduce me to her old man."

"What's her old man to you?"

Fitz said nothing, cautiously thinking over his next words. If he couldn't sell this lie, he and Erienne would both be dead by morning.

"Well?" Pruitt waved the knife back and forth in front of Fitz's nose. "I'm waiting, Fitzpatrick. Tell me."

"It's personal."

Pruitt and Maddox both burst out laughing. "Personal?" Pruitt laughed even harder. "Do you think I give a shit if it's personal? I'm ready to slit your fucking throat and you're worried about keeping a secret? Fine, have it your way. But if you're not going to share your secret, then you are going to share your girlfriend." He nodded back at Maddox, Cooney, and the others. "With all of us." He leaned in close to Fitz's face. "And after that, the real games will begin. So, what's it gonna be?"

Again Fitz held his tongue, although the stark raving terror on Erienne's tear-streaked face ripped his heart out. "Fitz, please! Tell him what he wants. I want to go home!"

"Aw, hear that? She wants to go home." Pruitt stepped back to her. "Maybe I'll just send her back to her daddy in little pieces. What do you think?"

"No!" Erienne cried. She tried to pull away, but Maddox held her tight. "Fitz!"

Pruitt grabbed her by the hair and yanked her head back. With a quick slash, he hacked off a slender length of her hair and waved it front of Fitz's nose. "That's your one and only warning shot. Tell me why you wanted to meet her old man or I start cutting you both." He pressed the knife to Erienne's throat, bringing forth a tiny bead of blood. She shook so hard Fitz was afraid she'd slice her own neck by accident.

"All right, leave her alone. None of this works if she's hurt."

"None of what works?" Pruitt kept the knife exactly where it was.

"Marcus Stuart killed my father."

Erienne's eyes went wide. "That's a lie! My father never killed anyone."

"You wouldn't know anything about it, you stupid, spoiled brat," Fitz snarled at her, hoping to shock her back into silence before she did something really stupid, like reveal the fact that she'd only met him a couple of hours ago.

"I've been working my way into her life," he went on. "She's been looking for a bad boy to piss off her daddy and get his attention. It was the perfect opportunity. I was going to get her to give me a job at her father's company. Hell, I thought maybe I'd even marry her. The point being to get my hands on the money that should have been my father's, and therefore mine. Once I had that, then I was planning to kill him."

Pruitt looked at him with a skeptical smirk. "That's a mighty big con."

"I could have done it. Like Maddox said, your boy Cooney was in the bar. He can tell you how she was all over me, eating out of the palm of my hand. Hell, she probably already picked out china patterns."

"Well, it doesn't matter." Pruitt jerked his head at Erienne. "She's onto it now. Besides, Tommy is still dead and it's still all your fault. So I really don't give a shit what revenge you were planning."

"It wasn't my fault your brother got pinched. He could have gotten away with me if he hadn't been so intent on shooting up the place. I'm sorry Tommy got shanked. I really am. But cutting her won't bring him back. And I can still get my revenge. But only if she's not hurt."

"I told you, I don't give a shit about your revenge. Only mine."

"But my revenge can put a lot of money in your pocket, too."

Fitz's stomach unclenched a sliver as Dave stepped back from Erienne. "Really? How do you figure that? And if I don't like what I hear, the next time you see this it will be cutting off her right nipple." He waved the switchblade toward Fitz before closing it and putting it in his pocket. "So make it good."

"It's no secret her father is a well-connected business-man, even if your best goons don't know who he is." He nodded his head at Maddox, earning himself a glare of hatred from the scarred face. Fitz didn't care. All the while he'd been working undercover he'd made it clear he didn't like Maddox. That was for authenticity. Making it look like he wanted to muscle Pruitt's right-hand man out of the oper-ation made Fitz look more like an opportunistic snake. Now more than ever, he needed to keep that image going. "Marcus Stuart may be a ruthless businessman, but he does appear to care a great deal about his daughter. He's gone to great lengths to keep her out of the public eye. I bet you didn't even know she existed until tonight. What does that tell you?"

"You tell me, wiseass."

"That Marcus Stuart protects his own. I did a lot of research on this before I even thought about approaching her. I paid a computer hacker to find out everything he could about their relationship. The bastard dotes on her. I knew if I could reel her into a relationship with me, hope-fully even knock her up, he'd have to accept me or risk losing her."

"Or he could have you squashed like a bug. His kind of money buys that sort of thing all the time."

"Not if it would make her unhappy." Fitz glanced back at Erienne before giving Pruitt a macho grin. "Trust me, I was making her *very* happy to be with me."

"Spare me," Pruitt said with a roll of his eyes. "I gotta say, so far you're not wowing me with anything."

"Well, it turns out Marcus's little girl isn't just a pretty face. She's got a brain and is going to run his empire someday. Not to mention she stands to inherit billions in cash and stocks when Marcus finally takes a dirt nap."

"So?"

"So she understands how important public image is to a large, publicly traded company like Stuart Enterprises. And in light of their recent troubles…"

A look of recognition dawned across Pruitt's face. "That's right. It was Stuart's company that was making headlines a few months ago. One of the executives raided the pension fund."

"Exactly," Fitz said. "A man named Kevin Stevens, the chief financial officer."

"Yeah, and Marcus fired his ass and then replaced every nickel out of his own pocket. Mr. Magnanimous Big Shot," Pruitt sneered.

"But Stevens still accused him of being in on it. He said her old man encouraged accounting fraud to keep the stock price high. The SEC and FBI are still investigating it all, aren't they, Erienne?"

Her pale cheeks blossomed with angry red blotches, but she kept her mouth shut, and Fitz plowed on before she could speak up and say something that would give the game away. "The public is already disenchanted with corporations screwing the little guy. What do you think will happen if a murder accusation gets thrown into the mix?"

"The stock price will drop like a stone," Pruitt said. "I still don't see what that does for me."

"I've got hard proof Marcus Stuart murdered my father. So in order to keep the company's stock out of the toilet, and keep himself out of jail, we insist that Stuart put you on the board of directors for the company. You'll be right on the front lines to get all sorts of insider trading information."

"A board member, huh?" A greedy glimmer grew in

Pruitt's eyes, and a matching glimmer of hope grew in Fitz's heart. Money alone wouldn't have tempted Pruitt, but the chance at being a board member of a Fortune 100 company? That was an opportunity the man would not dismiss so easily.

"What kind of proof do you have?" Pruitt asked.

"Sorry. That I'm not willing to share. You and I need to come to some sort of an understanding."

"Such as?"

"Such as I don't want to be looking over my shoulder every day for the rest of my life. I get you in on this deal, you stop trying to kill me."

Pruitt looked confused. "What's to stop me from killing you after I'm on the board?"

"The fact that you need me alive to stay on it. I'm never going to give you the proof I have on her father directly. That's just writing my own death sentence. Marcus Stuart will know I'm the only one with the information. And I'll also make sure he knows that if I'm dead there will be no reason to keep you on the board. He'll have you replaced before you even know you've been kicked off."

"Then why should I agree to this? If he killed your father, why wouldn't he just kill you, too? Then *I* don't get to kill you, *and* I don't get to be on the board. Pretty sucky deal for me."

"He won't kill me. I've already put procedures in place that in the event of my death, the proof goes public. I did that a long time ago in case I died before I could get close to him or his daughter." Fitz folded his arms. "So you see, both of you will need to make sure I stay alive."

Pruitt glared at him, greed and revenge waging a battle across his face. "I'll think about it," he said finally. "In the meantime, the two of you will continue to be my guests.

Maddox, show Fitzpatrick to his room. Keep someone watching him at all times." He turned to Anita, who'd been continually applying her feather duster around the immaculate room, and snapped his fingers at her. "Ms. Stuart will be staying with me. Take her to get cleaned up and give her something...appropriate to wear."

CHAPTER SIX

"No! The deal's off if you touch her."

"I thought you said she wasn't your girlfriend," Maddox injected himself into the conversation. "You sure keep acting like she's more important to you than you claim she is." He faced his employer. "I think he's lying about their relationship. He was hell-bent on getting us to leave her behind when we were at the Steel Horse. And every single thing he's said is all about protecting her."

"Mind your own business, buttlicker," Fitz snapped.

Maddox whipped his head back to him with narrowed eyes. Fitz would have given anything to be able to punch the sleazy, twisted fuck in the face. But now was not the time. "I've explained why I was with her. Her father murdered mine. And since this whole kidnapping scheme of yours has put an end to my plans to kill him, I'm going to have to take my revenge in other ways. The money angle is one, and you're getting access to that. His daughter is another. She belongs to me."

"You're not calling the shots here, Fitzpatrick." Pruitt

grabbed Erienne by the arm, pulling her away from Maddox. "If I want her, she's mine."

"Then take her. And kill me. But go ahead and forget about ever getting on the board of a prestigious company like Stuart Enterprises. Because if you take this away from me, take *her* away from me, there's no way in hell I'll help you with any of that. I've been waiting fifteen years for this opportunity, and I'm not giving it up to you just so you can scratch a momentary itch."

Maddox stepped forward with an arm raised, and Fitz braced himself for a fight. He was done taking shit from this mutant. "Bring it, asshole."

"Maddox, knock it off," Pruitt barked.

The big man dropped his arm. "Whatever you say, boss," he muttered. His eyes locked onto Fitz's, the promise of vengeance unmistakable. Fitz couldn't wait to put this jerk behind bars.

He turned back to Pruitt. "What's it going to be? A night with her or a seat on the board?"

Pruitt didn't even stop to think this time. "Fine. Take her. But neither of you are leaving here until the arrangements have been made."

He shoved Erienne at Fitz. She stumbled into his arms but bolted back from him as soon as she regained her footing. "Stay away from me!" she screeched.

Pruitt, Maddox, Cooney, and the other two jokers in the room laughed long and loud. "You two have fun," Pruitt said when he composed himself. "Maddox, lock them in the guest suite. Meet me in my office when you're done. I have another errand for you. Anita, go find that new maid and both of you wait for me in my room. I'll be there after I make a few phone calls. I need to talk to Buzz."

"Yes, sir." Anita actually curtsied before she hustled out of the room. Fitz barely stopped himself from shaking his head. Did the man really think this was how the upper-crust wealthy behaved, or was he just indulging in a teenage fantasy?

Fitz didn't have the time or the inclination to try and figure it out as he grabbed Erienne's arm and towed her along after Maddox, Cooney and the other two falling in step behind them. It wouldn't be long before Pruitt figured out everything Fitz had said was total bullshit. At best, he had a few hours to figure out a plan to escape.

If he didn't, they were both dead.

BUZZ KRUGER JOTTED DOWN the license plate numbers of the silver Mercedes and the SUV belonging to the two men talking to the crying woman. He had no idea who any of them were, but he was pretty sure all of them were related to what happened at the bar in one way or another. When Pruitt sent him with Maddox and Cooney, the plan had been to split up. Fitzpatrick had never met Buzz or Cooney before, so they'd been the point men inside the bar, along with one of the other men Pruitt sent along, the one that ultimately got shot. Buzz never knew that poor bastard's name.

Unfortunately, Fitzpatrick caught on to the fact that Buzz and the others were watching him almost right away. Impressive. If Buzz had been the one with an armful of gorgeous blonde on the pool table, he probably wouldn't have noticed a nuclear blast.

But Fitzpatrick *had* noticed. It didn't help that Buzz's hornet tattoo made him stand out, even in a place like the Steel Horse where more patrons were inked than not. So

Buzz hit on the first girl he could, some spacey chick who swore she could foresee the future in his palm. He ditched her as soon as it looked like Fitz and the blonde were leaving and went outside to wait in his car while Maddox and Cooney did their thing.

When they grabbed the woman and started shooting, Buzz ducked down in his car and waited until the van had torn down the road. While everyone crowded around the injured men, Buzz drove out of the lot and parked in a dark corner of the strip mall across the road to observe the proceedings. Being a known associate of Dave Pruitt's, Buzz figured the man wouldn't appreciate it if he got picked up by the police.

His phone rang and he knew without looking it was his boss. "What's going on there?" As usual, the man wasted no time on pleasantries. "Are the police going to be a problem?"

"Not as far as I can tell," Buzz answered. "Maddox and the rest of them got away clean. But some other guys showed up who might be undercover cops. And they're talking to a woman with a flashy Mercedes. I've got their license plate numbers." He rattled them off.

Computer keys clicked on the other end of the line. "Well, well."

"Who are they?" Buzz asked. "Cops?"

"No. Private detectives."

"What could they want?"

"Nothing for you to worry about."

"So Fitzpatrick is definitely a cop?" Buzz hadn't been sure, but Pruitt had ranted as much ever since his brother was shanked to death.

"It doesn't matter now. You've done all you can do for me there. Take off, and don't let anyone see you. I'll be in touch when I need you again."

The call ended, and Buzz tossed his phone on the passenger seat in disgust. He hated the dismissive way his boss talked to him. But the man paid well, and Buzz knew without a doubt he never wanted to get on the bastard's bad side. He almost felt sorry for Fitzpatrick.

"Better him than me," he muttered with a shrug. He started his car and headed for his girlfriend's house. At least the rest of his night wouldn't be a total waste.

ERIENNE WAS SCARED. No, make that terrified. At her father's insistence, she and Kylie had taken kidnap survival classes over the years, but they'd focused on cooperating with the kidnappers until the ransom was paid — her father had always been clear he would pay any ransom. This, however, wasn't a scenario they'd covered.

Instead of money, they wanted to blackmail her and her father to put a criminal on the board while she became the plaything of a revenge-driven hood. She couldn't let them do it, couldn't let them destroy everything her father had worked so hard for, nor let someone use her body for their own twisted ends.

Anger bubbled up beneath her terror. The lies Fitz spewed had turned that homicidal maniac Pruitt away from the idea of slicing her to pieces, so she'd kept her mouth shut. But she had longed to defend her father, tell all these vermin that he'd had nothing to do with the theft of the pension funds and that Kevin Stevens was lying through his teeth in an effort to save his own skin. The possibility that Fitz was lying to save them both niggled at her thoughts, but his obvious association with these criminals obliterated her ability to trust him. If an opportunity for escape presented itself, she was taking it, with or without Fitz. Preferably without.

Her wrath woke her brain, and snippets from her classes came back to her. Her instructors had told her to pay attention to her surroundings so she could give helpful information to the authorities when she was released. Now, she did so in order to find her own way out. She'd been in several Manhattan penthouses before for social engagements of one kind or another. And her father owned one just a few blocks from here, although she rarely went there. They usually had at least two entry points — the front door, and then a service entrance for the staff and deliveries, the latter usually located in or just off the kitchen.

With no idea where the kitchen was, she would focus her efforts on going out the front door. But with so many of Pruitt's thugs around, she didn't like her odds.

They stopped at a door at the end of the hall. "In here," Maddox said, pushing the door open and walking in.

Fitz followed him, but Erienne stood back. Pruitt had instructed they be housed together, but Erienne had no intention of spending the night in the same room as Fitz. She supposed it was possible Fitz had made up everything he'd told Pruitt to talk his way out of being beaten to death, but the fact remained that he was a part of Pruitt and the rest of these cretins. "I'm not staying with him." Her voice shook a little, but it was strong enough.

Not that it mattered. "Get in there," Cooney snarled, shoving her from behind.

She stumbled forward and would have fallen flat on her face if Fitz hadn't reached out and caught her. "Let go of me!" she hissed.

"Whatever you want, princess." He set her on her feet none too gently. "We'll get to what I want in a few minutes."

"Like hell!" She wrenched her arm away from his grasp and stepped away from him.

Cooney stepped forward to seize her arm. "Looks like she wants no part of you anymore, Fitzpatrick, so I'll take her. She still owes me big time for the mace. I can take it out in trade."

"No!" Fitz stepped in front of her. "She's mine. Nobody touches her but me."

Cooney glared at Fitz, and Erienne's terror returned as she saw the utter rage in Cooney's reddened eyes. If he took her, he would hurt her. She knew that in her soul. Fitz might be slime, but she didn't think he was vicious, and that made all the difference. She stepped away from Cooney "You know what? I'll stay here."

Fitz gave Cooney one of those patented male macho *I got her, you didn't* looks, and Cooney twisted his face into an angry scowl. "You're gonna regret that choice, bitch," Cooney sneered in a tone that more than confirmed his everlasting hatred.

She shuddered inside, praying this animal would never have the opportunity to get her alone.

Maddox smacked Cooney on the shoulder. "Not now. I'm sure once Fitzpatrick is tired of her, Pruitt will let you spend some time with her." He followed Cooney into the hall before turning back and grabbing the doorknob. "Hope you two enjoy your stay. Sleep tight," he mocked as he pulled the door closed, the click of its lock as loud as a gunshot.

Erienne whirled to face Fitz. "You keep your hands off me or I'll...I'll..."

"Relax, princess, we'll have time for that later. All night, in fact."

"Don't even think about it." Erienne dug deep for this

bravado. She really had no way to stop him if he chose to force himself on her. Ice formed in the pit of her stomach at the idea of her very first sexual experience being rape. She bit her bottom lip to stop its trembling, even as first one tear, then another rolled down her face.

Fitz looked at her with a lazy scowl as he peeled off his shirt. He went into the adjoining bathroom and shut the door. Erienne examined the bedroom doorknob, but she had no idea how to pick a lock. She hurried to the window, hoping for a fire escape. Of course not.

They were too high up, obviously, for her to climb out, nor would there be any chance of signaling anyone down on the street for help. And the window faced Central Park, so there were no other buildings facing her. No help there.

The bathroom door opened. "Erienne. Come here."

Wrapping her arms tightly around herself, she refused to face him. She stared out across the park, her tears falling freely now, turning the lights of the city into something that looked like blurry fairy lights.

"Erienne." His voice sounded sterner now, and icy shards of fear lanced through her. Try as she might, she could no longer stop herself from shaking. This was it, and she had no way out.

She spun to face him as he approached, raising her hands in front of her, ready to fight him with every ounce of strength she possessed. He crossed the room swiftly, easily dodging her hands and grabbing her wrists. She dug her feet into the rug and pulled back, but her Jimmy Choos just weren't designed for an extended session of hand-to-hand combat. He easily towed her across the room.

"Come on," he snarled. "I'd be very surprised if Pruitt didn't have the bedroom bugged. But he can suck it. I'm not doing this with an audience listening in." They reached the bathroom, and Fitz shoved her in and slammed the door.

She flung her arms out to stop the momentum, avoiding slamming her head into the mirror as she caught herself on the sink vanity. She barely had time to straighten up before he was on her. He spun her to face him and covered her mouth with his, muffling her screams. His arms whipped around her, pinning her arms to her sides.

Gone was the gentle lover from the Steel Horse. Instead he was a predator, punishing and lethal. He backed up, pulling her with him until his back was against the stall door of the shower. Steam filled the room, and she was oddly aware of her dress sticking to her thighs.

One of his arms slipped up her back and his hand cupped the back of her head, firmly holding it in place as he broke the punishing kiss and quickly pressed his lips to her ear. "Try not to worry," he whispered, "I'm not going to hurt you."

She struggled to free her arms and jerk her head away from him. "Let me go!" she screeched. He didn't, his hold on her like iron.

He laughed aloud. "Fight all you want, princess. Works for me."

"You're a sick maniac! Let me go!" She finally managed to wiggle one arm up from her side and she made a feeble attempt to slap his face.

He laughed again, dodging her hand easily, before pressing his lips back to her ear. "Erienne, listen to me!" he hissed urgently against her ear. "I'm not going to hurt you, I promise. But they have to think I will or we're *both* dead. Now listen!"

Something of his words penetrated her terror-induced

fury. She ceased struggling but she couldn't stop shaking. "Please," she whimpered. "Just let me go."

"I can't, not yet. I couldn't find any evidence of it, but there's a good chance this room is bugged, too. Maybe even a hidden camera." He broke off long enough to quickly shuck off his pants before seizing her lips in another punishing kiss. She squealed and struggled and tried going for his eye with her free hand. He blocked her effortlessly, as if he knew every possible attack she might make and was more than ready to counter each one.

"Stop it!" she cried when he tore his lips away.

"I'm sorry," he whispered against her ear, "but they have to think it's real." His hand slid up her back and began sliding down the zipper of her dress.

"No! Stop it!"

He ignored her and kept pulling. This was it. No matter what he'd been saying about not hurting her, he was going to strip her clothes away and rape her. And if anything he was muttering was to be believed, Pruitt and his filthy thugs were going to be listening, maybe even watching. She swallowed back the urge to vomit.

"Get in the shower," he said aloud. "Now!" His voice rose, but his eyes through the misty steam in the bathroom looked gentle and pleading. "I'm sorry," he mouthed silently, and he jerked her dress from her shoulders and whisked it down her body. It pooled at her feet before she could even register what had happened.

The steam had grown thick and hot, coating her body with perspiration. The lacy bra and panties she'd chosen so carefully with seduction in mind were now sheer and plastered to her damp skin, hiding nothing from his gaze. She crossed her arms over her chest and bolted for the door of the bathroom. He caught her easily, wrapping an arm around her waist and hauling her back against his chest.

"No, no, no, no, no," she keened as he turned her around and forced her through the door of the shower.

It was a huge space, and once inside it she realized it wasn't only a shower but also a large sauna. He shut the door and pressed her up against the glass, pinning her there with his big body. His hands took each of her wrists and pressed her palms against the glass. The steam enveloped them completely, and although she could hear shower water running nearby, she couldn't see it. She struggled to free herself, but the heat of the steam combined with her terror and exhaustion made it a losing battle. A wretched sob escaped her.

"Shhh," he whispered, "everything is going to be fine." He rubbed his cheek up and down against her face and neck. Though he still held her firmly, his thumbs were making slow circles on the inside of her wrists. He pressed a soft kiss to her temple.

"Erienne, we don't have much time. I need you to really listen to me. I'm not going to hurt you." He made no other moves, no attempt to remove any more of her clothes. Nor his own. He just stood there, murmuring assurances and gently caressing her face and wrists.

Gradually, her sobs decreased and he spoke again, his voice urgent. "I'm going to get you out of this, you have to trust me." He began moving his body up and down her back, pressing her even more tightly against the opaque glass of the stall. "I'm sorry to do this. I don't think there's a camera in here, but I can't be sure. So this has to look good, just in case."

Erienne could barely see anything with all the steam, but she could imagine what their silhouettes must look like they were doing to anyone on the other side of the glass. Visions of Maddox and Cooney watching them onscreen filled her head, and another wave of nausea swept through her.

"Please stop," she choked. To her surprise, he stepped back and slipped his hands to her shoulders, turning her to face him. The tenderness in his gaze gave her a small measure of relief. He might be a liar and a criminal, but he wasn't a rapist. Not that that made trusting Fitz any easier. He was the one Pruitt had been after in the first place.

Her skepticism must have been evident on her face. "Erienne, you are going to have to accept that I am the lesser of two evils here."

"Which still makes you evil."

"Fair enough. But do you really think you are going to get out of this mess on your own?"

She had no answer for that, other than the blazing determination in her heart to find a way out as soon as she could.

He sighed and stepped back. "Take a shower. It will help you feel better."

"I'm not showering with you!" she hissed.

He rolled his eyes. "That's not what I meant." He took her arm, gently this time, and pulled her deeper into the sauna. A tiled partial wall came into view through the steam, with an entry way to one side. He steered her toward it. "That's the shower. I'll stay on this side of the wall. There's a bathrobe hanging on a hook in there, so you can put that on when you're done." He released her arm with a gentle nudge. "Go on. I'll wait here. No one will come in."

She scurried around the other side of the wall. She didn't really care about taking a shower, but she was more than anxious to get the robe he spoke of. It was hard to think straight while standing there in underwear that was really nothing more than a few scraps of lace held together with some strategically placed elastic. She might as well have been naked.

As she reached for the robe, a few drops of water from the shower bounced against her hip. She turned and put her hand into the spray from the rainwater style shower head. After the heat of the sauna, the water was blessedly cool. A glance over her shoulder showed the back of Fitz's head through the steam. Could she trust him not to look?

Realizing he'd pretty much seen her naked already anyway, she decided to take the risk. She quickly unhooked her bra and slid her panties off. She eased her shoes off her aching feet, vowing to throw the lousy things away at the first opportunity. She'd get rid of the dress, too. She would keep absolutely nothing that would remind her of this awful night and her moronic plan.

There was a collection of body washes and hair products on a shelf, and she quickly lathered herself up. Except for the sting of a few scrapes she'd acquired this evening, the cool water felt like heaven, as did the welcome sensation of washing away the feel of all of those cretins — Fitz included — touching her, grabbing at her body and tangling their grimy fingers in her hair. But she didn't linger. The sooner she could get that robe on, the better.

She grabbed a towel from a stack piled on a shelf lining the wall above the shower head and quickly dried off before putting on the robe. She wrapped her hair up in another towel, picked up her shoes, and stepped back into the sauna. Fitz must have turned it off because, even though it was still muggy and misty, she couldn't hear the hiss of the steam anymore.

He stood leaning against the wall. She swallowed at the

sight of his naked chest, the heat rising within her not entirely related to the remaining steam of the sauna. His skin still held traces of a light summer tan, the moisture from his sauna-induced sweat giving it a golden glow. A droplet of water rolled down his front to his waist before disappearing into his royal-blue boxer briefs. She lifted her gaze to find him smirking at her, and she was glad she could blame the blush she felt in her cheeks on the steam.

"I won't be long," he said. "Stay in the bathroom until I'm done." This last was said a bit loudly and she realized he was still playing to their potential audience. She shuddered.

She moved out of the sauna and went to the mirror over the vanity. Using the sleeve of her robe, she wiped the moisture from the glass and looked at her reflection. She'd washed her makeup off and her skin was pale, except for the high red marks on her cheeks from the humidity. She looked like a cadaverous rag doll.

Forcing her mind back to thoughts of escape, she scanned the room, looking for a weapon. Nothing. She yanked open the vanity drawers to find them all empty. The cabinets beneath the double sinks held nothing but a few extra rolls of toilet paper. She straightened up slowly, the remaining steam of the bathroom adding lethargic weight to her limbs, and she couldn't think straight in all the mugginess. The water still ran in the shower, and she wondered how much longer he would be.

"Screw it," she whispered as she gathered up her clothes. She had no intention of wilting in this heat waiting for him to finish. Yanking open the door, she stepped into the air-conditioned bedroom. A startled squeak escaped her when she saw the maid from the living room seated on the foot of the bed.

"I came to see how you and Fitz were getting along. Can I get you anything before you go to sleep?" Anita asked.

"A taxi home would be good."

Somehow managing to look confident and in control, even in the ridiculous French maid's costume, the woman gave a sly smile. "What's the matter? Don't tell me Fitz isn't showing you a good time. I can't imagine he wasn't up to the task."

It did not escape Erienne's notice that Anita was the first one here to call him "Fitz" instead of "Fitzpatrick." And she all but purred when she talked about him. Erienne wondered if they'd been lovers. Not that she cared, but she had enough to deal with at the moment without adding a jealous lover to the mix.

"I told you to wait for me!"

Erienne jumped and whirled around. Fitz stood in the doorway. His chest was still bare, and though he had a towel slung low around his hips, he hadn't taken the time to dry himself at all.

"Hello, Fitz," Anita purred, eyeing him up and down as water dripped from his hair and ran down his arms and legs in rivulets. "You haven't changed. Still looking fantastic in a towel." She turned back to Erienne. "I assume he's still looking fantastic out of a towel, too?"

"Knock it off, Anita," Fitz said. "Leave her alone."

"Oooh, all protective and macho about her, are we?" She shook her head. "You should know better. Dave's going to take her from you. You know that."

"Over my dead body."

"I believe that would be his preferred method." She frowned. "And that would be such a shame."

She walked across the room and ran a finger across his wet, naked chest. Smiling up at him, she licked the moisture from her finger. For some reason, Erienne had an incredible urge to smack the woman.

"How about I help the two of you get out of here?" Anita asked.

Fitz raised a skeptical eyebrow. "Did Dave send you in here with that? What? Some kind of test? I'm not stupid, Anita. I'm sure he's got this room under constant surveillance."

"Yes, usually. But he's not watching now. He's on the phone with one of his goons. Then the new girl will make sure he's occupied as soon as he hangs up. And just in case, I set up the camera feed to play a continuous loop. It looks like you're spending a lot of time in the bathroom."

"What about sound recording?" He took Anita's wrist, stopping her as she reached out for another swipe at his water-laden chest.

She gave him a disappointed pout. "What? You don't like me touching you anymore? It didn't bother you before. Quite the opposite, in fact."

Fitz ignored this. "The sound recording?"

Anita took her hand back with an indifferent shrug. "Since you had both the sauna and the shower going, nothing much more than mutterings and a few screams got picked up. And nothing at all once you got down to business in the shower." She turned back to face Erienne. "So how was he? I hope you weren't disappointed."

Erienne's skin heated up, whether from anger or embarrassment, she wasn't sure. "We—"

"Shut up, Erienne," Fitz barked, making her jump. He ignored her as he spoke to Anita. "And you need to mind your own business."

For the first time, Anita lost some of her calm and calculating demeanor. "Look, Fitz, I'm your ticket out of this penthouse. You might try showing just a little appreciation. I need your help."

Fitz snorted. "In case you haven't noticed, I'm not really in a position to help anyone right now. And if I was, it would be myself."

"Please," Anita begged. "You're not like the rest of the slimeballs Dave and his brother bring here. Like any of them gave a damn if I came or not. You were different. For once, I made the choice. I chose you at that party before Dave or Tommy paired me off with someone."

Fitz flushed, and Erienne glared at him.

Anita went on. "Dave's right. You must be a cop. You have to help me. Isn't that pretty much the main function of your job? Helping people?"

Fitz shook his head. "I don't know who's been saying it, but I'll tell you what I told your boss. I am not a cop."

Anita planted her hands on her hips and stamped her foot. "Save it, Fitz! You're not fooling anyone. Least of all me. Why do you think I came on to you? I knew you were different. I even had hope you would fall for me and get me away from here..." Her eyes shimmered with unshed tears as her words trailed off.

"Anita, I—"

She swiped at her eyes. "That doesn't matter now. Dave is certain you're a cop, so it's only a matter of time until he kills you."

Fitz raised a sarcastic eyebrow. "If that's so, why are you here? What kind of help can you expect from a dead man?"

"I need you to save my daughter."

CHAPTER SEVEN

"You've got a kid?" Fitz looked doubtful.

"Yeah. Seven years ago, Dave knocked me up within six months of bringing me here. I thought he loved me. But as soon as I got pregnant, he kicked me out of his bedroom, and after Maisy was born, he treated me worse than dirt. You've seen that for yourself. And now Maisy's in danger."

"What are you talking about? Where is she?"

"I'm not sure."

"She's been kidnapped?"

"Not exactly. Dave got mad at me a few months ago and took her away to punish me. Took her to one of his country houses. I don't know where. He's never taken me to any of them."

"Not saying I would nominate him for father of the year or anything, but there's no law against a man taking his child to the country."

"No, you don't understand. While she's been gone, I thought it might be a good thing. Good that she be away from all this, away from seeing me being...passed around."

"Passed around?" Erienne echoed in horror. A small sliver of sympathy for Anita grew in her soul.

"I'm sorry," Fitz said softly. "I had no idea."

"I know you didn't, and I was too ashamed to tell you."

"Maybe it's better that your daughter is not living in this kind of environment," Erienne said.

"Yeah, I thought so until last night. We were alone in Dave's bedroom and he said he was planning to bring Maisy back here real soon. At first I was happy. I've missed her so much since he took her away. And I figured once she was back I would find a chance to take her and run. But then—" she broke off as tears filled her eyes again, and she caught her lower lip between her teeth.

"But then what?" Erienne whispered, fascinated in spite of herself.

Anita swallowed hard. "He said he'd bought her a present. I was surprised because he's never paid any attention to her since she was born. I asked what the present was and he showed it to me. It was a custom-made, child-sized costume. Just like this." She indicated her own outfit as her tears spilled over and streamed down her face.

Erienne's stomach dropped. The sick bastard! How could a man plan such a thing for his own daughter?

Anita wiped her eyes. "I can help you both escape here, but I won't unless you promise to save Maisy. Both of you."

"Me?" Erienne said. "Don't you think it would be better left to the police?"

"No. You can't involve the police. Other than him, of course." She nodded her head at Fitz. "And you have to go, too. Maisy is terrified of men, what with all the creeps who come and go through here. She won't go with a man willingly, and I don't want her traumatized by being forced."

"How can you help us get out of here?" Erienne asked.

Anita walked over to the door and opened it. There was no sign of Maddox or Cooney.

Erienne's heart leapt with hope. "Where is everyone?"

"Cooney was complaining about his eyes. He's lying down in one of the other guest rooms, soaking them with milk," Anita said. "Dave sent Maddox on some errand. The others either went to bed or are watching the loop on the monitors. So there's no one between here and the front door."

Erienne shook out her dress. "I'm leaving." She turned her back and pulled the dress over her head. Working her arms out of the robe and into the dress proved awkward until Anita walked over and helped her. Once she had the dress in place, she slipped on her shoes. "Thank you, Anita. My father has some very impressive investigators on his payroll. I'll get them to find your daughter."

Fitz had dried off and yanked on his clothes. "Wait for me," he said as he sat down to put on his socks and shoes.

"No thanks." Who knew how long the path to the door would remain clear? She wasn't risking losing the chance to escape waiting for Fitz, a man she hoped to never lay eyes on again anyway. In a state of near panic, Erienne bolted from the room, pulling the door shut behind her, hearing a satisfying click of the lock.

She hustled to the elevator. Once she got down to the street, she'd hail a cab and have the driver take her to the nearest police station. She pressed the call button for the elevator, sending up a silent prayer of thanks as the doors slid open with a hydraulic whisper. Remembering Maddox's remark about the building's security staff being on Pruitt's payroll, she hit the button for the garage rather than the lobby. Even though they might see her on camera, she could more than likely slip out to the street before they could stop her.

As the car traveled downward, Erienne took a few deep breaths and tried to ease her shaking. With a musical ding, the light above the doors announced the approach of the garage level. The elevator slowed to a halt and the doors opened.

Maddox stood on the other side. His horrid face registered surprise but he overcame it quickly, lunging toward the car just as she tried to bolt past him. "Oh, no, you don't," he said, grabbing her around the waist.

Erienne fought and screamed, praying there would be another tenant in the garage who would come to her aid, or at least call the police.

Maddox quickly overpowered her and slapped a hand over her mouth. He jerked her back into the elevator and pressed the button for the penthouse.

"Nice try, sweetheart," he chuckled.

Tear sprang to her eyes as she watched the doors close, killing all hope of her escape.

"Dammit, Erienne, wait!" Fitz shoved his feet into his shoes and bolted for the door. Halfway there, he heard a definite click. *No, she didn't!* But a quick twist of the knob confirmed that she had. She'd locked the damn door. "Son of a bitch!"

He whirled to face Anita. "I've got to get out of here. They'll kill her if they catch her."

"Relax. I already told you, everyone is otherwise occupied. She'll get out of here without any trouble. I promise. And I'll make sure you get out of here, too. But first you have to promise me you'll find Maisy and take her to my mother in Nebraska. Here's the address." She shoved a slip of paper into the front pocket of his jeans.

He opened his mouth to speak, but she placed her fingers on his lips. "Don't say you won't do it. You know what Dave is. How can you let him do that to her?" Anita's intelligent brown eyes, shimmering with tears, bored into his. She was right. He couldn't let that animal anywhere near the little girl.

"Okay. I promise. I will do everything I can to find her."

Anita closed her eyes and released a loud sigh. "Thank you," she whispered.

"What about you? Dave is bound to kill you once he finds us gone."

"No. Dave thinks I'm a frightened little idiot. He'll blame his goons for not paying attention." She pushed Fitz away from the door. He wouldn't have thought there was a pocket in that ridiculous outfit, but he was wrong. She pulled out a key and unlocked the door.

Fitz slipped into the hallway, and Anita watched him from the door. "I'm going to make the bed to look like you're both in it, and turn off the lights. Then set the cameras back live. With luck they won't realize you're gone until morning."

"Thanks, Anita. Be careful."

"Don't worry about me. I'll find my own way out when the time is right. Just find my little girl." She shut the door.

Fitz hurried down the hall and made it back to the foyer without passing anyone. The fact that the elevator doors didn't open right away told him that Erienne had already made it downstairs. *Shit!* He had to catch up with her. She was too vulnerable on her own.

A quiet ding announced the arrival of the elevator, along with the sounds of a struggle and Erienne's muffled screams. As soon as the doors slid open, he launched himself into the elevator car and slammed his fist right into the center of Maddox's face. The gratifying sound of cartilage snapping indicated Fitz had just broken his second nose of the evening. Good. Maybe it would improve the look of the ugly son of a bitch.

He didn't waste time relishing that satisfaction, though, not while Maddox was still on his feet. Fitz thrust himself between Maddox and Erienne, breaking the bastard's grip on her. He grabbed Maddox by the neck and swung the man's head into the wall of the elevator. Quickly reversing his momentum, he swung the man the other way and rammed his head into the opposite wall. Maddox went limp, and Fitz flung him out of the elevator. The big man fell to the floor of the foyer and lay there unmoving. Fitz quickly searched Maddox's pockets and came up with set of car keys and Erienne's cell phone.

Retreating back into the elevator, Fitz kicked Maddox's feet out of the car before jabbing at the garage button. He waited until the doors closed and they were descending before turning to look at Erienne. She was cowering in the corner, her hands over her face. "Are you hurt?"

She dropped her hands and shook her head. "Now what?"

"Now we get out of here."

"I'm not going anywhere with you." Color was returning to her chalky face.

"You *are* going with me. It's still not safe here."

"It's not safe being anywhere around a creep like you." She looked at the car keys in his hand. "You've got those. You'll have plenty of time to get away before I get to the nearest police station. I won't even look to see the license plate or the model. Just go and leave me alone."

The elevator reached the garage and the doors slid open. Erienne started to walk past him but he blocked her exit. "Listen to me," he hissed. "I know it's my fault you're in this mess, but if you keep fighting me, neither one of us is going to get out of here alive. Trust me. I really am one of the good guys."

She shook her head. "You're lying. You just want to keep me from going to the police so I won't tell them about you."

"Yeah. You're right," Fitz lied. She was too frightened to think clearly. He couldn't let her go unprotected, and it was easier to feed her the bullshit she already believed than to convince her of the truth. To stay in Pruitt's building any longer was madness. They'd been amazingly lucky so far, but that luck wasn't going to hold forever. "Let's go, princess."

He wrapped one arm around her shoulders and propelled her from the elevator. She struggled to get away from him, but he held on tight. "Knock it off," he ordered.

"Let me go!" She elbowed him in the stomach, right where Pruitt had punched him, and momentarily gained her freedom. Before she'd gone two steps, he caught her wrist and spun her around as if it were a choreographed dance move. She wound up with her back pressed against his chest and both his arm and hers wrapped across her middle. She kicked back at his shin but he dodged it, giving her a slight shake.

"Look!" he snapped, turning them toward the closing elevator doors. "Someone in Pruitt's penthouse just called for the elevator. Which means somebody found Maddox. They know we've escaped. So bigger evil or lesser evil? Do you want to fight with me until they get here? Or would you rather get the hell out of Dodge? Make up your mind. They'll be here in about thirty seconds."

She glanced at the elevator doors with panicked eyes. "Oh, hell. Get me out of here, Lesser Evil."

The words were snarled with hate. But Fitz didn't care. As long as she cooperated, it would save time. He pressed a button on the key fob in his hand. The horn beeped and the lights flashed on a red four-door pickup truck parked just a few stalls from where they stood.

They ran over and climbed in. Fitz pulled out of the space and headed for the garage door, relieved to see a remote door opener attached to the visor. The garage door slid slowly upward as they approached it. "C'mon, c'mon," he muttered, keeping an eye on the elevator door in the rearview mirror. The indicator light went on with a ding.

"It's opening!" Erienne squeaked from the passenger seat. Pruitt, Cooney, and two other thugs bolted out of the elevator.

"There!" Cooney shouted, pointing at the pickup. The four of them came running, and Fitz willed the garage door to open faster. Almost there. He slapped the button to lock the car doors a split second before Erienne did the same on her side. Unfortunately, her action reopened her lock just as Pruitt reached the SUV. He yanked her door open, and Erienne screamed as he grabbed her by the hair. Fitz leaned across and punched Pruitt in the face.

"You son of a bitch!" Pruitt yelled, letting go of her hair to grab Fitz's arm. Erienne dropped to the footwell and curled herself tight as Cooney banged the butt of his gun against the driver's-side window.

Fitz pulled his arm back, but Pruitt held on like a madman. The driver's-side window shattered, and Cooney's beefy arm groped its way around Fitz's neck. He saw a flash of blonde hair as Erienne seized Pruitt's arm and bit it. Pruitt howled and let go of Fitz.

Erienne dropped Pruitt's arm and launched herself between the front bucket seats and into the back. "Go, go, go!" she screamed at Fitz.

Good idea. He hit the gas and the pickup roared forward, the roof scraping a little on the still-rising garage door. Pruitt was spun away from the door and bounced off the wall of the garage. Cooney hung on for a few seconds before the speed of the vehicle forced him to release his grip or be dragged.

Fitz barreled out of the garage and up the ramp toward the street. He swerved a little to the right, knocking the passenger door against the wall of the ramp so it slammed closed. He smacked the door lock button once again, even though he knew Pruitt and his men weren't following. The door to the garage began to descend.

Thanks to the late hour, there were few pedestrians, and Fitz was able to pull onto the street without losing much speed, ignoring the angry blare of a taxi's horn as he cut it off.

"Are you all right?" he yelled over the wind whistling in through the broken window.

Erienne sat up in the back seat. "Yes."

He looked in the rearview mirror and saw her eyeing the door. He increased his speed slightly, not that that would do him any good for long. This was Manhattan, for mercy's sake. Pretty soon he was going to have to stop for a traffic light, giving her the perfect opportunity to jump out.

He glanced at the driver's-side door panel. *Yes!* There, under the chunks of shattered glass, he saw the child safety lock feature on the control panel. He clicked it on just as they were pulling up to a red light.

Sure enough, as soon as he stopped, she tried to open

her door. With a frustrated snarl, she reached for the lock to manually open it.

"I wouldn't do that," he said calmly.

"I'm sure you wouldn't," she snapped, "but I'm getting out of here."

"Without this?" He pulled her sparkly pink cell from his pocket, keeping it well out of her reach.

"I'll buy a new one." She opened the door.

"But I'll have all of your contacts."

She stopped and looked back at him.

"That's right. In a few minutes, I'll know everyone who's important to you. And I'll know how to find them."

She shut the door again. "You bastard."

Fitz felt like one, too. He hated scaring her like this. But he couldn't risk her leaving him now. Pruitt had her in his sights, and she needed to understand what such a threat meant. Not to mention that if she went to the police now, he had no doubt she would not only press charges against Pruitt and his goons, she would press charges against him, too. Straightening all that out would take too much time.

"Listen, Erienne, I really am a good guy. I—"

"Good guys don't hang around with people like Pruitt and Maddox. You've gotten me out of there, thank you very much, but now you're keeping me against my will. You're still a bad guy, Lesser Evil, and the sooner I can get away from you and never see you again, the better."

He sighed. She was still too terrified and angry to listen to reason, and after the events of the last couple of hours, he couldn't blame her. Fortunately, they weren't too far from OASIS headquarters. Soon he would be able to tell her the truth, and once she met the rest of his team, that would help to put her fears to rest.

And hopefully they could all work together to figure out the best way to eliminate the threat of Dave Pruitt for good.

———

COONEY LIMPED over and reached out a hand. "You okay, Boss?"

"I'm fine!" Pruitt snarled. "Get a car, you idiots!" One of the other men whirled and ran for another car in the fleet of vehicles Pruitt kept stored in the garage. He paid a pretty penny to keep all these parking spaces in the building, but it was worth the expense. Cooney helped him to his feet, and they all piled into the car. "Which way did they go?"

"I don't know," Cooney said, "I got thrown to the floor and they were gone by the time I got up."

"I think they went right," said the man at the wheel. He turned in that direction, and all four of them scoured the road. Pruitt spun and looked out the rear window. A stinging pain shot up his back. Shit! He'd probably strained or broken something when he fell.

He pulled out his phone and quickly dialed his personal physician. "It's me. Meet me at my penthouse right away. Take a look at Maddox. I'll be there soon. Wait for me." He disconnected without waiting for a response. The doctor would be there even if he had to wait for hours. And he could be trusted to keep his mouth shut.

They circled the area several times, but there was no sign of the pickup. "Take us back to the garage." Pruitt's back was throbbing now. Just one more thing he was going to make Fitz pay for.

And the blonde rich bitch, too.

CHAPTER EIGHT

Erienne was thrown to her side as Fitz took another turn practically on two wheels. She righted herself and fumbled for the seatbelt. As long as she was stuck here, there was no point in getting herself killed.

Think, dammit. There's got to be a way out of this.

Even in the dim light of the car, she could see the sinewy muscles of Fitz's arms, his biceps accentuated by his black tee shirt. She remembered how she'd found his physique so attractive back at the bar. Now it was all just an obstacle, and she had no idea how to get around it. She certainly couldn't fight him for her phone.

Nor could she charm it out of him. She had no experience in using feminine wiles to get what she wanted. Besides, shortly before all this madness started, Fitz had made it abundantly clear he was no longer interested in her. She didn't know what she'd done to turn him off, but she guessed it was her lack of experience. Had it shown in the kisses they'd shared? A lump rose to her throat and she fought off the sting of tears at the back of her eyes.

She forced her mind back to the task at hand, thinking

back to everything Fitz had said in the penthouse. He wanted to blackmail her father, so he was after money. Maybe that was the way to get to him.

"You know, it's true what I said before. My father will pay anything to get me back unharmed. Wouldn't that be easier than some complicated revenge plan? Let me call him and have him wire the money to your account. You've got an account set up already, right? Then we can part company. I can go home, and you can go start a new life somewhere."

"You think Pruitt's just going to leave us alone?" He shook his head, a derisive smirk on his lips. "Never gonna happen. He's going to be after both of us with a vengeance."

"My father can afford the best security money can buy. And you'll have enough cash to disappear."

Fitz ignored her as he stopped at another red light. He pulled out her phone again and dialed a number. "It's me," he said into the phone. Erienne heard a woman's voice and while she couldn't make out the words, the tone left nothing to the imagination. Whoever she was, she was pissed off.

"I couldn't help it!" Fitz responded. "But I'm nearby. I'll be there in a few minutes. I'm not in my car, though, so I'll need someone to let me into the garage. I'll explain everything when I get there." He disconnected and returned the phone to his pocket.

Erienne folded her arms across her middle as the light turned green and Fitz sped along. "That was your wife, I suppose. Look, if you let me go right now and give me back my phone, I won't say anything to her about what happened at the bar."

Fitz snorted and kept driving.

"Really. Not a word," she persisted. "Is all of this really worth ruining your marriage over?"

"Princess, I told you before. I'm not married."

"Well, your girlfriend then. It's clear you have a relationship with whoever that was. Just drop me off and go see her. They're not following us anymore, so I won't go to the police. I'll just call a car service and go home." A lie, of course. She was calling the police the first chance she got. "Please, Fitz. Your girlfriend never even has to know about me."

He gave another one of those annoying snorts. "Trust me, my *girlfriend* is going to want to know all about you."

Great. He had a kinky girlfriend. "Look, nothing's going to happen between us. Not even with your girlfriend around. I'm not into that."

This time he gave an uproarious laugh. "Ha! That's priceless. Wait 'till I tell Tobie *that* one." His eyes met Erienne's in the rearview mirror. "Relax, okay? Tobie is very much a team player, but not the way you're thinking. I know it's hard, but you're just going to have to trust me a little while longer."

"Trust you? Are you out of your mind? You're the one that's gotten me into this whole mess to begin with. Why should I trust you?"

Something that might have been guilt flashed in his eyes before he looked at her with that haughtily raised eyebrow of his. "You don't have a choice, do you?"

No, that couldn't have been guilt after all. He was too damned smug and sure of himself. It didn't help that he was right. As long as he had her phone, she couldn't make a clean break from all of it. Couldn't just go home and forget this awful night.

He drove the pickup toward another underground garage. A woman with a thick mane of hair dyed an eye-catching gradient of pinks, blues, and purples stood just inside the entrance. She wore leather pants and a vintage

Sex Pistols tee shirt with the sleeves rolled up over her shoulders. Fitz rolled the pickup past her. "Nice getup."

She flipped him the bird and turned a key to close the garage door again. Fitz parked the vehicle and opened his door. "Let's go, princess."

"Stop calling me that!" The nickname had been fine back at the bar but had long since lost its endearment factor. Erienne shoved her door open and climbed out.

"Who's the princess?" Rainbow Hair asked as she joined them, and Erienne wanted to strangle her.

"Maddie, meet Erienne Stuart. Erienne, this is Maddie Barnes."

Maddie gave her a long, scathing look up and down. "Charmed, I'm sure."

"Knock it off, Maddie. It's been a rough night, and I'm not in the mood for your crap."

"Like I care?"

Fitz rolled his eyes before turning to Erienne. "Ignore her. She's training to be an Olympic-level pain in the ass."

Maddie opened her mouth to retort, but Fitz turned his back on her and took Erienne's arm, towing her toward the elevator. She yanked her arm free. "Don't touch me!"

"Ha!" Maddie snorted. "Looks like you'll have to put a little effort into charming this one."

Erienne whirled and glared at the woman. "Shut up."

"I'm warning you, Maddie," Fitz said at the same time.

Maddie smirked at them both. "C'mon. Tobie's waiting."

They piled into the elevator. "Have Jake and Ian checked in?" Fitz asked.

"Yeah. They're on their way." The doors opened, and Maddie stepped off first. "Tobie's in the conference room."

She led the way down a richly carpeted hall, the walls lined with stunning black-and-white photographs of the

Manhattan skyline and architecture, as well as prints of the city's streets back in the day when trolley cars and horse-drawn wagons were the popular modes of transportation. They turned left into a conference room dominated by a long oak table surrounded by at least a dozen plush chairs.

A blonde woman with snapping green eyes shot out of her chair at the head of the table as they entered. "Dammit, Fitz! Where the hell have you been? What's going on?"

"Nice to see you, too."

"*Fitz!*"

The woman's wrath rivaled Erienne's. Fitz, on the other hand, merely looked bored as he pulled out a chair and gestured for her to take a seat. Erienne wanted to throttle him and wondered if her fellow blonde would help her. She sat down, thankful to get off her shaky legs.

Fitz took a seat on her right. "Erienne Stuart, meet my boss, Tobie Armstrong. Tobie owns and operates October Armstrong Security and Investigation Services."

Private investigators? Erienne's thoughts tumbled in a thousand different ways, with a thousand different questions leaping to mind. Before she could articulate one, Fitz turned to face Tobie.

"Erienne and I just met tonight. Unfortunately, Pruitt's goons targeted her to get to me. They assumed we were in a relationship."

"Gee, I wonder why," Maddie snorted from the door.

"Not now, Maddie," Tobie said absently. "Miss Stuart, are you all right?"

"Not really. I'd like to go home, but this Neanderthal won't let me."

"It's not safe for her to go home," Fitz said.

"Why don't you fill—"

Tobie was interrupted by the entrance of two more men.

As large and imposing as Fitz, they were dressed similarly in black tee shirts and blue jeans. One of them — auburn-haired, gray-eyed, and taller than Fitz by a few inches — smirked at Maddie as they passed her on their way through the door.

"Stuff it, Ian," Maddie said. "You know I was undercover downtown at that club."

The one called Ian took a seat at the table. "Yeah, I knew that. It's just that I never thought such a girlie rainbow dye job would have been your style. I was wrong. It suits you."

Maddie looked as if she was about to spout enough steam out of her ears to power a locomotive. She took a step forward with murder in her eyes.

"Maddie!" Tobie barked. "If you don't dial back the atti-tude this instant, I'm placing you on indefinite leave, effec-tive immediately."

Maddie turned and glared at Tobie, who glared right back. "I'm not kidding, Maddie. It's late, and I just don't have the patience for your crap tonight."

Muttering something under her breath as she redirected her glare at Ian, Maddie sat down in the chair on Erienne's left. Erienne could actually feel the hostility coming off the woman in torrents.

"Now then," Tobie said as she picked up her phone and sent off a quick text, "since we are all here, will someone please tell me what is going on? And why is Tanner Mont-gomery calling me. Just how the hell did he get involved?"

"Tanner?" Erienne was startled. "Tanner Montgomery called you? Why?"

"That's what I'd like to know. How do you know him?"

Tobie's eyes were like lasers boring into hers, but Erienne didn't care. She'd had enough. "I'm not telling you anything until I get some answers. Just who the hell are you people? And who the hell is Dave Pruitt?" She turned to Fitz, extending her hand. "And I want my phone back. Now."

Fitz hid a grin. Not many women stood up to Tobie like that. Maddie was something of an exception, but then again, Maddie often seemed to have a death wish, so she wasn't the best benchmark for comparison. Seems his initial observation of Erienne at the bar was spot-on. She had a boatload of spunk. Too bad he wasn't going to get to explore that spunk on a more personal level. He'd really love to, but the situation had changed. She was a client now, whether she wanted to be or not.

He pulled out her phone. "I'll give it to you in a minute. You have to hear us out."

"I don't have to do anything of the kind. Like I said before, you're keeping me here against my will. If you don't give me my phone and let me go right now, I will press charges. My father's attorneys will come after everything you own."

"I can afford excellent attorneys, too, Miss Stuart," Tobie interjected. "Lawsuits don't frighten me. But if Fitz says you need to be here, then you do. The sooner we can all talk this through, the sooner we can figure out what to do and the sooner you can get back to your normal life."

Erienne dropped her hand and folded her arms across her chest again. "All right. You first. Who are you people?"

"As I said, this is Tobie's firm," Fitz answered. "And just like the name says, we provide investigation and security services. We recently wrapped up a case against Tommy Pruitt, Dave Pruitt's younger brother."

"What kind of case?"

"We're not at liberty to say." Tobie leaned back in her

chair and folder her arms. "Client confidentiality is of the utmost importance to us."

Fitz looked at Tobie. "We have to tell her. She's involved now, and she needs to know what she's up against. We don't need to give her our client's name, but she needs to know the rest."

Tobie hesitated a moment and then nodded. Fitz turned back to Erienne. "Not long ago, while working on another case, we came across some video tapes involving young women being auctioned off in a twisted human trafficking sex-slave operation. Women — mostly in their late teens to early twenties, but some as young as fourteen — were being kidnapped and sold to the highest bidder. These bidders were wealthy men, many of them with highly public profiles, all of them with a predilection for brutalizing young women."

Erienne shuddered "You're talking about the Iceman Tapes." Reports of those horrid tapes had hit the media several weeks ago and had dominated the news cycles ever since.

"That's right."

"So what does that have to do with you now? With what's happened tonight? All those men were arrested," Erienne said. "I saw that on the news, too. It's in the hands of the court system now."

"Not all of the men were arrested. Just the ones who were easily identified. The politicians and the celebrities. We're still looking for the rest of them, the ones that aren't so publicly well-known."

"Isn't that a job for the police? Or the FBI?"

"Normally, yes. And they are working on it. But their process is slow and often underfunded. Our client approached us after the initial arrests were made. His daughter was one of the girls on the tape. He didn't want to wait for the police or the FBI. He wanted us to find the man who...purchased... his daughter. That sick bastard was not one of the ones immediately identified."

Erienne's eyes went wide. "Your client didn't pay you to kill this man, did he?" She threw a panicked look around at all the occupants of the room. "My god! You're not paid assassins, are you?"

Tobie sat up straighter in her chair. "Of course not! How dare—"

Fitz held up a hand. "Give her a break, Tobie. She's been through a lot tonight." He faced Erienne. "No, we're not assassins. We're just able to operate a little more freely than the local and federal authorities. Plus, we have a wide network of informants. We're able to pay them off better than the police, too, so we can collect a lot of information when we need it. One of our informants recognized Tommy Pruitt from one of the auctions. I went undercover and worked my way into his inner circle."

"Why didn't you just give Tommy Pruitt to the police?"

"Because he wasn't the man our client hired us to find, but Tommy was sitting next to our target on the tape, and the two of them looked pretty chatty. Tommy could lead us to the man who brutalized our client's daughter."

"And did he?"

"It took over a month but, yes, he finally did. Turns out the man is an arms dealer. I found out that he and Tommy would be meeting for a large gun buy, so I alerted the authorities. Both the arms dealer and Tommy were arrested after a gun battle at the scene. An ATF agent was killed in the fight, so Tommy was in boiling water up to his neck. The authorities were hoping that would be enough to get him to turn on brother Dave. Unfortunately, Tommy was killed in custody earlier tonight without giving up anything useful. And now Dave Pruitt wants revenge. On me."

"Why you? How does he know it was you who turned his brother in?"

"That's something we need to figure out. I never revealed any kind of personal information. And I never went near the Steel Horse while I was undercover. I don't know how they knew about it."

Erienne arched an eyebrow at him. "Wait, let me get this straight. I'm supposed to trust you when you are obviously so incompetent that you've made yourself the target of this man?"

"We're not incompetent, Ms. Stuart," Tobie said stiffly. "We suspect a leak from one or more of the authorities."

"Pruitt is bound to be even more pissed off now that we've escaped," Fitz said. "And don't forget he knows who you are. Believe me. You need our protection."

"Ha. You can't even protect yourself. You nearly got us both killed tonight!"

Fitz bristled. "Hey! Maybe if you'd left the bar when I asked you to, you never would have been involved. And don't forget who it was that got you out of that penthouse."

"I believe that was Anita."

Fitz folded his arms across his chest. "It was Anita who took care of Maddox in the elevator?"

"It was still your fault that—"

"Do either of you think this is helping?" Tobie asked. Her phone dinged with an incoming text.

Erienne glared at him another few seconds, her blue eyes crackling with fire. "No," she said to Tobie. "But I want to leave."

Tobie looked up from her phone, an irritated scowl on

her face. "Tanner Montgomery is on his way up. He wants you to wait for him."

"Who the hell is Tanner Montgomery?" Fitz asked, not missing the look of relief sweeping across Erienne's face at the mere mention of the guy's name.

"He works for my father," Erienne said.

"Doing what?"

"Whatever is needed, not that it's any of your business. He doesn't have an exact job title. How did he know I was here?" she asked Tobie.

"I texted him that information a few minutes ago."

"But how did you know to contact him? And why is he here already?"

The third man at the table, dark-haired and wearing horn-rimmed eyeglasses in a rounded Wayfarer style, spoke up. "Ms. Stuart, my name's Jake Hooper. Ian and I met your cousin, Kylie, at the Steel Horse earlier. She was worried sick about you, and she contacted Tanner."

"Oh no! I have to call her. She must be frantic." She extended her hand toward Fitz. "Phone. Now!"

He handed it over just as a tall, dark-haired man entered the room. "It's already taken care of, Erienne. I called Kylie and your father as soon as Tobie texted me. They both know you're unharmed and in a safe environment."

"Tanner!" Erienne jumped up and hugged him. Fitz ignored the urge to separate them. Maddie caught his eye and gave a slight nod toward Tobie. He looked at his boss, surprised to see the intense interest on her face as she watched Tanner and Erienne embrace. Tobie swallowed hard before schooling her features back to a look of professional neutrality.

"I've never been so happy to see anyone in my life," Erienne said. "Can we please get out of here?"

Montgomery examined the finger-sized bruises Pruitt had left on her jaw, and Fitz cringed inwardly. Erienne had been hurt tonight, and it killed him that he hadn't been able to prevent it.

Tanner kept an arm around her waist. "Not just yet. I need to hear everything that's been going on. What were you doing at the Steel Horse? Kylie said you were implementing a plan? She wouldn't say what it was."

Erienne cast a quick glance at Fitz and turned a light shade of pink. "It doesn't matter now, I promise."

Tanner looked at Fitz. "Did she go there to meet you?"

The challenge in the man's tone was unmistakable, and Fitz's hackles rose. "She said it's none of your business."

"Ignore him," Erienne said to Tanner. "It's not important why I went there. But you can rest assured I won't ever go there again."

A flash of her supple body beneath his on the pool table flitted through Fitz's brain. It was a damn shame he wouldn't have the opportunity to repeat that. *Why do I even care?* He shook his head, not wishing to analyze the thought, and brought his attention back to the conversation.

"Erienne, sit down. You look like you're ready to fall over." Tanner guided her back into her chair. "So," he addressed the table at large, "just what exactly happened tonight? How did Erienne wind up being kidnapped? And who is responsible?"

Fitz glanced at Tobie, waiting for her nod of approval before answering. "Erienne's abduction was a simple case of being in the wrong place at the wrong time. Dave Pruitt was behind it."

"Dave Pruitt?" Tanner faced Tobie. "You're investigating Dave Pruitt? Are you crazy?"

"Hardly," Tobie said. "And who we investigate is none of

your business. We're very sorry Ms. Stuart was involved, but that wasn't our fault. And although I haven't heard the whole story yet, I have no doubt Fitz did everything he could to keep her safe and get her out of there."

Tanner walked to the other side of the table and sat opposite Erienne. "Okay, fill me in. All of it."

Fitz and Erienne related the events of the evening, starting with the scene in the parking lot. Neither of them mentioned the steamy details of what had transpired in the bar. Fitz saw no reason to embarrass Erienne on top of everything else.

"We have to report this to the police," Tanner said.

Fitz nodded. "Agreed. I wasn't able to pin anything on Dave while I was going after his brother. But now Erienne and I can both file charges for kidnapping and put him away for a long time. And we can testify about Maddox shooting those two men at the bar. We'll put him away, too."

He turned to Erienne. "Assuming, of course, you're willing to do all this?"

"Absolutely. I won't sleep a wink until I know each and every one of them is in custody."

"I'll contact the police," Tanner said. He turned to Tobie. "If it's all right with you, I'll have them come here. I'd rather she not have to go to the station."

"That's fine." Tobie faced the rest of them while Tanner made the call. "What about the child? Do we know if she even exists?"

"I never saw a little girl at the penthouse anytime I was there," Fitz said. Considering what went on at the few parties he'd attended there, he was damn glad of that fact, too.

Jake clicked away on his laptop. "Do you know Anita's last name?"

"Ward."

A few more clicks. "Okay, I've found a birth certificate for a Maisy Ward, born a little over six years ago. Mother is listed as Anita Ward, father listed as 'unknown.' Guess Pruitt didn't want to be on the hook for child support."

"Or he just didn't want to be reminded he was the girl's father, considering what he has planned for her." Fitz saw one advantage from tonight's kidnapping. As upsetting as it had been for Erienne, at least it would lead to Pruitt's arrest before he could molest his own daughter.

"And Anita didn't have any idea where Maisy is now?" Tobie asked

"She said Dave took the girl to one of his other residences, but that she didn't know where any of them were because she's never been to any of them."

"All right. Jake, do whatever it takes to get a list of all of Pruitt's real estate holdings. I mean anything and everything, not just residences. Warehouses, business locations. He could be holding her anywhere."

"I'm on it." He stood and gathered up his laptop. "If you need me, I'll be in the tech center."

"We could use Reeve on this one," Ian said.

"No." Tobie's voice was firm. "He and Jessie are still on their honeymoon, and he needs the downtime. I want you and Maddie to stay focused on tracking down the unidentified men on the Iceman Tapes. Did you get anything useful at the club?"

Maddie shook her head. "No, not tonight. But I want to go back. Most of the regulars weren't there. It seems they all took off for some secret house party. The few people I spoke to tonight said that happens every couple of months. It's strictly by invitation only to a very select list."

"Okay. Until they get back, you and Ian see if you can track down any leads on the other men on the tapes."

"Got it." Ian got up and headed out of the room, Maddie slouching out behind him.

Tanner pocketed his phone. "The police are on their way."

Fitz glanced at Erienne. She looked tired but determined. *Good.* He wouldn't have blamed her if she wanted to just go home and try to forget any of this ever happened. But Pruitt damn sure wasn't going to forget anything about tonight. He would be out for blood now, hers included. The sooner they got the police involved, the sooner Pruitt could be neutralized.

Then both he and Erienne could forget they'd ever met.

"SON OF A BITCH!" Dave Pruitt flung his phone across the room, just missing Maddox's head. The big man didn't even flinch. "We have to get out of here." He stood, wincing at the pain in his back. The doctor had left painkillers, but Dave couldn't afford to take them. Not now. He needed a clear head.

"What's going on?" Maddox asked, his voice nasal, the bandage across his broken nose making him look even more grotesque.

"That was my contact at the local precinct. Fitzpatrick and his little rich bitch girlfriend are pressing charges. The police are on their way here, and they've got warrants already. Get everyone out of here now. You, Cooney, and Anita will come with me. Tell everyone else to get out of sight and lay low until they receive further instructions. And have the tech guys look up the name Mordecai Fitzjames. That's the name he gave to the police, not Fitzpatrick."

Dave seethed as they drove out of the city, his wrath and humiliation masking his pain. He'd *known* Fitz was a cop, and Dave couldn't believe he'd made the rookie mistake of not listening to his gut. The prospect of being given a seat on the board of a prestigious company had awoken inside him that slumbering need for legitimate respect. Not the kind of respect he received from those he'd dominated as he fought his way to the top. Those people feared him more than respected him, really.

No, as much as he would hate to ever admit it out loud, he craved the respect of those who had always looked down on him.

Somehow, Fitz had seen that need, though, and had dangled that board seat so convincingly that Dave gave up avenging his baby brother, as well as a night of fun and games with the blonde rich bitch — who Dave would bet money on *was* Fitz's girlfriend. They'd both played the whole thing too smoothly not to be in on it together.

They weren't going to get away with it. Oh, hell no. They were going to give Dave what they'd promised. He deserved that spot on the board. He was just as good as anyone else, just as smart. Hadn't he clawed his way up from the gutters of New York? Stupid people couldn't do that. Stupid people bought the drugs Dave sold and let themselves wallow in the squalor they were born in. Not him. He'd seen a way up and out and he hadn't looked back.

His fury continued to boil in his stomach. He should be sitting in his beautiful penthouse right now, drinking the finest brandy money could buy and fucking his women to his heart's content. But instead he was on the run, acting like a criminal once again.

Damn Fitz and his girlfriend! When Dave got his hands on them, they would see how stupid they had been. It would be days, weeks even, before he would grant them the mercy of death.

Maybe even months.

CHAPTER NINE

"I TOLD you it was a stupid idea." Kylie's voice was sharp, her expression reproachful as she sat on the edge of Erienne's bed.

"And you were right." Erienne leaned back against her propped-up pillows, sipping the coffee Kylie had brought. Normally she would feel like a lazy slug for staying in bed so late, but after the events of last night, she felt she owed it to herself. She planned to spend the day in her most comfortable sweats. She might not even leave her bedroom suite all day.

"Are you sure you're all right?" Kylie asked. "Maybe I should cancel my trip. I could keep you company."

"No, don't do that. You've been looking forward to this trip for months." Kylie and some of her friends from college were taking a hiking tour through the North of England. As the departure date drew closer, Kylie had been speaking of little else. "I'd feel terrible if you backed out now. Go and enjoy yourself. I'll be fine. Tanner and his team will take good care of me."

"Yes, I'm sure they will. But you have to promise me you won't do something like that ever again."

"Well, I can pretty much guarantee you I won't set foot in the Steel Horse any time soon."

"Why do I feel like there's a 'but' coming after that remark?"

Erienne fell silent. How could she explain? Last night had been awful, beyond her worst nightmares. Yet...the time spent with Fitz before everything went to hell had exceeded her best expectations. She'd slept dreamlessly once she'd returned to the familiar safety of the estate, her exhaustion barely allowing her to stop and talk to her father and Kylie, other than to show them she was physically unharmed.

But as soon as she'd woken up this morning, images of Fitz had occupied her brain, front and center. Until Kylie arrived, Erienne had been reliving their pool playing and slow dancing over and over in her head. And those kisses...

"Erienne? Hello?" Kylie waved her hand in front of Erienne's eyes.

She shook her head, dispelling the sexy images. "Sorry."

"What are you thinking about? Don't tell me you're coming up with some other ridiculous idea. I swear, you're turning into another Carol DiMarco."

"Ugh! I don't know if I can ever forgive you for that one." Carol DiMarco, born to a wealthy family in the hotel business, had been Erienne's high school nemesis. Throughout their four years at Candlewood Academy, Carol had been inordinately jealous of Erienne. In her quest to be the most popular girl in school, Carol had tried every conniving trick in the book to make Erienne's life miserable.

"Well, don't give me a reason to say something like that," Kylie went on. "Now spill. I know you've got something going on inside that methodical brain of yours."

"No, not really. But I still wish my plan had worked."

Kylie sighed deeply. "You know I love you, right? But you're worrying me lately. I wish you wouldn't let what happened with Kevin have so much control over you. He was the one with the hang-ups, not you."

"This is not about Kevin."

"The hell it isn't. Ever since he said what he said to you, it's like you're a different person. Forget him. He's a loser jerk who was only using you. I'm sorry to be so blunt about it, but I can't stand watching you tie yourself up in knots because of him. And let's not forget he's going to be in jail soon for stealing those funds."

"As if I could. You have no idea what it's like to know your boyfriend is an embezzler."

"He's not your boyfriend."

"Not anymore, but that doesn't make it any easier." Erienne still felt a sting in her heart over Kevin. As their romance had blossomed, he'd seemed like a dream come true. Intelligent, funny, hardworking, and handsome. The whole enchilada. But it had all been an illusion. He'd been systematically stealing from the employees' pension fund and using his relationship with Erienne to get ahead of anyone finding out about it. She'd thought nothing of him always talking about the business and her father since she worked for the corporation, too. It seemed natural they would talk about it. But the whole time, Kevin had been using her for information.

She should have known better. He was the first man she'd dated in years who hadn't tried to get her into bed in the first weeks of the relationship. She'd thought it chivalrous and romantic. But when she'd finally shared with him her sexual status, he changed.

Initially, he'd acted like it was no big deal, but then he

started to pull away from her. He became more intense whenever they discussed work, grilling her on any conversations she'd had with her father, and he never wanted to hug or cuddle anymore. On their last date, he actually yelled at her, telling her she had no right to put so much pressure on him to make their first time pleasant for her. He'd dropped her off and sped down the driveway as if she were carrying a deadly infectious disease.

The next day her father told her he'd been stealing and had been fired.

"I know what you're thinking. It's not your fault, you know," Kylie said.

Erienne sighed. "I know. But I still can't believe I didn't see him for what he was."

"None of us did. Not even Uncle Marcus. Kevin was good. If he hadn't been such a greedy bastard, he could have had a very successful, lucrative career. Listen, let's not talk about him anymore. He's not worth it, and the courts will take care of him soon enough. Are you going into the lab today?"

"No, but I'll be there bright and early tomorrow."

"After what you've just been through, I wish you'd take a few days off."

"You know I can't. I have to finish the CS180 project so Dad can announce it at the costume carnival."

"You're the only one who's insisting on that deadline."

"I know. But CS180 is Mom's legacy. It would mean so much to Dad if he could make the announcement at the carnival. And it would mean even more to Mom if she were still here," Erienne said, swallowing the lump in her throat.

"Aunt Cassie wouldn't want you to kill yourself to do it." Kylie tilted her head and gave Erienne an exasperated look.

"But I'm sure I'm wasting my breath telling you to take a few days off."

"You are. But I love you for trying." Erienne pulled her cousin in for a quick hug. "You should go back to practicing medicine with real patients. You're too much of a people person to be spending all of your talents on research, even if it's for a good cause."

Kylie stiffened for a moment but said nothing, and Erienne was sorry she'd said it. Her cousin refused to discuss her decision for leaving patient care in favor of doing research at Stuart Industries' pharmaceutical R&D department. Erienne knew why she did it but didn't agree it was the right course of action. Her cousin had been born to do hands-on medical care.

"Speaking of the carnival, I brought this along to help cheer you up," Kylie said as she let go of Erienne and rose from the bed, her tone bright and cheerful as if Erienne had said nothing awkward. "I finally picked the mask I'm going to wear."

She retrieved the shopping bag she'd left by the door. "I love it. What do you think?" she asked as she withdrew a Venetian mask and slipped it on. The right half of her face was hidden behind a large, elaborate butterfly wing shaped from a deep blue metal filigree and set with large dark-purple gemstones along the upper edge of the wing. The rest of the mask crossed to the left side of her face in a stunning combination of jewel-tone blues and purples. Short feathers of the same colors lent a small balance to the butterfly wing as they swept up against her left temple and nestled against her white-blonde hair. Tiny crystals dotted the whole mask, and they glittered happily in the sunlight streaming through the window.

"Oh, Kylie," Erienne gasped. "It's gorgeous. It will be perfect with your blue gown."

"Thanks." Kylie smiled as she removed the mask. "Did you get yours yet?"

"No, I haven't had time. I'm not even sure what I'm going to wear."

"Wear your green gown. I'll take care of getting a good mask to go with it."

Erienne smiled. "You're a lifesaver. Thanks."

"Anything for you. You've got enough on your plate at work. Plus, I can't imagine you can even think straight after all that happened last night."

Erienne couldn't disagree, and her scattered thoughts were the main reason she'd stayed away from the lab today. If she wasn't reliving those awful moments in Pruitt's living room, Erienne couldn't force her mind on anything beyond those moments with Fitz's lips on hers. She wished she could dismiss the memory. It had been one thing to be attracted to him when he was just a "bad boy" in a vague, unknown yet sexy kind of way. It was something else entirely knowing he spent most of his time in the company of people like Dave Pruitt. Fitz might be on the right side of the law, but he was far too thuggy for Erienne's peace of mind.

She sighed. "Don't worry about me, Kylie. I'll be fine. I'm going to stay here and take it easy. Go catch your plane and have a great trip."

"All right. I'll check in with you. Call me anytime if you need to."

"I promise."

Kylie left, and Erienne finished her coffee over the small lump rising in her throat. She missed Kevin. Not actually Kevin, of course, but she missed the idea of him, the idea of having that special closeness and, eventually, intimacy. Would she ever find someone to share that with for real? Someone to share her soul with as well as her body? Considering the way things were going, she thought not.

Images of Fitz reappeared. He definitely could have handled the body part, but she had no illusions he would be her emotional soulmate.

She flopped over onto her stomach. Why even waste her time thinking about him, anyway? Except for possibly testifying against Dave Pruitt, she was never going to see Fitz again.

Her phone rang, flashing Tanner's name on the readout. Her stomach clenched. She hoped he was calling with the news that Dave Pruitt was in custody and had admitted to the kidnapping and the whole ordeal was over and done with. "Hi, Tanner."

"Hello."

That one word told her she'd been kidding herself. "What's wrong?"

"Dave Pruitt is missing. There's no one at his penthouse and no trace of where he might have gone."

Erienne scrambled to her knees, icy fear coating her stomach. "How could he just disappear?"

"He was seen leaving his building in a gray Jaguar sedan. That same vehicle was found abandoned in Hunt's Point in the Bronx. He could be anywhere by now."

She stood and paced her room. "So what do we do?"

"We're going to do everything we can to find him. In the meantime, you're getting extra security. You are not to go anywhere without a bodyguard. Understood?"

"For how long? I can't live my life surrounded by bodyguards."

"Yes, you can. Presidents do it all the time. Besides, it

won't be forever. But it's non-negotiable. Your father and I have already discussed it. We're bringing in outside help."

"What's wrong with your team?"

"Nothing, but we need a lot of manpower for this. We won't just be watching you — we also need to be looking for Pruitt and his men. It makes sense to work with a firm that already knows a lot about him."

Warning bells went off in her head. "You're talking about OASIS, aren't you? I don't want any of them for my detail."

"Sorry, Erienne, but that's the way it has to be. We're putting extra security on your father, too. We'll have to make the schedules work for everyone involved. Tobie Armstrong has put together an excellent team and built OASIS into a top-notch organization." Tanner sounded as if he were proud rather than impressed. "Plus they are highly motivated to get their hands on Pruitt. He's threatening one of their own."

Erienne had no trouble believing OASIS team members would be motivated. Fitz especially. His life was in danger every moment Pruitt remained free.

"And they know you're a target now, too," Tanner continued.

"Don't remind me." Erienne shuddered at the mere memory of those horrific moments at the penthouse.

"I *will* remind you. Often if necessary. Not only will you be guarded, you need to be *on* your guard at all times until this threat is removed."

The absence of Tanner's usually laid-back, unflappable tone unnerved her. Tanner was *worried.* A bucket of ice water couldn't have shocked her so much. In all the time she'd known him, Tanner had exuded an unshakable confidence.

"Of course, Tanner. You're right. I'll be careful."

"Good. And play nice with Tobie's team. I know you're not happy with any of them right now, but they really are good at what they do."

"How do you know Tobie Armstrong so well?"

There was a brief pause before he answered. "We're both in the same business. Her reputation is stellar."

Erienne believed there was more to it than that but didn't press. Considering the threat, she didn't want Tanner's attention diverted.

"I don't want you to leave the house today." Tanner went on.

"I'm not planning to go anywhere. But tomorrow morning, I'm going back to work. I can't take time away from my project."

"Got it. We'll beef up security at the lab. And you will have a personal detail escorting you to and from work every day. I'll call you later with more details."

She crawled back into bed and pulled her covers over her head. Damn Dave Pruitt anyway. But it was really herself she was mad at. Kylie was right. Erienne had let the things Kevin said to her cloud her thinking. In the right frame of mind, she never would have gone to that stupid bar, and the resulting effects of that mistake wouldn't be haunting her right now. She still hadn't lost her virginity, but she had lost her freedom. Until Pruitt was caught, she was in a terrifying prison just as surely as if he still had her locked up in his penthouse.

She hoped Fitz would not be assigned to look after her. While she had no trouble entertaining visions of his handsome face in her mind's eye, she was far too embarrassed and angry with him to see him in person. What might he think of her in the cold light of day? Some ditzy blonde who was willing to jump into the sack with the first guy she met at a bar? She hadn't worried about that before because one of the plusses of her original plan had been that after the deed was done, she'd never have to see the guy again.

Her eyes drifted shut as drowsiness overtook her. Procrastination wasn't her style, but she just couldn't think about this anymore. Her subconscious, however, worked against her.

As sleep claimed her senses, Fitz's devilish smile claimed her dreams.

As the sun's early rays announced the coming of a beautiful day, Fitz and Maddie drove up the long, winding drive of the Stuart estate. Erienne wasn't scheduled to leave for work for another hour or so, but they were getting there early in order to be briefed and given a tour by Tanner Montgomery. They had already been to Stuart Laboratories with one of Tanner's men yesterday, and now knew its floor plan and grounds by heart.

"So Tobie didn't say *anything* to you about why we're taking orders from some other firm's team?" Maddie asked for what had to be the umpteenth time.

"No. And we're not taking orders. We're working together."

"Yeah, yeah, yeah. But why?"

"You know as much as I do. Tobie says she knows Tanner Montgomery, and that he's trustworthy and competent. Her word is good enough for me."

"Yeah, me too," Maddie admitted grudgingly. A mischievous tone crept into her voice. "I think they were involved. You know, lovers even."

Fitz suspected the same. The tension between Tobie and

Tanner was subtle but definite. Maybe it wasn't sexual, but there was some sort of history there. Tobie, however, wasn't saying a single word about it. Her only statements had been strictly about the case at hand and the working out of logistics and assignments.

He couldn't say he was thrilled with his role at the moment, but Tobie flat-out refused to let him work out in the field looking for Pruitt. She'd wanted him to go to a safe house and lay low for the duration, but he balked at that notion. Bodyguard detail for Erienne was a compromise he and Tobie had both come to grudgingly.

He had a feeling Erienne wouldn't be too thrilled with his presence here, either. He'd done what he had to do to fool Pruitt, but Fitz still mentally slapped himself every time he thought about how he'd treated her in the shower. If Erienne *actually* slapped him on first sight, he wouldn't blame her. He could only hope that someday she would realize he'd been protecting her with the only means he had at the time.

"Some spread they got here," Maddie remarked as they approached a six-car garage attached to the large main house.

"Yeah, nice digs."

"Really makes you wonder what the little princess was doing at a place like the Steel Horse." There was a sing-song needling to Maddie's voice.

"Stuff it, Maddie. Don't bring that up in front of her."

"Who, me?"

"Yeah, you. We're here to protect her, not embarrass her."

"I don't see why I got stuck with babysitting the princess. I'm sure Ian and Jake could use my help tracking down the Ward kid or going after the next jerk on the Iceman Tapes."

With the memories of Erienne in his arms all too fresh in his mind, Fitz had his own reasons for not wanting to be on this detail. But Tobie knew her team inside and out. Jake had no competition when it came to computer hacking. He'd already compiled an impressive list on Dave Pruitt's holdings. Maddie was competent on a computer, but she would slow Jake down. Any of the team would. They all worked at it, but it would take time for them to reach Jake's level.

And as for Maddie and Ian collaborating on the Iceman Tapes, that only worked in small doses before they were at each other's throats. Fitz didn't know the details about their shared past, but they had a weird dynamic. Though they would lay down their lives for each other, extended periods of civility were a problem for them, especially Maddie. She was more or less like that with everyone, but it was worst with Ian.

Hence today being Fitz's lucky day to work with his prickly partner. He trusted her implicitly, but conversations with her could be tedious. She already suspected something between him and Erienne and would be circling like a shark, looking for any excuse to attack with tactless teasing.

They drove past the garages to park before the wide front steps leading up to the front entry. The door opened, and Tanner stepped out. "Erienne will be ready to go shortly. I'll show you around inside in the meantime. I hope you've studied the map of the grounds I sent you. The usual house security teams have stepped up their surveillance routine, but you should still be aware of the layout."

"Gee, you think?" Maddie said sweetly. "You know, we *have* done this sort of thing before."

"Ignore her," Fitz said.

"Yeah, Tobie already warned me. But she also said Maddie's good and can be trusted."

"She is and she can."

Maddie scowled at them both. "I just love it when people talk about me like I'm not here."

Tanner scowled back. "Don't give people a reason to." He led them into the house.

The tour was thorough, Tanner showing them all the possible entries and exits. He introduced them to the house staff which consisted of a manager, a cook, and two house-keepers. "The staff is live-in. They've all been here for years and have been completely vetted. They can answer any questions you might have about the deliveries and routines around here," he said. "They aren't bodyguards, but they'll know if something is out of the ordinary."

Fitz was pleased to learn that each bedroom suite came equipped with a panic room and that there was an additional one located on the ground floor next to Marcus Stuart's home office and another in the servants' quarters. "They're all state of the art," Tanner explained. "If the door to any of them is shut, a call automatically goes to my office as well as 911. Help will arrive within minutes."

"Good to know," Fitz said. "Let's hope we never have to use them."

"Agreed."

"Tanner?" Erienne's voice floated from the intercom speaker on the wall of Marcus's office. "I'm going to the kitchen for a quick bite. I'll be ready to leave in fifteen minutes."

Tanner pressed a button. "Okay. I'll meet you there after I show the team around upstairs."

Fitz forced his mind to pay attention to everything Tanner pointed out, memorized the security codes for each panic room, downloaded the necessary software to his phone so he could access the security cameras for the grounds. But it was hard to concentrate, knowing he would see Erienne in a few minutes.

When they entered her suite of rooms on the second floor, Fitz knew it was hers the second he'd walked in without Tanner having to tell him. The subtle scent of her perfume and the memories it invoked sent a surging message to his groin. Her large, four-poster bed looked so inviting, and he had no trouble imaging himself there, worshiping every inch of her exquisite body.

Damn, he needed to get a grip.

This wasn't the first time he'd been the bodyguard of an attractive woman. He'd never kissed any of them before, though, never slow-danced with them, never held them against a shower wall while they were all but naked. Even so, he didn't understand why she had this effect on him. He'd been with plenty of beautiful women. None of them haunted his memory like Erienne.

Could it be because they hadn't actually slept together? Had he become that callous? Seeing every woman as a conquest and then dismissing them from his mind once he'd been with them? Shit, he didn't even want to think about what that might say about his character.

Tanner led them back downstairs, and Fitz kept repeating the security codes in his head. Anything to keep his mind off the fact he was about to face Erienne in person. If he was feeling this uncomfortable, he could only imagine what she might be going through. He was the one with experience, so it would be up to him to make her feel comfortable. Especially in front of his partner. Erienne didn't deserve the sharp side of Maddie's tongue.

In the kitchen, Erienne sat at one end of the large central

island, sipping a cup of coffee while thumbing through messages on her phone.

"The team's ready to go when you are," Tanner said. Other than a slight nod of her head, she didn't even acknowledge their presence.

An uncomfortable silence settled over the room as Erienne drank her coffee, never lifting her head from her phone. Finally, she drained the cup and put the phone into a slim briefcase. "Let's go," she said, avoiding eye contact with everyone.

Yep, just as Fitz suspected, Erienne was not happy with his being here.

Maddie looked at Fitz with a raised eyebrow and barely concealed smirk but, thankfully, kept her mouth shut. Erienne brushed past him, leaving another delicate cloud of her perfume in her wake. He followed her to the front door and stopped her as she reached for the knob.

"Wait. Always let one of us go out first."

She finally lifted her head to look at him, and the power of those sweet baby blue eyes was as strong as he remembered. "Surely you don't believe Dave Pruitt is wandering around the grounds here unnoticed?"

"No but that doesn't mean he hasn't hired a sniper to take you out from a distance."

Her face went white, and he regretted his blunt remark. He hadn't meant to scare her, but the way she ignored him rubbed the wrong way. Still, he knew better than to let his temper get the best of him.

Color returned to Erienne's face as anger danced in her eyes. "What about you, then? You're pressing charges, too. Doesn't that make you just as much of a target?"

"Yeah, but I'm a target with training."

She turned to Tanner. "Are you certain this is a good

idea? Wouldn't it be better if someone from your team was assigned to me? Someone who isn't a target?"

"We've already been through this. If I didn't believe this was the best course of action, they wouldn't be here," Tanner said.

Fitz didn't know the man well, but he was pretty sure Tanner was fighting back a smile. Great, someone else who was getting a laugh at their expense.

"I'm asking you to trust me," Tanner continued, "and trust them, too."

Erienne's lips twisted into a pretty pout, but she finally nodded her agreement.

"Well, now that that's been settled, why don't I go first?" Maddie didn't wait for an answer but walked past both of them and opened the door. She looked around for a full minute before motioning them to come out.

Fitz took a last look at his phone and checked the property perimeter that could not be seen from the front door. Satisfied all was clear, he held the door for Erienne. She swept through with the confidence of an invincible warrior, walking quickly down the stairs and getting into the back seat of the SUV.

They drove a few miles in silence, Fitz determined not to make Erienne feel uncomfortable in any way. If giving him the silent treatment helped her get through their forced proximity with a minimal amount of aggravation, he'd deal with it. It was better this way for him, too. He'd already spent far too much brain power reliving those moments of Erienne stretched beneath him on the pool table, or pressed up against him as they danced...

It had been maddening, actually, how often those memories distracted him from his work. Like plenty of other guys, Fitz enjoyed indulging in sexual fantasies, some of them purely imagination, some of them from actual experience. But, with the exception of his first real crush at age thirteen on his overly-endowed math teacher, he'd never had trouble putting a woman from his mind before. He told himself it was because Erienne had gotten wrapped up in his case through no fault of her own, but that didn't make it any less distracting.

Maddie drummed her fingers on the armrest for several moments before she spun around and faced Erienne. "What is it exactly that you do at this laboratory?"

Fitz glanced in the rearview mirror. Erienne looked surprised by the question. He would have preferred Maddie to stay silent, not wishing to intrude on Erienne's privacy any more than they actually had to, but now that it was out there, he found himself curious. Occupation was not a topic that had come up at the Steel Horse.

"I'm a chemist," Erienne said.

Maddie whistled. "Really? I never would have guessed chemist." The remark was a bit tactless, but Fitz could tell Maddie was impressed. Her own area of expertise was explosives, where a good knowledge of chemistry was a critical job requirement.

"Why does that surprise you?" Erienne asked.

"I don't know. I just figured you had a more of a desk-type job. You don't seem like the brainiac type."

"*Mad-die*," Fitz warned.

"It's all right. I get that a lot," Erienne said. "Most people think I just live off my father's money and that I have a token office at the company. They see blonde hair and blue eyes and automatically think I'm just a spoiled little rich girl."

"Tobie complains about that, too," Maddie said. "Her family has money. She says it takes forever for people to take her seriously sometimes."

Erienne made a noncommittal noise, apparently not wishing to discuss someone else's finances. Fitz steered the subject in another direction. "What made you go after chemistry for a career?"

"My mother. She was a chemist, too," she said softly.

"What are you working on now?" Maddie asked.

"It's a project my mother was researching before she died. We've been working on a formula that converts everyday grass into fuel for combustible engines."

"Like for cars and stuff? A synthetic gasoline?"

"Yes, only CS180 would be a lot cheaper and run a lot cleaner than gas. And it has the potential to improve air quality nationwide by over eighty percent."

"Wait a minute," Fitz said. "Aren't they already making biofuels? From corn?"

"Yes, from corn and several other organic materials," Erienne said. "But, after a lot of trial and error, we have come up with a formula that's easier to make, using any of the most common grasses grown in the world. And CS180 doesn't require as much of it."

Maddie whistled again. "Wow. I'll bet that's gonna put the oil companies' noses out of joint."

"There's a problem, though," Erienne continued.

"What's that?"

"There are couple, actually. We are trying to speed up the process and convert the grass into significantly larger amounts of fuel than has been accomplished so far. But in so doing, the resulting product contains a couple of very undesirable side effects. In liquid form, CS180 burns the skin on contact and causes respiratory difficulties. Too much of it absorbed by the skin can be lethal. Second, in its current stage of development, CS180's emissions from a combustible engine are acting as a defoliant. They kill off any vegetation within at least a mile radius, possibly farther with the right weather conditions."

"So you're saying that a formula derived from grass is actually killing the grass?" Maddie rolled her eyes. "Brilliant."

"Yes, I realize the irony, thank you," Erienne said, and Fitz admired how she didn't back down from Maddie's bluntness. "But we've been working on both of those issues for some time now. We're very close to isolating and removing the toxins. However, until we do, CS180 is very dangerous. It can't leave the lab."

"Tanner explained the lab is under very tight security. I figured it was to keep competitors from filching information," Fitz said as they stopped at a red light, and he glanced at her in the rearview mirror. "He never mentioned you were working with something so toxic."

"I only told you because I believe everyone who goes into the lab should be aware of what they may come in contact with, even accidentally. I'm sure Tanner had everyone at your organization sign a confidentiality agreement. He didn't tell you anything about CS180 because he signed that same agreement. I expect you to take it every bit as seriously as he does."

She finally met Fitz's eye in the mirror. Her disdain for him practically bounced off the reflection and punched him in the face.

Yeah, this was shaping up to be a great day.

CHAPTER TEN

Erienne sat on a stool, looking through her microscope at the sample on the slide for what seemed like the millionth time in the last hour. She hadn't made one single decent observation from this latest derivation of CS180. Her concentration was shot, and knowing that Fitz was monitoring her every move from his laptop as she worked in the secured lab didn't help. She never knew one could lose one's mind in such a brief space of time.

Five days. Five long days spent in Fitz's company, at home, in her office, and the constant proximity was getting to her. She'd thought not speaking to him more than the bare minimum would help keep thoughts of him at bay.

It didn't.

Try as she might, she just couldn't ignore the man. Not when every time she saw him, an electric jolt comprised of embarrassment and desire coursed through her. As far as she knew, he'd said nothing about her behavior at the bar to anyone else, and she appreciated his tact. But that didn't change the fact that *he* knew all about it.

Every infinitesimal, clinging detail.

She'd never know it by his behavior, though. Not by so much as a flicker of an eyelash did he betray the fact that they had almost wound up in bed together and that she had practically begged him to take her there. She wished she could put it from her head as easily as he had. But every time she saw him, her mind's eye was assaulted with the images of his face so close to hers, of how his honey-colored eyes had darkened to whiskey just before his lips met hers, of the intoxicating pleasure of his powerful body pressed against her as they danced.

It was late, and everyone else had gone home long ago. She might as well have, too, considering how little she'd accomplished. Giving up on the sample, she declared mental defeat with a heavy sigh. She'd look at it with fresh eyes tomorrow. Tonight, she would go back to her office and review the day's notes from the rest of her team before going home and getting into bed. Sometimes sleeping soon after reading through the notes allowed her to wake up with new insights.

After safely storing the sample, she removed her protective jumpsuit, gloves, goggles, and respirator. Outside the lab, she stopped to slip on the cardigan she'd hung up by the door. A shadow flickered down the hall as she ran a hand behind her neck to clear her hair from her collar. "Fitz? Is that you?"

A slight squeak, a whisper of a sound really, reached her. She looked directly down the hall as she tugged her cardigan tighter against the chill of the air conditioning. Nothing moved, but still a frisson of nervousness ran through her. She stood a moment longer until she saw the shadow flicker again, clearly this time as one of the overhead lights sputtered briefly.

She released the breath she didn't realize she'd been

holding. Yep, she was definitely losing it, jumping at shadows. It didn't help that no one, not the police, not Tanner, not OASIS, had come up with a single solid lead on the whereabouts of Dave Pruitt.

His name and picture had been plastered everywhere. Every day there was a fresh news story about him or his brother or his business holdings and associates. How could someone so much in the public eye remain so hidden?

She walked down the hall and mentally braced herself as she headed to her office. Fitz would be there. Alone.

Yawning, she stopped in the small kitchenette on the way, intending to fortify her wits with a jolt of caffeine. The room was dim, with only the lights of the three large vending machines along one wall illuminating the room with a low glow. Someone — Fitz, probably — had recently put on a fresh pot of coffee, its aroma welcome after the powerful, acrid burnt-paper odor of CS180. She took a mug from an overhead cabinet and poured.

Another squeak sounded from the hallway. She went back to the door of the kitchenette and looked up and down the hall. Nothing. The light did its fluttery thing again, a slight buzzing noise accompanying it.

"Take it easy, Erienne," she muttered, reminding herself she was in the most secure part of the building, with a highly trained bodyguard just two doors down. "Stop jumping at light bulbs."

She went back to the counter, and added sugar and cream to her coffee. Grabbing a cookie from a plate of them one of the employees had brought in, she turned to leave. A scream erupted from her throat and she dropped the cup and cookie, clapping her hands over her mouth.

A man, broad and tall, stood just inside the doorway. "I'm so sorry, Miss Stuart," the man said. "I didn't mean to scare you." He turned to the hallway at the sound of thundering feet approaching.

Fitz skidded to a halt behind the man, gun drawn and pointed at the man's head. "Hands up. Now!"

"Whoa! It's me, Marty Wagner. I work here!" He threw his hands up over his head. "You know me. You just saw me walk past your office."

"That was before you made her scream," Fitz said.

Erienne's heart still raced like she'd run a mile but she found her voice. "Fitz, put the gun down! He's okay."

Fitz stepped back but kept the gun trained on Marty. "What happened? Why was she screaming?"

"Fitz, please," Erienne said, "it's all right. Marty's been part of security here for years. He just startled me, that's all."

Fitz lowered his gun and Marty dropped his arms. "I just got here. I was going to grab a cup of coffee before I got changed and clocked in," Marty said. "I'm sorry for frightening you, Miss Stuart. Usually there's no one here at this hour, so I didn't think I'd be disturbing anyone."

"It's fine, Marty. It was an accident and could have happened to anyone." She grabbed some paper towels and set about wiping off the coffee that had splashed all over her legs while Fitz and Marty cleaned up the broken mug and spilled coffee.

Erienne prepared another mug of coffee and headed for her office. Fitz followed close behind. Her spine tingled, a slow prickle that started at the nape of her neck and traveled down the path she knew his eyes currently roamed. "Stop looking at my butt."

She turned to face him, just catching the guilty grin before he wiped it off his face. "Sorry," he said, not looking sorry at all. She shouldn't be surprised. He was a player, she knew that, and a part of her envied him for it. She wished she could turn it on and off like he did. Right now, it was all she could do to try to convince herself she didn't want him to kiss her again.

She whirled around, Fitz's laptop the first thing she saw as she stepped into her office. One of the Iceman Tapes played, a terrified young woman's tear-streaked face filling the screen. Horror congealed in Erienne's stomach.

"Sorry," Fitz said again, sounding like he meant it this time. He crossed the room and shut the laptop. "I thought you were in trouble, so I didn't bother to close the file."

She took a seat behind her desk. "I can't fault you for doing your job," she said absently, trying to get the girl's face out of her head. How he could maintain his sanity after looking at that horror show all day long? And she knew he looked at it a lot. She'd overheard enough conversations between him and Maddie to know the entire OASIS team was one hundred percent dedicated to tracking down as many of those men as possible. She admired their perseverance, but she didn't know how they could stomach looking at those sordid images day in and day out.

Or maybe she did, in Fitz's case at least. His emotions just didn't run that deep. How could they? She may have been the one looking to hook up at the bar, but he was the one who really would have made it happen. She thought of the first boy who'd spoken to her when she got there, the drunk one and his friends. They all may have been very nice young men, but she had trouble believing any of them would have been able to relax her, never mind seduce her, with Fitz's incredible ease.

Fitz had obviously been at that sort of thing for a long time, perfecting his method, thoroughly seducing a woman in a minimum amount of time. Getting what he wanted — what he would make sure his chosen partner would want —

and then walking away without a backward glance. She couldn't fault him for that, either, especially since that had been the exact type of behavior she'd been looking for. *Shallow* had been her watchword.

She imagined the ability to turn emotions on and off were an asset in his line of work. Acting, too. He'd spent months acting like a criminal to gain the confidence of the Pruitt brothers. But maybe it wasn't all acting. She'd found him in a bar known for its somewhat seedy reputation, and he wasn't there for work. He lived like a hood on his own time. Maybe not to the delinquent degree he projected when undercover, but definitely enjoying life on the darker side of the street.

Fitz returned to his seat and opened his laptop. She pulled a file toward her, reminding herself she was in no position to judge him or anyone else on how they lived their life. She'd indulged in deprecating thinking in the past and wound up being sorry for it. Painful as that had been, she'd learned some valuable lessons, one of which definitely applied here — don't let your happiness be dependent on the behavior of others.

His brow furrowed as he looked at the screen, and she dropped her eyes back to her files. *Better him than me.* Frustrated as she was with her research at the moment, she wouldn't trade jobs with Fitz for anything. One brief glance at the Iceman Tapes had been more than enough.

One hour and two cups of coffee later, and Erienne had finished looking through all the days notes provided by her subordinates. As usual, her team had done impeccable work. She jotted down a few ideas about paths they could pursue over the next few days. After a good night's sleep, she would likely come up with several more, one of which, she hoped, would provide the answer they were looking for. She so wanted to give her father great news when he returned from his business trip to Brussels.

"You ready to go?" The rich timbre of Fitz's voice was like warm caramel.

"Yes. I'm sorry to have kept you here so late."

"Not a problem." He closed his laptop and slipped it into its case while she grabbed her jacket from the back of her chair. They met Maddie in the lobby, and the three of them rode back to the Stuart estate.

They arrived without incident, and Fitz led Erienne inside while Maddie opted to do a perimeter check of the grounds. The house was dimly lit, and much as she would hate to say it out loud, Erienne was glad Fitz was with her. The fright Marty had given her earlier had frayed her nerves more than she'd cared to admit, and she still wasn't quite herself.

"I'm going to have a glass of chardonnay," she informed Fitz, hoping the wine would help her sleep without tossing and turning. "Would you like one?"

"No thanks. I'll just have lemonade or some orange juice."

They got their drinks and moved into the living room. The huge bay window with French doors on either side offered a lovely view of moonlit gardens surrounding a large koi pond. "This is one of my favorite rooms in the house," Erienne said quietly. "The view is so gorgeous all year round."

"Considering the amount of time you put in at the lab, I'm surprised you've had the time to notice."

"There's nothing wrong with working hard," she said, perhaps a little more strongly than she intended. But his comment brought back memories of the nasty remarks Kevin had made the last time they'd been together. He'd accused her of not having the good sense to enjoy all the wonderful things her life of privilege afforded her. "Money is wasted on the rich," he'd sneered.

"I'm sorry," Fitz said, jerking her out of her thoughts. "I didn't mean to imply—"

She waved her free hand at him. "No apology necessary. I'm just on edge all the time. It's making me too sensitive. And it's true, I do work a lot, especially over the last several months."

"Have you had any success eliminating those side effects?"

"That depends on your definition of success. There's a quote by Thomas Edison that says, 'I have not failed. I've just found ten thousand ways that don't work.' Well, by my estimation, my team and I have found at least five thousand ways that don't work." She raised her glass. "Here's hoping we don't have to go through another five thousand to find our solution."

Fitz raised his glass in response. "Here's to it."

She sipped her wine. "I really am anxious to find the answers soon. We're running out of time."

"I wasn't aware there was a deadline."

"There's always a deadline. We're not the only company working on something like this. And anyone who's working on it wants to be the first to get it to market, so doing so would be a real coup for Stuart Enterprises. My father would be so pleased."

"You're very close to your father, aren't you?"

"Yes. We always have been, and grew even more so after my mother died. It would mean so much to both of us to see my mother's dream come true. And it would be even more special to announce it at the charity carnival because my mother founded that event. She was always looking to raise money to educate children in the sciences" She leaned back and gave a brief shake of her head. "Enough about me. I feel like all we've done for the past week is talk about me and monitor my every step. I can't take much more of it. Tell me something about you."

"That's a pretty dull subject."

"Oh, come on. No one reaches your age — and especially in your line of work — without having something interesting to say about themselves."

He drained his orange juice and placed the glass on a side table before giving her a sheepish smile. "Okay. I can run a mile in six minutes."

The wine was doing its job relaxing her, and she found herself enjoying his playfulness. But she wasn't letting him off the hook that easily. "You're going to have to do better than that. C'mon, Fitz. You know so much more about me. Some pretty darn personal stuff, too. That's not fair."

He raised his hands in mock innocence. "Hey, you were the one who chose to reveal your sexual status to a complete stranger. I never asked you a thing. As for the rest of it, we need to know your movements in order to do our jobs."

"I don't care. It's still not fair. You've got to give me something. Something simple is fine. How many brothers and sisters do you have?"

"None."

She waited for him to enlarge upon the statement, but he didn't. He just sat there, his honey-colored eyes never leaving hers. "You're really going to make me work for this, aren't you?"

"Sorry. I don't like to talk about myself."

"Why not?"

"It's part of my training. The less I tell people about

myself when I'm undercover, the less likely I am to trip up and make a mistake."

"But this isn't an undercover job. I already know your real name, what you do, and who you work for. And I'm certainly not looking to" — she raised her fingers to air-quote — "*trip you up.*"

He leaned back in his chair. "Call it force of habit if you like. I spend a lot of time undercover. It's best that I follow the training procedure at all times."

Something in his tone told her there was more to it than that, but she decided not to press. She wasn't even sure why she'd invited him to sit and talk with her anyway, instead of taking her wine upstairs and curling up with a book for a few minutes before calling it a night. Except maybe because over the last few days she'd let go of her anger with him, realizing his behavior at the penthouse had been warranted in order to save their hides. And in so realizing, she now wanted to know more about him. Him, personally. Not the act he put on for his job.

His evasiveness increased her curiosity. He was definitely hiding something. Or was self-conscious about something. She really would have expected someone like him to be more forthcoming, more braggy. Still, her recent loss of privacy and personal space made her far more respectful of that of others. "All right. Have it your way. I won't ask again."

"I appreciate that."

"Have you had any luck in identifying more of the men on the Iceman Tapes?"

"Not me, personally. But Ian may have a lead. One of his informants thought he recognized someone. Ian is chasing it down."

There was a wistfulness to Fitz's tone, and she wondered if he would rather be doing more active work than bodyguard detail. She couldn't imagine that five days of sitting with her in her office or monitoring her movements in the sterile lab held much appeal for him. For his sake, she felt a little guilty that she didn't have a more glamorous, exciting occupation.

She rose to her feet. "Come with me. I've got an idea."

They went out the French doors to the garden, the scent of lilies perfuming the air. She led him around front to the garage and punched in the key code. One of the double-wide doors rolled up silently, and the overhead light came on. He faced her with a charming, lopsided grin as the receding door revealed what was inside the garage space.

"You're a Harley collector?"

"Not me, my dad. He loves them."

"Can't blame him." He nodded his head toward the motorcycles. "May I?"

"Of course."

He smiled a bit wider and entered the garage. Eight Harley-Davidson motorcycles of various vintages were spaced evenly in two rows. Fitz took his time, examining each one thoroughly, rubbing his hands over the leather seats, the chrome handlebars. She smiled inwardly, glad she had brought him here. His appreciation of the vehicles was obvious, just as she'd known it would be. Very unlike Kevin's reaction, which had been to give the bikes a quick once-over before declaring them collectibles that would probably bring in a small fortune.

Erienne had hidden her disappointment at the time. She herself didn't know much about motorcycles, but she loved them because her father did. She should have known in that moment that Kevin wasn't the one for her. Somewhere deep inside, she knew she had to marry a Harley man.

"Pick one," she said, "and take me for a ride."

He jerked his head back to her. "You want to go for a ride? Now?"

She walked over to the side wall where a pegboard held an assortment of keys hanging from Harley key rings, next to a stack of shelves holding an array of motorcycle helmets. "Yes, now. My father used to take me for short rides when I was a little girl. It's been years since then, though. I miss it. You know how to ride a motorcycle, don't you? Don't disappoint me by saying no."

"We can't. Maybe we can go tomorrow. After we've had time to set up security."

Her face drooped in disappointment, and Fitz had to admit to himself he felt the same way. These hogs were priceless, and he had no idea if he'd ever have the opportunity to ride one again. Not to mention the thought of having Erienne pressed up against his back held its own appeal. But they couldn't do it, not now.

Maybe not ever. Their main priority was safety. Pruitt's whereabouts were still unknown. The popular consensus among all involved was that Pruitt had left the country. But even if the bastard had fled to foreign soil, he still had the means and the motive to try to silence them. They were both determined to testify against him, even if the trial was held in absentia, meaning the son of a bitch could still be convicted whether he was present for the proceedings or not. If so, he could never return to the United States without serving a prison sentence.

Pruitt issues aside, Fitz was still reeling from the heart-pounding terror he'd felt when she'd screamed back at the lab. Even though he'd been keeping a close eye on her, monitoring her with his laptop surveillance while she was in the lab. Even though he'd just seen the well-vetted security guy, Marty, walk by the office. Even though Fitz knew she was safe and there was no one else in the building, in that heart-stopping moment after she screamed he'd thought he'd lost her. If he was that on edge in a secure, controlled environment, he didn't want to think about how he'd feel in an uncontrolled one.

So no bike ride, no matter how much they both wanted it.

Erienne plucked a set of keys from the pegboard. She faced him, her look of disappointment morphing into one of calculated temptation. "C'mon, Fitz," she purred, spinning the key ring around her index finger. "We don't have to go far."

He shook his head. "We can't. I'm sorry."

A sound like muffled popcorn popping reached them from somewhere on the estate. Fitz whirled around and looked toward the entrance to the drive just as all the lights went out, plunging the entire estate into eerie darkness.

CHAPTER ELEVEN

"Fitz?" Erienne's voice held a multitude of fears.

"Quiet," he hissed as he hurried to the garage door. He could see nothing out of the ordinary in the shadowy, moonlit night. His phone vibrated in his pocket. He pulled it out to find a text from Maddie.

Get her out of here. Hostiles coming over the wall. Back entrance still looks clear.

He spun around and ran back toward Erienne. "Which one are they for?" he asked as he snatched the keys from her fingers.

"The '77 FXS Low Rider." She pointed.

"Grab a helmet. We've got to go."

He yanked a helmet on his own head, not bothering with the straps. The Low Rider stood second in line in the first row. He threw a leg over, jumped on the starter, and the engine roared to life. Erienne climbed on, wrapping her arms around his waist.

With a twist of the throttle, the bike surged out into the night. He turned left and headed for the far side of the garage where a narrow paved lane led to the rear entrance of the property. Just before he reached the end of the building, shots sounded, much closer this time, and sparks flew up from the pavement in front of him.

Erienne shrieked and tightened her grip on him as she buried her face against his back, the edge of her helmet biting between his shoulder blades. He barely slowed down as he made the turn around the building, skating one foot on the pavement to keep the bike upright. The sounds of gunfire tore through the night, this time unmuffled, and hope surged through his veins with the realization that the security team was answering the assault and would fight to keep the intruders engaged long enough for Fitz to get Erienne to safety.

They raced down the narrow road, and the gates of the rear exit appeared in the distance. Fitz slowed a bit as he pulled his phone from his shirt pocket and keyed in the security code. The gates swung open and he roared the bike through.

A set of headlights flashed on either side of him as they hit the road. *Shit!*

He twisted the throttle and the Harley's powerful engine responded like a dream. The metal beast catapulted forward and roared down the twisty street. The two cars followed but had nowhere near the agility of the Harley. Fitz lost them within minutes.

He slowed to a halt, taking cover behind a parked minivan, and killed the engine. "Are you all right?" he asked over his shoulder.

She nodded against his back but didn't loosen her hold on him.

"Okay, good." He rubbed a hand over the knuckles she held locked in a death grip around his waist. "But we've got to get off the road and out of sight."

"Yes," she squeaked out. "Let's go."

The nearest place he could think of was the Oak Motor Inn. They took cash and neither asked nor answered questions. He could even wheel the bike inside the room. He fired up the Harley and took off. Twenty minutes later, they rode into the parking lot of the motel. Fitz pulled out his phone and called the front desk.

"You have this motel on speed dial?" Erienne asked as she slid off the bike, a note of critical astonishment in her voice.

He ignored the sting of embarrassment at her remark, arranging for the clerk to meet them at the door of a ground-floor room. "Open the side door there," he instructed as he pushed the heavy bike toward the building. They went inside, and the clerk didn't even bat an eyelash at the sight of a motorcycle being wheeled into a room normally rented by the hour. Why would he? Fitz had been here often enough to know that a lot of strange shit took place at the Oak.

Fitz paid for the room and generously tipped the clerk before locking the door and throwing the dead bolt. Erienne slid the helmet from her head and shook out her hair, running her fingers through the golden strands. She made as if to toss the helmet on the bed but stopped herself as she took a good look at the dingy, slightly stained bedspread. Flipping the helmet upside down in her hands, she laid it on top of the dresser, careful to make sure the edges of the helmet that might ever directly touch her head had no contact with the dresser's surface.

He looked around the room, trying to imagine how it looked from her point of view. Had the bedspreads here always had those spotty stains? Had the bathroom mirror always been so pockmarked? After seeing where Erienne lived and worked, he could only imagine what she thought of this place. And worse, what she thought of him.

No doubt she'd figured out by now this is where he would have brought her the night they met. She could only be relieved it hadn't come to pass. What woman would actually want to lose her virginity in a place like this?

And how sad was it that he'd never really noticed what a dump this place was? He'd always known it was no five-star resort, of course, but he'd never realized the extent of its shabbiness. The bed linens were always cleaned and sterilized — he'd checked into that long ago — and the place was exterminated regularly. He drew a firm line at vermin. But even with the basics of clean sheets and roach-free rooms, there was no getting around the fact that the Oak was a low-class dive.

To her credit, Erienne said nothing, but guilt and shame still nibbled inside him. When had he become that guy? The kind of man that brought women to such a cheap joint just to scratch an itch? He'd never wanted to take a woman to his home, partly because of his work and partly because he didn't want the women he hooked up with to know where he lived. But it's not like he couldn't afford to do better than the Oak. OASIS paid well, and he lived fairly cheap.

Thugs took women to junk motels. Thugs didn't want women invading their personal space. A niggling little feeling inside made him wonder if he was beginning to enjoy living like a lowlife.

He couldn't deny he liked living on the edge. That was one of the main reasons he'd joined the military. And while OASIS had plenty of boring assignments and paperwork, it had more than its share of exciting ones, too. He enjoyed the edge of being undercover, the idea of beating criminals at their own game. The longer he'd done it, the better he'd gotten at it. No one ever suspected he was anything other than the persona he presented.

What's more, he found he enjoyed showing that edgy, streetwise persona to others, even when he wasn't under-cover. Gradually, he'd been spending an ever-increasing amount of his free time at places like the Steel Horse, hanging around with the kind of people who had lots of leather in their wardrobe and plenty of crude jokes in their repertoire.

Really, when the hell did I become that *guy?*

An image of his mother floated across his mind as guilt gave a firm yank on his heart. She'd died when he was a teenager, but he knew without a doubt she would not approve of his recent behavior. His father had also been rough around the edges, but his mom had been the one to smooth those edges. Fitz remembered clearly how all it took was a raised eyebrow from his mother to make his father rethink a crude story he might be telling to dinner guests. Or how she had convinced her husband to head off to the tattoo parlor to get a tasteless ink of a woman's boobs reworked into a badass-looking owl. And the old man had done it all with a smile.

Not to say his mom was a controlling prude. Fitz remem-bered many times when his dad would roll his Harley out of their garage and hold out the spare helmet to his wife. She'd always laugh, drop whatever she was doing, and hop on. Fitz noticed how happy and cuddly his parents were whenever they came back from a ride.

"Now what?" Erienne's soft voice interrupted his thoughts. "When can we go back home?"

"Let's find out." He called Maddie. "What's going on there? Is the estate secure?"

"More or less," Maddie responded. "The police are here now. Once the two of you took off, the assault on the estate stopped. I think it's safe to say that getting their hands on you guys is their only mission. Where are you? Do you need backup?"

"We're at the Oak Motor Inn, and we're fine for now. You stay at the estate and work with the police. Any information you can find on the shooters will be one more nail in Pruitt's coffin. I'll call Tobie and work out our next move."

He dialed Tobie and filled her in on what happened.

"I don't think you should take Ms. Stuart back to the estate," Tobie said.

"I agree. I'll take her to my uncle's cabin and we can lay low there. Meet me here with a four-wheel drive vehicle. Bring Jake or Ian with you. One of them needs to take Mr. Stuart's motorcycle back to the estate."

"What makes you think I can't do it?" Tobie disconnected without waiting for a response.

"How do you know we'll be any safer at your uncle's cabin than at the estate?" Erienne asked.

"For one thing, it's not in my name or yours. And Sully's not really my uncle, just an old and close family friend. So there's no paper or electronic trail to connect him to me. He retired to Florida but still owns the cabin. He lets me and my dad use it whenever we want in exchange for looking after it for him."

"Then your father might be there? Won't that put him in danger, too?"

"No. I spoke to my dad two days ago. He was on his way to Vegas to meet some of his old army buddies. He won't be back until next week."

She still looked unconvinced. "It's only a couple of hours until dawn. Why don't we just stay here?" Her eyes darted about the room, and she barely suppressed a shudder as she spoke.

Nope. Definitely not staying here.

"We're not going back to the estate for a while. We need to get you to a place those assholes won't find. And trust me, the cabin is much better than this dump."

"But what about work? My team and I are so close to a solution. I can't stop the momentum."

"Look at what's happened tonight. Pruitt's getting desperate. I know it sucks, but it's no longer safe for you to go about your normal routine. Believe me, if he is attacking your home, he'll have no problem attacking your offices. Do you want to put your employees in that kind of danger?"

Her shoulders slumped. "No, of course not."

"Hey, it's not all bad. The cabin has Wi-Fi. You can stay in touch with your team."

Before long, Tobie called, indicating her arrival. Fitz wheeled the bike out to meet her, Erienne right behind him.

"Ms. Stuart, I've contacted Tanner Montgomery and your father. They know you're safe and have been advised of the current plan. Is there anything else I can do for you?" Tobie asked as she got out of a dark-gray Jeep.

"Just whatever you can to find Pruitt."

Tobie nodded as she handed Fitz the car keys. "Call me when you get settled." She put on Erienne's helmet, then threw a leg over the Harley. With practiced ease, she started it up and took off.

"Huh. Just when you think you know a person," Fitz chuckled.

They got into the Jeep, and Erienne lowered her window a crack. As they cruised out of town, they passed the Steel Horse. Strains of the song she and Fitz had slow-danced to reached her ears. Her cheeks warmed, and she chanced a quick glance at Fitz. He was watching her with a small grin tugging up one corner of his mouth.

"You probably don't want to hear this, princess, but that's always going to be one of my favorite songs now," he said.

Her cheeks burned, but even more disconcerting was the pool of heat that formed at the base of her stomach. She could well remember the feel of being in his arms and how close she'd actually come to surrendering everything to him. Even though she could no longer actually hear it, the love ballad played on a constant loop in her head. And with that soundtrack already in place, her memory betrayed her will by broadcasting the image of them plastered against each other over and over again. She knew she shouldn't still want him, but she did. And she really hated that Fitz seemed to know it.

"You're right," she snapped. "I don't. And don't call me princess."

He drove her out of town, taking a series of twists and turns on some dark and narrow back roads. Before long, he turned into a narrow driveway that led to a small wood cabin. The isolation of the place leapt out at her, making her extremely conscious of the fact that she and Fitz would be here all alone. Most likely for several days, maybe even a few weeks. She hoped to heaven it wouldn't be that long, but she hadn't forgotten what Fitz had said earlier. With Pruitt waging such full-on assaults, she had to abandon her home and office. She couldn't put others in jeopardy.

But would she be putting herself in a different kind of jeopardy by staying here alone with him? She had no doubt he would never force himself on her, but the man oozed charisma like a volcano oozed lava, and he had the bad boy thing down to a science. It was hard for her to remember he wasn't just some biker dude who spent his time partying and chasing women. Hard to remember he was part of an elite organization that was working on a very worthy cause.

Maybe that's why it irritated her so much when he called her princess. It had been different when she thought he was someone who would never actually fit into her life. She hadn't cared then if he thought she was a spoiled little heiress. And truthfully, she shouldn't care about that now.

But she did.

No matter how much she'd tried to ignore him during their forced proximity, his constant presence had made it impossible to forget not only that hot and incredible evening at the bar, but that he was fighting to right a terrible injustice. All in all, it was a potent combination.

Fitz parked the Jeep under a lean-to next to the cabin, and she followed him up the two steps to the front door. As he keyed in a security code on the small panel mounted under the doorknob, she reminded herself to just keep her distance from him as long as they were here.

The enormity of the challenge that would be hit her when they entered the cabin. It consisted of one large room with a galley kitchen on one end. A small round wooden table and four mismatched chairs near the stove was the only eating area available. A huge flat-screen TV took up most of the wall opposite the kitchen area, and several large armchairs and recliners, as well as a long sectional couch, took up the rest of the space. Stairs along the wall opposite the entry led to what appeared to be a large loft.

"Are there bedrooms up there?" she asked.

"Not exactly. Sully bought this place to use as a getaway from his shrew of a wife. He stayed here mostly alone, but sometimes he had his buddies join him for a weekend of fishing and poker. The place is really just a man-cave in the woods. You may be the first woman to ever set foot in it."

"I'm honored. But really, no bedrooms?"

"The sleeping area is upstairs, but it's just an open space with four beds." Her face must have conveyed her horror because he quickly added, "The bathroom has a door and it locks. I promise."

She raised an eyebrow.

"And I'll sleep on the couch down here, if that will make you feel better," he finished.

"Thank you."

He reset the security code, and she memorized the numbers as he recited them to her.

"Do you want something to eat? Coffee? There's whiskey, if you want something a little stronger," he said.

Bone-deep weariness set in, and she shook her head. "I just want to get some sleep."

He nodded and led her up to the loft. Four stripped double beds were spaced evenly along the wall, each with a trunk at its foot. Fitz lifted the lid of the first one. "There are clean sheets, blankets, and towels in each trunk. I'll take these for downstairs." He pointed to a pine dresser tucked in a corner. "Sully keeps tee shirts in there. He won't mind if you borrow one to sleep in."

"Okay, thanks."

He gave her a piercing look, and despite her exhaustion, a tingly little yearning danced low in her belly. She stared back, saying nothing. He took a small step toward her before shaking his head and moving quickly around her and down the stairs. "Good night, Erienne."

"Good night," she whispered, unable to determine whether she was relieved or disappointed.

Actually, she was both.

"NONE OF PRUITT'S men were caught, boss. They all got away. But so did the Stuart woman and her bodyguard. Pruitt is furious."

"Pruitt is a fool. Sit tight and wait for my next instructions." Mitchell Cochran disconnected, barely resisting the urge to fling the burner cell phone across the room. That little cockroach, Dave Pruitt, couldn't get anything right. His need for vengeance overruled rational thinking, and the moron actually ordered an armed assault on the Stuart estate. The media was in a frenzied hysteria.

Mitchell had been studying OASIS, searching for ways to trip them up and bring them down ever since they'd had the audacity to interfere with his vengeance on his traitor of a daughter. The Iceman would have snatched her up with no problem if it hadn't been for OASIS operative Reeve Buchanan. He and his coworkers ruined a perfect plan, and Judith — or Jessie, as she called herself now — had gotten away without paying the penalty for her betrayal. Even now, she was on her honeymoon with Buchanan, living her life as if she were beyond retribution.

She wasn't.

Both she and her new husband would be made well aware of that in time. Mitchell was formulating a new plan of revenge. The details were still in flux, but no matter what plan he settled on, it would involve a great deal of pain and humiliation for them both. In the meantime, he was going to put an end to that intrusive investigative agency. Reeve and Judith never would have escaped without the OASIS team.

Toward that end, Mitchell had been the one to tip off Pruitt about Fitzjames being responsible for Tommy Pruitt's arrest, although he'd strongly hinted that Fitzjames was a cop, not a private investigator. Mitchell hadn't wanted Pruitt nosing around OASIS.

When Pruitt had called Mitchell in a fury about having to leave his penthouse, Mitchell had been tempted to hang up. It was the idiot's own fault for letting Fitzjames escape. As Pruitt had continued his raving and demanded Mitchell do something about the kidnapping charges, Mitchell had bitten back his laughter. Pruitt seemed to think they were a team. Equals, even. The worm had no idea what a ridiculous notion that was.

Mitchell had no equals.

But the mention of Erienne Stuart had put a different spin on things. Having vanquished just about every corner of the financial arena, Mitchell was eager to make a name for himself in the scientific and pharmaceutical sectors. So far, the results of his efforts were small potatoes compared to Stuart Enterprises.

Mitchell had long been looking for an opportunity to bribe or blackmail his way into that company. But while Marcus Stuart was a fierce businessman, he was also a frigging saint. Not even that internal scandal with the pension fund was going to leave any lasting harm since the do-gooder had replaced every cent of the embezzled money.

Over the last few months, Mitchell had been following Stuart Enterprises' progress on biofuels. Their CS180 looked especially promising, and if they were successful with it, Mitchell would be left eating Stuart dust once again.

The Stuart woman's entanglement with Pruitt could be a game-changer if Mitchell could figure a way to appropriate CS180 while Pruitt took the blame for the theft. Once he had CS180 in his possession, Mitchell would hire the best scientists in the world to perfect the formula. He'd bring it to market first and make a killing. Another arena conquered.

Mitchell's temper subsided as he warmed to the idea. Pruitt so desperately wanted to be accepted into the super-elite circle, he was willing to do anything. The idiot could be useful for a good while yet as long as he did as he was told. And he would. Mitchell would make sure Pruitt understood how dangerous to his health it would be if he screwed up again.

And despite Pruitt's fuck-ups, Mitchell would see to it Fitzjames wound up dead soon, the first step in taking down OASIS. Tobie Armstrong and her cohorts would regret having interfered in Mitchell's personal family business. Perhaps he'd "invite" Armstrong to be a guest at one of the auction events. She was a little older than most of the women they used, but she was a stunner. Hell, Mitchell might bid on her himself. He'd enjoy having her at his disposal for a few months.

The thought made him smile.

CHAPTER TWELVE

Erienne woke to the sound of birds chirping and the scent of bacon frying, surprised she'd managed to sleep at all. Between the craziness of last night's events and the awareness that only a staircase separated her and Fitz, she'd been sure she wouldn't sleep a wink. But the mattress had been surprisingly comfortable, and she'd gone out the second she'd put her head to the pillow, her exhausted body demanding she rest it.

She got out of bed, spying her overnight bag lying on top of the trunk. She walked to the railing and looked down, swallowing hard at the sight of Fitz's bare back and jeans slung low on his hips. His hair was damp, and a towel was draped around his neck. She must have been out like a light. She'd never even heard him come up and use the shower.

"Good morning," she said. "How did my bag get here?"

"Maddie dropped it off. One of your household staff packed it for you. Breakfast will be ready soon, but you've got time for a quick shower if you want."

"Okay." She opened her bag, her heart sinking when she saw it had been packed with enough clothing and toiletries to last her at least a week or more. A small knot of tension grew at the base of her neck at the thought of all the work she'd miss.

Much to her surprise, the shower had plenty of pressure and hot water. This Sully person might not care if the furniture matched, but he definitely didn't skimp on the creature comforts. She let the water go to work on her neck, kneading away some of the tension until her stomach growled, reminding her she'd skipped dinner last night. Leaving her wet hair wrapped up in a towel, she dressed quickly in a pair of gray sweatpants and an oversized pink sweatshirt. She chose the outfit for the express purpose of cancelling any impression she wanted to pick up where they had left off at the bar.

Would that be such a bad idea?

"Yes, it most certainly would," she muttered to herself firmly as she descended the stairs.

"Did you say something?" Fitz asked as he gestured to the pair of mugs he'd set by the now full coffee maker.

"Just talking to myself." She poured the coffee and took both mugs to the small table, sitting down just as Fitz slid a plate with a large fluffy omelet on it in front of her. He grabbed his own food and joined her.

"Do you do that a lot?" he asked. "Talk to yourself?"

His eyes held that endearing, teasing twinkle, and she quickly turned her attention back to her breakfast. "Sometimes. When I'm working out a difficult problem, it helps me if I hear my thoughts aloud." She risked another glance at him. "You should get used to it. Since I can't go to the office, I'm going to have to work here as best I can."

"I figured as much, so I also had your staff send your briefcase and laptop." He nodded toward a desk tucked into the corner of the room, her laptop sitting on top. "We've got a secure network set up here. I had Jake install it because I occasionally answer work emails from here."

A wave of relief swept through her, and that little knot of tension at the base of her neck loosened even more. Lab work would be out of the question here, but at least she could stay up to date with her team and advise them on the next steps.

"Look at you," Fitz teased. "You're already chomping at the bit, aren't you?"

"You bet." She finished her breakfast and stood, reaching for her plate.

"Leave it. I'll take care of it. Go get to work."

FITZ LOOKED up from his laptop, the view of Erienne sitting across the room from him far preferable to the sordid images of the Iceman Tapes he'd been looking at all afternoon. After she'd dispensed with the towel turban, she'd piled her hair up into an adorable messy bun. And who knew that slouchy sweat clothes could look so sexy? Up until today, he'd have said form-fitting and tight was what rocked his world. But now? The sight of the neckline of her sweatshirt slipping down, revealing a creamy shoulder, was fast becoming one of the hottest things he'd ever seen.

With a sigh he forced his eyes back to his work. If only he could catch a break. He'd been studying the same video clips for what seemed like forever and was no closer to identifying anyone — either perpetrator or victim — on the tapes. The only satisfaction he took from his current work was that he had memorized all of their faces and was confident he would recognize them anywhere should fate throw them in his path.

A few of the men who had already been arrested for their participation in the Iceman's twisted auctions had turned on some of their fellow buyers in return for a deal with the DA's office. But many chose to remain silent. Either they legitimately couldn't identify anyone, or they were too afraid. Not of the Iceman, seeing as how Reeve had sent that white-haired bastard to hell, but of the other men on the tapes. Everyone involved in the investigation agreed the participants in the auctions were powerful men, with an obvious disregard for their fellow human beings. They would stop at nothing to protect themselves from prosecution, and those who had already been arrested knew it.

Erienne shifted in her seat again, arching her back and rolling her head from side to side. Fitz wasn't surprised she had a few kinks in her neck. After sitting on the couch, leaning over to the coffee table to work on his laptop all day, his own neck protested the inactivity with a few kinks of its own. "What do you say we go for a walk before it gets dark?" he asked.

She started at the sound of his voice, as if she'd forgotten he was even there. He admired how she immersed herself so deeply in her work, but at the same time his ego muttered a silent *thanks a lot*.

Jeez, he needed this assignment over. His brain was turning to mush.

She looked out the window, a wrinkle of concern appearing just above her nose. "Are you sure it's safe? I mean, what about bears and things?"

"Bear sightings are pretty rare around here, and usually they want nothing to do with people so they just take off. But we'll bring a rifle and we won't go far. Just enough to shake off the kinks and the cobwebs."

"Okay. Let me just send this last email and I'll be ready."

As she typed away, he went to Sully's gun cabinet and selected a Remington 870 pump-action shotgun. He loaded it and put a box of shells in his pocket before stepping out onto the cabin's front porch. Erienne joined him a moment later, and they walked down the steps together.

"There's a deer trail over this way," he said, pointing to his right. "We'll follow that for a little while. It's an easy walk."

"Sounds good."

They walked in silence, the twitter of birds the only sound. Fitz's stomach fluttered as if they were teenagers on a first date, which was ridiculous considering how much time they'd already spent together.

The night they met, he'd been beyond confident. Cocky, even. And he'd managed to get her pressed up against him in the most delicious way. So why now, when he had every intention of keeping his hands off her, did he feel nervous? Why couldn't he treat her just like any other client?

Because she's not like any other client, you idiot.

Sex had never been on the table with other clients. But he'd damn near slept with Erienne the very night they met. That little factoid colored everything about their relationship no matter what.

Still, he could at least try to have a pleasant conversation with her. What about, though? Sports? Harleys? Occasionally he and the guys at OASIS talked about weaponry. Typical guy stuff. Tobie and Maddie only talked about work lately — the Iceman Tapes and capturing Pruitt, so scratch that, too. Thinking of his regular hookups didn't help either. All he ever discussed with them was where they should go for privacy and what positions they wanted to try. He wracked his brain to recall what he talked to his other female friends about.

What female friends?

With a shock, he realized he didn't have any, and that realization rankled, even though there were plenty of other guys in the same boat. Fitz knew quite a few that didn't believe it was possible to be "just friends" with women.

He wasn't one of them, though. He'd been friends with several girls in high school without it leading to anything more, and even still touched base with some of them now and then. But between the military and OASIS, he spent most of his time with men, some of them downright lowlifes. Except for Tobie and Maddie — who were really more like family — any women he spent time with these days were either criminal suspects or someone whose pants he wanted to get into.

Hell, no wonder he couldn't talk to Erienne. He was way out of practice, making him doubly motivated to start a conversation. His mind flashed back to her remark about bears. "So, I take it you don't spend too much time in the woods."

She smiled. "No, not really. I'm a city girl at heart. I enjoy nature, but with the limited amount of free time I have, hiking or camping has never been my first choice of how to spend it."

"What is your first choice?"

"Oh, it depends on my mood. A spa day at the salon. Lounging on the beach — which counts as nature, by the way," she laughed. "Or sometimes curled up in a chair by the fireplace and reading a good book. What about you? How do you spend your off time?"

Looking for a bed partner. Nope, couldn't say that out loud, and it pissed him off that was the first thing that popped into his head. "Tinkering with my Harley," he said at last. "I like to read, too."

"What kind of books do you like t—" The harsh crack of wood interrupted her. Eyes growing wide and wild, she whirled toward the source of the noise. "What's that? Is it a bear?"

He slung the rifle from his shoulder as he scanned the area. A rustling noise came from the trail ahead. Two deer darted across the trail. The sound of their passing faded as they headed deeper into the woods.

Erienne clutched his arm. "Do you think a bear is chasing them?"

Fitz chuckled. "No, I think we're the ones that frightened them into running. What's your obsession with bears?"

She blushed a light pink. "It's silly."

"Sometimes phobias are. But they're real. How did your bear one start?"

She bit her lip, her eyes hesitant.

"I won't tell anyone. Cross my heart and hope to die." Fitz made an X on his chest before kissing two fingers and holding them up toward the heavens, completing the time-honored ritual.

"Kylie and my father are the only other people who know."

"I'll take it with me to the grave." He lifted one hand. "Want to pinkie swear?"

"Ha ha, very funny." Her lips twisted into a sheepish grin as they started walking again. "Okay. When I was very small, my dad used to call me Goldilocks all the time. So much so, I believed it was my name as much as Erienne. When my mother finally read me the story of the three bears, I was convinced the story was truly about me and I've been terrified of bears ever since." Her eyes narrowed as he swallowed a chuckle. "Don't you dare laugh."

"Okay," he said, barely suppressing a snort.

"I mean it!"

Despite his best efforts, he laughed. "I'm sorry. I understand it. I really do, but it's still kind of funny."

"I knew I shouldn't have told you," she said, stopping and planting her hands on her hips.

He laughed again and she rolled her eyes before she let out a little giggle, and then gave him a playful punch on the arm. "Jerk."

"Acknowledged. Let's head back." They turned toward the cabin. "How's your research going?"

"Good. We've found several other ways that don't work, but a couple of them have pointed us in a very promising direction."

"That's great."

"It really is. If it keeps going this well, I'm confident we'll be able to announce our success at the charity carnival. That will mean so much to Dad. And to me, too. It will be great to see my mother's work come to fruition."

"Isn't this your work?"

"Mom was always looking for ways to help the environment, and this was her life's project. I'm just finishing what she started. I owe her that."

"What do you mean?"

Her face grew wistful and he regretted asking. But she spoke before he could apologize.

"When I was a teenager, I went through that awful period where I loved my parents but they always seemed to embarrass me, especially my mother. I thought I was so cool and knew it all. I hated the way she dressed most of the time, like she was a throwback to the hippie era. I never gave it much thought in grade school. But in high school, well...I heard snotty remarks about Mom from other kids. I shouldn't have let it matter, but I did."

"Sounds like she and your father were an odd match."

"Not really. Dad has a great head for business, but he's a bit of a free spirit, too. And Mom could play the part of chic society woman when necessary. They loved each other very much." A tear rolled down her cheek.

"What happened?" Fitz whispered.

"One day I had a group of friends over, hanging around by the pool. Mom came home early to get ready for a fundraiser in the city. She swept out to the patio in her tie-dyed tank top and batik skirt, looking like she'd just spent all day hugging trees or something. I was mortified. When my friends went home, Mom and I had a big fight before she left for the fundraiser. I told her how much she embarrassed me and why couldn't she be like everyone else's mother? I hurt her feelings but I didn't care. I was so mad."

"How old were you?"

"Fifteen." Another tear rolled down her face. "Those were the last words I ever said to her. She was crossing a street in Manhattan and was hit by a taxi. The final report said the driver ran a red light, but I always wondered if she might have avoided it if she hadn't been so upset by what I said. Maybe she hadn't been paying attention."

Fitz opened his mouth, but she waved him off before he said anything. "I know, I know. *I shouldn't blame myself. There's no way to know. She wouldn't want me to be unhappy.* Believe me, I've heard it all before. And most days I try very hard not to blame myself. But on other days, well..." she trailed off.

"Is that why you became a chemist?"

She nodded. "Mom got me a chemistry set when I was a little girl, and we did all sorts of fun experiments together. I drifted away from it when I got to high school. Fashion and boy bands took more of my attention. But after Mom died, I swore I would continue her legacy. I started paying more attention in my science classes and found I still loved it. So no more boy bands for me. From then on, I had posters of Marie Curie, Rosalind Franklin, and Louis Pasteur on my walls."

"And it's paid off," Fitz smiled. "You're doing some great work. You should be proud."

"I am. But it's a trade-off. I threw myself into the work so deeply, both in school and after. As a result, I had virtually no social life. Dad tried to get me to ease up, but I just couldn't. I'd date occasionally, but it never amounted to much. And before I knew it, I was a something-year-old virgin." She blushed. "I don't know why I'm telling you this."

"At the bar you said you were 'kind of' a virgin. What does that mean?"

Her blush deepened. "I can't believe I told you that."

"I'm sorry. I shouldn't have asked."

"No, don't worry about it. I'm the one who brought up the topic of my sexual status." She gave a sigh. "It's not a big deal, really. I was born without a hymen."

He blinked in surprise. "I've never heard of such a thing."

"A lot of people haven't. It's rare, but it happens. So, I've never had sex with anyone, but I physically don't possess the body part that generally provides the proof. In high school some of my girlfriends started sleeping with their boyfriends, and word spread around the school pretty fast when they did. A few of the not-so-tactful guys liked to gloat when they got lucky, and bragged about popping a girl's cherry."

Fitz grimaced. "I apologize for my gender. We can be crass assholes sometimes. Especially in high school."

"No kidding. But girls can be pretty crass, too, and

vicious besides. I didn't have a steady boyfriend, mostly because after a few dates they would start pressuring me to have sex. I wouldn't do it. It never felt right. Plus, at that age I was too afraid they wouldn't believe I was a virgin because there wouldn't be any visible sign that I was. I know now how ridiculous that belief was, but as a teenager I was terrified I would be branded a whore and wanted no part of the gossiping and name-calling that would have resulted.

Fitz hesitated. "I know it's none of my business, so tell me to shut up if you want, but what about after high school? Someone as nice as you are must have been beating the guys off with a stick in college. You were never once tempted to...?"

"Not really. My head was totally into my studies. I went on a few dates when a girlfriend would fix me up. They were nice guys, but none of them ever interested me enough to have the awkward conversation about my status. I suppose I could have kept the information to myself, but I figured my inexperience would show. Besides, I knew I didn't want to be in any kind of relationship where I had to lie to my partner. So, I graduated college with my sexual experience no further advanced than it had been in high school."

"I see. So what brought you to the Steel Horse?"

"It's kind of complicated. After college, I threw myself into working on CS180 and didn't give much thought to anything else, telling myself I had plenty of time to find Mr. Right when my work was complete. And then Kevin came into my life. It all happened so fast and I was sure I had found 'The One.' But when I finally told him I was a virgin, he started treating me like a freak and actually blamed me for putting so much pressure on him. Of course, it turned out he was only using me so he could steal from the company, so he never cared about me anyway." She gave Fitz a sheepish glance. "I can sure pick 'em, can't I?"

"Don't blame yourself. He was a con man. Fooling people is what they do. But that still doesn't explain why you were at the bar."

"Well, even though Kevin turned out to be a complete jerk, I'm afraid I let some of his remarks about my virginity get to me. So I figured what the hell? Just take it out of the equation. A simple matter of getting over the awkward part and figuring it all out, in a way. I thought it would be a good learning experience. Pretty stupid idea, huh?"

"Yes and no," he said. "I understand your logic, but you could have gotten hurt. And I don't understand why you thought telling me you were a virgin would be a turn-on when Kevin made you feel so bad about it."

"I was kind of desperate," she said with a sheepish grin. "I really didn't want to let you go. And I guess I sort of thought since Kevin lied about everything else, he wasn't a good benchmark for that either." She shook her head. "Honestly, Fitz, I realize now that I was so confused and misguided that night. I really wish I could forget it ever happened."

Fitz ignored the small pang of disappointment that poked at him. He should be glad she wanted to forget it, but instead the idea stung a bit. Especially since he was having a hell of a time putting it from his own mind.

As they entered the cabin, her stomach growled, and his own echoed the sentiment. "I'll start dinner. There's wood laid in the fireplace. Light it up if you're feeling chilly."

She rubbed her arms. "Sounds good to me. Then I'll set the table."

As they puttered around the kitchen area together, a surprisingly welcome feeling of warmth and domesticity stole over him. If anyone had asked him a month ago, hell, a *day* ago, if he would have enjoyed cooking a meal for a woman while she laid out placemats — a shock that she'd even found any of those in Sully's place — and set a nice table, he would have laughed his ass off.

Sure, he'd sort of done it before. On the rare occasions he'd spent the night at one of his hookups' places, he sometimes cooked breakfast. But that was largely out of necessity. After the vigorous night spent together, they'd both wake up hungry. And he'd discovered he was usually the better cook. Not that he cared about any of that. He hadn't been with them for their culinary skills.

But on this twilit evening, in this remote and cozy cabin, he couldn't deny the warm feeling of contentment. He found himself thinking of that Goldilocks story she'd told him, and he loved the idea that he knew something about her that only her family knew. He loved how she made him laugh.

When his mother passed away, a part of his father died, too. Laughter became a thing of the past, and his father no longer even tried to maintain any sort of respectability. He drank a lot, although never to the point of really falling down drunk. He continued to earn a living as an auto mechanic, and he made sure his son graduated high school, but he'd lost the one person whose good opinion meant the most to him, the one person who made him truly happy.

Erienne breezed behind Fitz on her way to the overhead cabinet that stored the glassware. The floral scent of her perfume teased him, sending a tantalizing wake-up call to his groin. No surprise there. He'd been kidding himself thinking he could treat her as a friend or client.

He wanted her. And, with a throwback, caveman

emotion he never would have guessed he was capable of, he wanted to be her first.

Dave Pruitt watched the news report, fury and disgust warring in his gut as his name was liberally mentioned in connection with the shooting at the Stuart estate. Why the hell hadn't Cochran suppressed the story? Dave would love to rip the man a new one, but right now he needed the son of a bitch too much to piss him off. Without Cochran's help, Dave could never come out of hiding. As high as he'd climbed out of the gutter, he still didn't have the kind of clout Cochran had.

The TV screen switched to yet another angle of the Stuart estate, the reporter all but gleefully pointing out bullet holes in the trunk of a large tree just outside the estate wall.

"After two days, you'd think they would have moved on by now," Buzz said.

"Bastards," Pruitt muttered. "I donated a million dollars to the children's hospital last year. They never bother to report *that*."

Buzz shrugged.

Pruitt clicked off the TV. "Here," he said, passing Buzz the manilla envelope Cochran had sent over earlier today. "There's an ID badge in there. You are to report there for work as a security guard."

Buzz peeked in the envelope. His eyes widened as he looked at the company name on the credentials. "What am I supposed to do there?"

"Nothing yet. Just learn the lay of the land." Pruitt didn't want to reveal that he didn't actually know the plan.

Cochran hadn't shared anything beyond the badge and a dismissive "wait for further instructions." Being treated like a lowly foot soldier pissed Pruitt off, but he knew how to be patient. After all, Cochran was the one who had reached out to Pruitt in the first place, providing information about Tommy's murder and Fitz's part in it. A man like Cochran wouldn't do something like that unless he saw value in having Pruitt as an ally.

Recent events aside, Pruitt was sure he wouldn't have to hide out in this dump much longer, and he was optimistic about the future in general. He might have lost his little brother, but he would exact his revenge on the man responsible. And if he made a good enough impression on Cochran in the process, Pruitt would soon be moving in the circles he'd been aiming for his whole life.

Buzz left, and Pruitt turned the TV on again. The news had moved on to the story of some goody two-shoes actor and his waifish yet angelic-looking wife donating their time and money to a local food bank. He leaned back in his chair, dreaming of the day it would be his name mentioned so favorably on TV, and how he would be the one people looked up to and admired.

But all that would have to wait until Fitz was dead.

CHAPTER THIRTEEN

"Hallelujah!"

Erienne followed this exclamation with a war whoop of delight. She reread the email from her assistant, joy and excitement bubbling through her to the point she thought she might explode.

Fitz came running in from outside where he'd been chopping wood to replace what they'd used over the last couple of days. He'd taken off his shirt, and the light sheen of sweat highlighting his incredible pecs momentarily drove all thought from her head. He held the ax diagonally across his chest as his eyes scanned the cabin in search of a threat. "What's wrong?" he asked.

"Wrong?"

"Why were you screaming?"

"Oh, that. Oh my god!" She jumped up from her chair and started doing a happy dance. "Put the ax down. It's good news. We did it!"

He looked at her as if she'd gone mad, but did lower the ax. "Who did what?"

"We did! Me and my team. We isolated the toxin and

stripped it from CS180!" He leaned the ax by the door as she danced over to him and clutched his arms. "Do you realize what this means? It's safe now. We did it. My mother's dream has come true!"

She pirouetted in place before throwing her arms around his neck. "I can't believe it! I'm going to burst." Without thinking, she kissed him. An excited, close-mouthed happy kiss that lasted a few seconds. His arms slid around her waist. She leaned back, her breath catching as his eyes darkened from honey to whiskey. She hadn't been this close to him since the night they met.

All those memories came flooding back. How good his arms had felt around her. How soft his lips had been. How he reduced her to a molten jelly of need with nothing more than a look. Just like he was looking at her now.

"That's great," he whispered. "I'm very happy for you."

"Yeah, me too." She studied his face, so close to hers. Her mind was a tumble of emotions. Happiness, excitement, pride. And a touch of regret that her mother wasn't here to see the fruition of her dream. But there was something else.

Desire.

For him.

Keeping her eyes locked on his, she closed the distance between them. Her lids fluttered shut as he took what she offered, his tongue gently probing her lips and easing them open. Heat flashed through her as she met his tongue with her own. His arms tightened around her and every raging, wonderful feeling she'd felt at the bar came roaring back.

A tiny part of her brain laughed at her. Why had she stayed away from him? She'd known from the very beginning that being with him would be fantastic. Having him as her first wouldn't be a mistake. Not following this through would be the real regret.

He pulled his mouth from hers and they stared at each other, each breathing heavily. "We shouldn't do this," he said.

"Yes, we should. And you know as well as I do we were destined for this from the moment we met. Don't ask me how I know this is right. I just know that it is."

"No, darlin', I'm sorry. You're going to have to give me more than that."

She took a deep sigh as he pressed his forehead to hers. At least he wasn't pulling away. If he backed out again, she'd go mad. "It's kind of hard to explain."

"Try."

"I understand your concern. But I need you to know that this is what I want."

"How can you be sure? You're on an emotional high right now. This moment should be about your work. We should break out the bottle of champagne I know Sully has stashed here someplace and celebrate your victory."

"There's champagne? Good to know."

"I'm serious."

"So am I." She slid her fingers through his hair. "Look, Fitz, you're right. I am riding a great high right now. But having reached this milestone has only made me realize that life is too short not to enjoy all it has to offer. I've spent too much of my life letting this cloud everything else. What's more, I want the first time to be good. And I know you'll make it good."

He arched an eyebrow at her. "How do you know that?"

"Because you already make me feel good. Don't say no. I get what you're saying about how I should be celebrating my success. But what I don't think you get is that this is the perfect way to celebrate it. This success was a long time coming and involved a lot of hard work, and I had so many doubts and fears. Wondering if I would ever be able to complete my mother's work. But after every scary and disappointing setback, I brushed off the fear and tried again. And you know what? I'm not afraid anymore. I know I can do anything I set my mind to."

"And you've set your mind to having sex, huh?"

She smiled at him. "Damn straight. Look, I realize it may not be perfect — although I think you will come pretty damn close — but it will be worth it."

"I can't promise perfect."

Her heart did a little victory jig. He might not realize it, but he'd just about admitted they were going to do this. "Fair enough." She kissed him again before he could say anything else. Kissing, at least, was something she had experience with, and she drew on every ounce of that experience now. A growl sounded low in his throat, and she smiled against his lips.

He broke the kiss and pulled his head back, a small grin tugging at the corners of his mouth. "You're not scared at all, are you? Not of me? Of what we're about to do?"

"Fitz, I have never been scared of you. Not even when we first met. You looked a little dangerous at first, but you didn't act dangerous. Not really. You never pushed me at all. You gave me hints of what it would be like for us and then you let me be the one to decide to take it to the next level."

He lifted his eyebrows slightly and gave her a direct look. "I would never force you — or any woman for that matter — to do something you don't want to do. I never want to see fear or uncertainty or pain in your eyes. That would eat me alive."

"I know." She understood his hesitation. He was a man who, for a living, did his best to spare people from suffering. Now he was staring down the age-old belief that a woman's first time was painful. She could tell him all the scientific and biological reasons why that belief wasn't always true, particularly in her case, but she had a feeling such a clinical discussion of a woman's lady bits would kill the mood faster than a bucket of ice dumped over his head. Reassurance would be the faster route. "If I get scared or uncomfortable in any way, I'll tell you. I promise. If I need you to stop, you'll stop. Won't you?"

"Of course. Even if it kills me."

"Then there's nothing in our way."

She caught a brief sight of his trademark devilish grin just before he swooped down and claimed her lips. With one arm he held her close to his granite chest. His other arm slid up her back, his fingers threading their way into her hair at the nape. Erienne tightened her hold around his neck, unable to deny the need to try to be even closer when already every inch of their bodies were seamed together.

Not breaking the kiss, Fitz walked backward, pulling her with him. As they passed the open front door, he swung it shut, lifting his mouth from hers just long enough to flip the deadbolt and set the alarm. She used the time to plant sucking little kisses on his neck. Fitz scooped his arm behind her knees and carried her to the stairs, climbing them two at a time.

Up in the loft, he laid a knee on her bed and dropped his arm from her legs. Her knees hit the mattress and they clutched each other, chest to chest, face to face. Their breath intermingled for just a moment before they smiled at each other. As if a silent bell chimed for both of them, they leaned in and fused their mouths together once more.

Liquid fire heated her body wherever it touched Fitz's. Memories of their evening at the Steel Horse were mere embers to the roaring flames consuming her now. Pressure built like a hot coiled spring at the confluence of her thighs. He eased her onto her back and she wrapped her legs around one of his, pressing her sizzling desire against him and instinctively rubbing herself up and down.

He moved his lips from her mouth, nipping and suckling along her jaw and down to her neck. She whimpered with need as she pressed herself even harder against him. "Shhh," he whispered. "We'll get there, darlin', don't rush it."

"I can't help it," she rasped. "It's too much."

"No, babe, it's just the beginning."

He pushed himself back up to his knees, and she whimpered with frustration at the separation. He straddled her hips, pinning her to the mattress as he slid his fingers underneath the hem of her tee shirt. He locked his gaze on hers, and she quivered as he slowly grazed his fingertips up her belly to the bottom of her bra. His hands slid slowly up, up until they cupped her breasts through the bra. She pressed up against his palms, her nipples hardening as his hands rasped the lacy fabric against her skin. His nimble fingers found the front clasp and deftly snapped it open.

She laughed as she rubbed her hands along his forearms. "You *have* done this before, haven't you?"

He smiled back. "Once or twice, maybe."

Swooping down for another searing kiss, he pulled her up to a sitting position. The friction of their jeans rasping against each other undid her. "Fitz, please."

"Trust me, darlin'." He pulled her shirt and bra off and immediately brought his lips to her breast as they lay back down. She clutched his head, gasping as even more heat coiled and tightened between her legs. Grinding her pelvis against his, she searched for a release from this exquisite torment as Fitz slowly made love to her breasts with his mouth. He suckled and nipped and licked first one, then the other until she thought she would lose her mind.

He slid his mouth from her breasts, and she reached for his face to pull him back up for a kiss. But Fitz had other ideas. He held her wrists in his hands as he kissed way down to the top of her jeans. Releasing her wrists, he undid the snap and zipper before sliding her jeans and silk panties off her legs. Tossing them to the floor, he picked up one of her feet and pressed a soft kiss just below her ankle. He continued, marching a line of soft kisses up the inside of her calf, then her thigh. Reaching the top, he draped her legs over his shoulders and dipped his head between her thighs. When his tongue touched her pulsing nub, flicking over it again and again, incendiary sensations blazed through her from head to toe, culminating in a fiery explosion that all but burst through her skin as she cried out her pleasure.

Fitz lifted his head and gave her a lazy smile as he got to his feet. He quickly shed his jeans, retrieving a condom from his wallet before tossing them aside. He sheathed himself and returned to the bed, lowering himself on top of her and pressing her into the mattress.

Reclaiming her mouth, his long, deep kisses rekindled the embers within her. Shifting the bulk of his weight to his elbows, Fitz slid into her with one slow, sensuous stroke. Her eyes slid shut as her body adjusted to this intimate penetration. There was no pain, but there was a pressure she found a little uncomfortable. He held himself rigid, not moving within her, and she opened her eyes.

His gaze, warm and amber, held a trace of worry as he searched her face. "Are you all right?" he whispered.

His worry and thoughtfulness touched her. She smiled at him as she nodded. "Yes. It's just all so..." The right words wouldn't come, but she smiled up at him again, and relief flashed in his eyes. She moved first, placing her hands on his hips, holding him still as she slowly rocked her pelvis back and forth, easing her body into accepting him. Tiny beads of sweat broke on his brow, and he gritted his teeth as a low moan escaped him.

She stilled. "Is this not okay?"

He growled out a deep chuckle. "Darlin', this is the most okay thing to ever happen to me. You're doing fine."

Encouraged, she pulsed against him again, her movements growing faster as her discomfort faded, replaced by a pooling warmth where their bodies joined. Fitz continued to hold himself still, letting her take the lead, but she knew she needed more from him. "Help me, Fitz. Help me get there again."

"You got it," he groaned as he lowered his head for a searing kiss. He met her thrusts with his own, deep and sure. Instinctively, she wrapped her legs around his thighs as their tongues danced in rhythm to their hips. Faster. Hotter. The fire flared up to an inferno, engulfing her until once again she exploded with a release that devastated her senses. Fitz uttered a deep, wordless moan as his body pumped its own release. Erienne melted back into the mattress as he collapsed on top of her, one thought and one thought only flaring across her brain.

"Why the hell did I wait so long?"

FITZ STARED at Erienne's sleeping face. So beautiful. So delicate, as if she'd shatter like a china doll. An illusion, of course. This woman was one of the strongest people he'd ever met.

His thoughts drifted back to what they'd shared just a

few hours ago. If he hadn't known it was her first time, he never would have guessed it. In fact, *he'd* been the nervous one, afraid to move, afraid to do anything that might cause her harm or embarrassment. But as his efforts to make the experience as pleasant as possible were rewarded with her assurances she was not in any pain, it was soon her boldness that blew him away.

With a smile, he recalled how he'd laughed when she said she didn't know why she'd waited so long to have sex. A nice little boost to his ego, that. But after a short rest, she'd initiated another go round. "It's my turn to please you," she'd whispered before lowering her head to his groin. "Let me know if I'm not doing it right."

"Don't worry," he'd rasped after a few minutes, "you're a natural."

But it wasn't just her lack of inhibition that laid him flat. It was the trust she'd placed in him, and the things she'd said about him — things that had nothing to do with sex — that had knocked him for a loop. Like how she'd known he wasn't dangerous. That she knew he would take care of her and protect her. That he would always do the right thing. He wouldn't have thought anyone beyond his OASIS team-mates could see those sort of qualities in him.

His thoughts drifted to his parents. Except for their very small, close circle of friends, most people had given his father a wide berth. But his mother brought out the best in his dad. Maybe Erienne was the one to do the same for Fitz? Because he always found himself wanting to be a better man around her.

So maybe there was hope for him. Maybe he wasn't a complete thug after all. Maybe he could have a wife and a family. A happy one like he'd had before his mom died.

His eyes drifted shut with dreams of rolling his Harley

out of a suburban garage as the sound of children's laughter drifted from the attached house, and a beautiful blonde wife with sweet baby-blue eyes dashed off the porch to join him for a ride.

SEATED AT THE KITCHEN TABLE, Erienne finished her coffee while she waited for Fitz to pack up the last of his things. He'd yet to put on a shirt since his morning shower — a shower she'd been all too happy to share with him, just as she had for the past three mornings. An uncontrollable smile took hold of her lips as she thought about the last few days. That night at the Steel Horse, she hadn't given any thought beyond the basic missionary position. Thanks to Fitz's seemingly bottomless experience coupled with his patient tenderness, she'd not only learned about and enjoyed a variety of positions, he'd introduced her to all sorts of fun and games in the shower.

The buzzing of her cell phone penetrated her musings, and she answered it absently as she stared at Fitz's magnificent torso. "Hello?"

"Erienne, thank god I've reached you!" Kevin's voice crashed over her like ice water. "Darling, you've got to listen to me."

Anger surged up. "No, I do not. How did you get this number?" She'd changed her number shortly after the scandal broke to avoid his constant calls begging for her forgiveness and asking her to convince her father to drop the charges.

"That's not important," Kevin said. "I need your help. You've got to tell the authorities that I was authorized to use those funds."

"Are you crazy? I'll do nothing of the kind." *It's okay,* she mouthed to Fitz as he joined her at the table, a scowl on his face.

"Darling, please," Kevin went on. "You have to help me. And I've missed you so much. I need to see you."

"No. I have no desire to see you, Kevin."

Fitz's eyes narrowed and he extended his hand. "Listen, jerk off," he growled into the phone when she handed it to him. "I don't know how you got Ms. Stuart's private number, but I'm warning you right now to never use it again. Bother her one more second and I will hunt you down and give you the beating of your life." He disconnected without waiting for a response, and returned her phone.

"Well, that was rather primitive," she said.

He shrugged. "A man's gotta do what a man's gotta do."

"I hope he got the message. I really don't want to have to change my number again."

"If he calls back, I'll make sure to repeat the message to him. In person."

Erienne had to admit she liked him being so possessive and territorial. A flicker of hope that Fitz might see this relationship as a *relationship* sprouted within her. Lord knew she felt very possessive about him. While she was quite happy to benefit from all his previously acquired experience, the thought of another woman touching him now made Erienne see red and entertain vengeful thoughts of ripping said woman's hair out by the roots. She'd never felt that way about Kevin.

Dismissing Kevin from her thoughts, she got to her feet. "Are you ready to go? I can't wait to see you in a tux at the carnival tonight."

He waggled his eyebrows. "Wouldn't you rather stay here and see me out of a tux?"

"Nice try. We're going."

They gathered their bags and went outside. Erienne tossed her bag in the back of the Jeep and turned to look back at the little cabin. When she'd first arrived here, she hadn't thought much of the place, but now it was the most precious and adorable cabin in the world. "Think your friend Sully might be interested in selling?"

Fitz came to stand behind her, slipping his arms around her waist and pulling her back against his chest. "Why do you ask?"

"I like it here. I wouldn't mind coming back again."

He buried his face in her neck and she felt his lips form a smile. "I know what you mean. But you don't have to buy it to come back. I told you before, Sully gives me free run of the place. Besides, I'm not too sure he'd ever want to give it up altogether. It's meant a lot to him over the years."

"Well, it means a lot to me, too." She dropped her voice to a fake rasp. "I'll make him an offer he can't refuse."

Fitz laughed. "You do a lousy godfather. And you don't know Sully. If he really doesn't want to part with the place, no amount of money will make a difference."

She shrugged. "Doesn't mean I can't try."

"True." He kissed her neck. "Let's go. We're running late as it is."

They drove down the driveway, and Erienne couldn't resist one last look at the little cabin where her life had changed in so many ways.

Fitz chuckled. "I am definitely bringing you back, no matter who owns the place. Are you sure you don't want to come back here tonight?"

"It's tempting. *Very* tempting," she purred. "But I can't keep hiding out here. I still have work to do to get CS180 ready for market, and I'll need to be at the lab for that."

His face wore an expression that was a combination of disappointed schoolboy and concerned bodyguard. Later on tonight, she'd take care of the schoolboy. He might believe they had to sleep apart now that they were going back to the real world, but Erienne had other plans. As for his bodyguard concerns, she understood them but couldn't completely eliminate them. "Your team and Tanner have doubled the coverage at the carnival event, right?"

"Yes, and at the house, too. But Pruitt is still on the loose. I wish you would reconsider going to this thing tonight."

"Absolutely not. I'm not letting anyone take this night away from me or my father. This means as much to him as it does to me."

"I'll bet keeping you safe means more to him than some party."

"Dad would never want me to cower in fear. He's always taught me to stand up to bullies."

"Pruitt is not a bully. He's a cold-blooded killer."

"I know that. But if he keeps me living my life afraid, keeping me in hiding, he might as well kill me."

"It's not forever, Erienne. Just until he's caught and put away."

"And what if he's never caught? Am I supposed to hide in that cabin with you forever?"

"Would that be so bad?"

"It would be a heck of a lot of fun, but it wouldn't be enough. For either of us. Not forever."

Something about the way she said *not forever* rankled. He wasn't sure when he started thinking in forever terms, but he had. And if he'd been hanging on to any doubts about that, the phone call a few moments ago had sealed that deal. He'd never once cared when he saw one of his hookups talk to or flirt with another guy at the Steel Horse.

But when he heard another man's voice call Erienne "darling," when he realized it was Kevin Stevens on the phone, Fitz had been rocked with a possessive fury he'd never experienced before. The mere thought of someone trying to take Erienne away from him shook him to his core.

He should have anticipated she might not feel the same way. She liked him, sure, but hadn't she been clear from the very beginning of their acquaintance that he was nothing more than a means to lose her virginity? And if it had gone the way she planned that night, he probably wouldn't have cared whether he ever saw her again or not.

Although maybe that wasn't quite true, either. He'd been feeling pretty possessive of her even then, warning off all comers with a look. He recalled when that drunk kid tried to make a claim for her. Fitz had felt a caveman level of possession about her right from the start. And that feeling had only strengthened over the time he'd spent with her.

Fat lot of good it did him since she didn't feel the same way. Why would she? Their lives and backgrounds were so different. She would never see him in her world. Hell, he couldn't imagine himself in her world. And how could he expect her to spend time in his? That's not where she belonged.

He pushed those depressing thoughts aside as the Manhattan skyline rose into view. Time to get his game face on. Between the OASIS organization and Tanner Montgomery's protective detail, security for the event was tripled. And knowing how important this night was to Erienne, Fitz had every intention of making sure it went off without a hitch.

They arrived at the hotel hosting the event and checked in, and a bellman took their bags. Erienne glanced at her watch. "Oops, I'm already five minutes late for the hair salon." She hurried across the lobby, Fitz right beside her. "Are you really going to stand there in the salon while I get my hair and makeup done?"

"We talked about this. No matter what, where you go, I go. Even if that means risking my manly reputation being seen at a salon."

"It's not your reputation I'm worried about, it's my appearance. Once Philippe gets a look at you, he won't be concentrating on my hair."

"Philippe?"

"My hairdresser. He's not shy talking about his love life and believe me, you are just his type."

Fitz snorted with laughter. "I'll do my best to stay out of his line of sight."

They arrived at the salon, where a frantic-looking man dressed in black from head to toe hurried forward, tapped at his watch, and cast a shaming eye at Erienne before glancing at Fitz. His feet slowed their steps as his eyes widened before giving Fitz a very thorough raking from top to bottom.

"Too late," Erienne giggled. "He's already setting his mantrap. I'm just going to have to make it clear to him which team you play for." She pressed against him and wrapped an arm around his neck, pulling his face to hers. The kiss she gave him burned straight through to his groin and lasted an eternity. When she pulled her lips from his, he rested his forehead against hers.

"Kiss Philippe like that and he just might switch teams," he whispered.

"No thanks. Our team of two works just fine for me."

CHAPTER FOURTEEN

"I HATE WEARING THIS GETUP."

Erienne looked up from her phone. Maddie stood at the glass doors leading to the suite's terrace and scowled at herself in the thin reflection.

"You look great," Erienne said. And it was true. A simple black gown hugged Maddie's generous curves in all the right places. At Erienne's insistence, Philippe had done Maddie's hair, including touching up her dye job. The vibrant streaks of pinks, purples, and blues now played peek-a-boo from a cascading waterfall of curls and stood out against her black mask with its upsweep of black feathers. Erienne had loaned her a pair of small diamond stud earrings that sparkled daintily in the light. "Although I still think the chandelier earrings would look better. They'd give you just the right touch of pizzazz."

"Nope. Pizzazz is not for me. The slit in this torture device of a dress is the only thing I like about it." She swept the front flap of the dress skirt aside, revealing a gun in a holster wrapped around her upper thigh. "Easy access."

She dropped the flap and returned to examining herself

in the glass, tugging at the neckline in a futile attempt to have it cover more of her cleavage. "He just better not say a damn thing about this dress," she muttered.

"Who?"

A hint of color crossed the woman's cheeks. "Nobody. Never mind."

A knock sounded. Maddie hustled to the door, looked out the peephole, and let out a sigh of martyrdom. She opened the door to Fitz and Ian, both of them striking in sharp tuxedos. Ian took one look at Maddie, opened his mouth, and then shut it again. Maddie grew pink, quickly turning away and muttering something about getting her communication device.

"I'll help," Ian said hoarsely as he followed her to the other side of the room.

Erienne lasered her focus on Fitz. His hair was slicked back and tamed into a discreet, short ponytail. He'd trimmed his mustache and shaved the scraggly, sexy stubble he'd accumulated over the last several days at the cabin. Still, even groomed and attired in a knockout tux, his raw animal wild side was blatantly evident. He didn't walk into the suite so much as prowl into it.

She slipped her phone into her silver-sparkled clutch purse and got to her feet. A shiver of desire ran through her as she watched his eyes trail a blazing path from her toes to her face, taking in every detail of her emerald-green sheath with a mermaid skirt. The heat of his gaze as it lingered at the gown's deep sweetheart neckline burned straight through to her soul. For the first time ever, she seriously considered ditching the carnival. Another night alone with Fitz was far more appealing.

"You're beautiful," he whispered.

"So are you," she breathed.

She had no idea how long they might have stood there if Ian and Maddie hadn't joined them. "Are you two ready?" Ian asked.

Fitz blinked and then cleared his throat. "I am. Erienne?"

"Yes," she said, grateful she was able to force something more than a whisper through her mouth. She put her mask on and draped her matching green wrap over her shoulders, adjusting it so it fell just so. Fitz donned his own simple, black eye-mask before offering his arm, and the four of them took the elevator to the mezzanine level. Sounds of an upbeat dance remix of a waltz reached them as the doors opened and they walked to the ballroom.

The giant room was awash with color. Women wore gowns of every hue, and their bejeweled, feathered masks flashed like paparazzi cameras in the strobe light spinning above the dance floor. For the most part, male guests wore black tuxedos, but their masks were just as diverse and colorful as the ladies'. A few men wore plague doctor masks, their long pointy noses and narrowed eyes appearing a bit sinister compared to the others.

At one end of the room was a stage where paid performers in harlequin-patterned leotards displayed limber dance moves combined with stunning acrobatics. Many guests were on the dance floor, while more paid performers — these ones arrayed in elaborate flashing or glow-in-the-dark costumes — mingled among them, dancing and clapping, ensuring the guests were enjoying themselves.

A woman in a tight red dress with a V-neck that plunged to just below her navel approached. Erienne stifled a groan. Even with half of the woman's face obscured by a red satin mask, she had no trouble recognizing Carol DiMarco. Erienne had known the woman would be here — the DiMarcos owned the hotel, after all, and Carol's father was a good friend of Erienne's father. Yet while Erienne was fond of Bruno DiMarco, she couldn't say the same about his spoiled brat daughter.

"Hello, Erienne," Carol purred as she stood in front of them. "And just how were you able to find yourself these two fine specimens?" she asked, eyeing Ian and Fitz up and down while completely disregarding Maddie.

Erienne ignored the question. "No escort tonight, Carol?" she remarked with a sympathetic tilt of her head. "That's too bad. But leave it to you to show everyone you are a strong and confident woman on your own. And..." She paused to give a pointed look at Carol's nearly bottomless neckline, "I'm sure you won't leave alone."

Carol reddened, and her eyes shot daggers from the crimson mask. "Oh, I'm not alone. My escort was more than eager to join me and has hardly left my side. He only just excused himself when you arrived. He had no interest in renewing his acquaintance with you."

Erienne refused to give Carol the satisfaction of asking for the identity of her escort. Especially since Erienne had no doubt it was one of the boys from high school that both she and Carol had crushed on. Several of their names were on the guest list.

"Well," Erienne said brightly, "I hope you and your friend enjoy the carnival. But you have to excuse us. I see my father and Kylie, and I need to say hello."

"Well, meow," Maddie said when they'd walked away from Carol. "No love lost between the two of you, huh?"

"She does tend to bring out the worst in me. It's been like that between us since high school," Erienne admitted.

"But tonight is much too important for me to waste one more second thinking about her."

They crossed the ballroom and Kylie met them halfway, her butterfly mask perfectly complementing her royal-blue gown. She drew Erienne into a hug. "Uncle Marcus gave me the good news about CS180 as soon as I got back last night. Congratulations!"

"Thanks. I'm so glad you made it back in time for this."

"I wouldn't have missed it for the world. Come on. Uncle Marcus can't wait to see you."

After Erienne quickly introduced Kylie to the OASIS team, they continued across the room. Erienne soon spotted her father standing amid the usual small crowd of divorcées, widows, and trophy-wife wannabes that flocked to him at every gathering. She smiled inwardly. Her father was tall, and his dark-blond hair showed only the faintest touches of gray at the temples. Regular workouts kept him as fit as a man half his age. Since the death of his wife, he'd become the target of every unattached woman in their social circle. But beyond social niceties, her father paid little attention to any of them.

"Erienne, sweetheart! I'm so glad you're here." Much to the disappointment of his admirers, Marcus Stuart excused himself and drew his daughter into a gentle embrace, placing a fatherly kiss on her cheek before pulling back and holding her at arm's length. "You look fantastic, as always. Your mother would be so proud."

"Thanks, Dad. Although I hope Mom would be more pleased about the announcement we're going to make tonight."

"Of course she would. I can barely keep my shirt buttons from popping, I'm so proud of you. But your mother would be out on that terrace with a megaphone, shouting her pride in her daughter to the world."

Erienne blinked back tears as she saw a sheen of them in her father's eyes. He looked at her a moment longer before gruffly clearing his throat. "Well, well, now. This is a happy night. Not a night for tears." He kissed her forehead before turning and extending a hand to Fitz. "I'm Marcus Stuart. I understand you are the young man who has been looking after my daughter?"

Fitz shook his hand. "Yes, sir. Mordecai Fitzjames."

"I can't thank you enough for all you've done already. Tanner has kept me informed of all the events. I'm counting on you to keep up the good work. Nothing on this earth is more important to me than my daughter."

"I promise you, Mr. Stuart, that no one will get to her as long as I am alive."

The two men stared at each other, and Erienne warmed inside as she saw the mutual admiration and respect building between them. Fitz introduced Maddie and Ian.

"Yes, Tanner has spoken of you, as well," Marcus said. "I must say, I'm very impressed with the entire OASIS team. I've instructed Tanner to call on Ms. Armstrong whenever he needs outside help."

"I'm sure our boss will be happy to hear that," Fitz said.

Marcus nodded before placing Erienne's hand in the crook of his arm. "Sweetheart, I'd like you to say hello to Congresswoman Wyatt. She's very interested in writing an energy bill that will focus heavily on environmentally friendly fuels. She's eager to hear about CS180 from you firsthand."

After a brief conversation with the congresswoman, Marcus whisked Erienne off to another group of his friends and colleagues, followed by another. Through it all, Fitz was never more than one foot away from her, the heat of his body against her back a soothing comfort. Ian and Maddie were always circulating nearby, and at various times throughout the evening Erienne spotted Tanner and members of his team throughout the room.

At one point, Tanner appeared to be in an uncomfortable conversation with Tobie Armstrong, further convincing Erienne that the two of them shared a past and boosting her curiosity about what that past might be. She adored Tanner and had always thought he would make some lucky woman a great husband. However, he'd gently rebuffed any attempts Erienne or Kylie made to fix him up with someone. She mentally shrugged. Tanner and Tobie were grown-ups. Whatever was going on between them didn't appear to affect their work, so it was none of Erienne's business. Though a small part of her smirked at seeing the usually unflappable Tanner Montgomery a little out of sorts over a woman.

After dinner, a hush fell over the crowd as Marcus strode up to the stage, where a microphone had been set up. "Good evening, everyone. On behalf of Stuart Enterprises, myself, and my daughter, I would like to thank you all for coming. Thanks to your generosity, this gala has raised seventeen million dollars for Chemistry for Kids, an organization founded by my late wife, Cassie Stuart." He paused as everyone gave a hearty round of applause.

"Thank you. You've exceeded our expectations. In addition, my daughter, Erienne, and her team at Stuart Enterprises has been working diligently to carry on her mother's legacy to create cleaner fuel. Toward that end, my daughter has an announcement to make. Erienne, please join me."

More applause swept through the room. Erienne met her father's gaze as she approached the stage, overjoyed to be sharing this fantastic moment with him. She kissed his cheek before facing the crowd. "Good evening. I echo my father's thanks to you all for coming tonight. Several years ago, my mother started working on creating cleaner fuel made from grass. When her life was cut short, so was her work. Since that tragic day, I made it my number-one goal to see my mother's work done. I'm thrilled to announce that after a lot of trial and error, my team and I have realized her vision. Our new fuel, to be trademark named Cassoline in honor of my mother, will now go through the proper procedures for governmental approval. We will be bringing it to market as soon as possible."

The applause this time was thunderous. Confetti dropped from the ceiling as the chorus of "We Are the Champions" played from the speakers, and the lights flashed in a jubilant celebration. Erienne sought out Fitz among the crowd, and he was on his feet with everyone else. He winked at her, and tears clouded her eyes. Who knew that meeting him that night in the Steel Horse would have such an impact on her life? He was fast becoming central to her world, and she was beginning to have trouble imagining her life without him.

Her father came up beside her and drew her into a tight hug, lifting her off her feet and spinning her around, much to the delight of the crowd. He set her down, and she looked out across the room. Carol stood at her table, clapping slowly and staring daggers at Erienne. Same old, same old. But it was the large man standing next to Carol that snagged Erienne's attention. He was bald and still wore his mask, so Erienne could not see his face but something about him was incredibly familiar, confirming her earlier assumption he was an old high school classmate. Considering his size, he was probably one of the football players. Carol had dated most of them at one point or another before graduation.

He whispered something in Carol's ear, eliciting the woman's trademark scowling smirk. Tossing a look of smug triumph at Erienne, Carol turned and intimately kissed the man on his neck before taking his offered arm and disappearing into the crowd.

Erienne dismissed the couple from her mind as her father took her hand and raised it above their heads in triumph. Arm in arm, they left the stage. Erienne stopped first at the table where her team was seated.

"I want to thank all of you. This is your victory, too," she said.

"You're the one who did it, boss. They were your parameters. We just followed your instructions."

A grateful lump rose in her throat. "Thank you for saying that, but I never would have found those parameters without your help. This is a team victory, and I can't thank you enough."

"I agree," Marcus added. "You can all expect a damn good bonus with your next paychecks. Now, if you'll excuse us, I'm going to dance with my daughter."

The festivities continued. Erienne was in high demand and before long, one of her father's business associates cut in on their dance, seeking to learn more about CS180. Additionally, she and her father circled the room, greeting the attendees and thanking them for their donations to Chemistry for Kids. Fitz remained close, and the rest of the team were always circling nearby, keeping a close eye on both of them, reminding her that Fitz was a target as well as a bodyguard. The team was guarding him just as much as they sought to protect her. The realization both comforted and frightened her. If anything happened to Fitz, she would be devastated.

Kylie caught up with her at one point. "Forgive me, cuz, but I'm going to take off. Jet lag is catching up with me."

"Of course, I understand." As Erienne hugged her cousin, an unmistakable flash of red caught her eye. Carol and the bald man were dancing on the other side of the room. Erienne was certain she knew the man, but he still wore his mask, the strobe lights made identification that much more difficult. "Kylie, do you know who Carol's escort is? He looks familiar."

Kylie turned and looked. "No. But who cares? She always dated those pompous jocks. It's probably just one of those jerks that she keeps dancing on her string."

"Yes, I'm sure you're right." She hugged Kylie again. "I'll see you tomorrow."

"Is everything all right? For a second, you looked concerned about something, " Fitz whispered close to her ear, tickling her lobe with his breath.

"I'm fine," she answered as Ian and Maddie joined them. "I saw Carol's date and I thought he looked familiar. Probably just another former classmate of mine."

"But you didn't recognize him? Are you sure it wasn't one of Pruitt's goons?" Fitz raised his head, agitatedly scanning the room.

Erienne shuddered. "No, definitely not one of them. I'm positive. Like I said, it's probably just an old classmate. But with the mask I couldn't see his face."

"Where is he?"

"I don't see them now," she said, scanning the room.

"I'll call Jake," Ian said. "and see if we can get the name of Carol's escort from the guest list."

"I'm sure it's nothing," Erienne said, smiling up at Fitz.

"Dance with me." She took his hand and led him to the dance floor.

As if on cue, the band struck up a slow number. Although they couldn't drape themselves all over each other as they did at the Steel Horse, they were able to be in each other's arms. Erienne reveled in the warmth of his eyes as they turned around the floor, dissolving into the feeling they were the only people in the room.

The song ended and fatigue caught up with her. Erienne made her excuses to her father and let Fitz escort her out of the ballroom. "I can't wait to kick these heels off," she sighed as they reached the elevator bank, smiling at a toddler waiting for the elevator with his parents. He smiled back sleepily as his mother said something about it being way past bedtime.

The bell dinged, and the doors to the car opened. The family entered first. Erienne followed, rooting around in her clutch purse for her key card. She slipped it from the purse, but dropped the clutch and it skittered across the hall. Fitz walked over to retrieve it.

"I press! I press!" the toddler squealed. He pulled against his mother's hand and pressed the *close door* button and two floor buttons before his mother pulled him back.

Fitz hurried back but the doors shut before he could get there. Erienne smiled at him from through the glass wall of the car. "I'll go straight to the suite," she mouthed as the car began its ascent. He nodded, pressing the button for the next car. She saw Ian and Maddie approach and then head for the stairwell after a few words with Fitz.

She let herself into the suite, shutting the door behind her. She flicked on the lights just as someone grabbed her and pushed her against the wall. Terror sliced through her, and a hand clapped over her mouth.

CHAPTER FIFTEEN

"Hello, Erienne. Surprised to see me?"

The bald man she'd seen with Carol earlier smirked at her, and as Erienne looked into his all too familiar eyes, anger swiftly replaced her fear. She dragged his hand from her mouth. "Kevin! Let go of me!"

He released her but didn't step back. "We need to talk," he said as he removed his mask and flung it to the floor.

"No we don't! How did you get in here?"

"Carol was all too willing to help me as long as I kept telling her all sorts of crap about you. She laughed long and hard when she found out you were still a virgin. In exchange for any goods on you, she's been letting me stay in her private suite here at the hotel for the last few months. No one, not even the staff, knew I was here. And as daughter of the hotel owner, the crafty little minx has a master key to every room and elevator in the place. I just slipped it out of her purse while she was getting dressed tonight."

Amidst her anger and disgust, Erienne made a mental note to never stay at this hotel again, never mind her father's friendship with Mr. DiMarco.

Kevin's tuxedo was impeccable — as always, vain about his appearance. But gone was the smartly styled sandy brown hair he'd always been so proud of. The bald look did not suit him at all.

Kevin glared at her as her eyes returned to his. "Yeah, thanks to you and your father, I had to shave my head. I knew your old man would have found an excuse to get me thrown out of the carnival if he'd recognized me. Fortunately, he was so wrapped up in making such a fuss over you he didn't have eyes for anyone else."

She pushed against his chest, but he didn't back off. "Get out of here."

"No." He planted his hands against the wall on either side of her head. "You've got to help me."

She laughed. "Help you? You stole money from hard-working people and smeared my father's reputation. The only thing I'm going to help you do is go to prison!" She ducked under his arm and moved away from him, but he grabbed her and dragged her back.

"Not so fast." He slammed her back against the wall. Seizing her wrists, he pinned them above her head as he pressed himself full-length against her. Tendrils of fear wrapped themselves around her spine.

"Kevin, don't you think you're in enough trouble? Let go of me and get out of here!"

"No! It's your fault I'm in this mess. You've got your father wrapped around your little finger. You could have told him to let me pay the money back and not to press charges. But you wouldn't. Not to mention how many nights I went to sleep with blue balls because you're such a stuck-up, self-centered, frigid little cocktease."

She stared at him in disbelief. *He'd* been the one to act as if she and her vagina were radioactive, but now he was calling her a tease? The man was truly unstable. "Please just go, Kevin," she said shakily.

"No. You owe me, and tonight it all comes due."

He ground his lips against hers. Erienne held her mouth shut and twisted her head away. Kevin grabbed her jaw and turned her head back, forcing his tongue into her mouth. Her stomach roiled as she struggled against him. She twisted and fought as hard as she could, painfully twisting an ankle in the process. Finally, she wrenched a hand free and wasted no time scratching his face.

"Ow!" Kevin let go of her other wrist and staggered back, putting a hand to his cheek. He looked at the blood on his fingers before unknotting his bow tie and pulling it from his neck. "You'll pay for that, you bitch!"

Erienne spun for the door, but he caught her before she got two steps. He hauled her to him, pinning her arms to her side as he wrapped one arm around her and pulled her back to his front. She opened her mouth to scream, but he shoved the wadded-up tie into her mouth and clapped his hand over it. Lifting her clear of the floor, he hauled her to the bedroom and flung her facedown on the bed. She pushed to her knees, but the slim skirt of her gown impeded her progress as she attempted to scramble to the other side of the bed.

Kevin laughed. "Give it up, Erienne. You're not getting out of here until I get what I want."

"I hate to disappoint you," Fitz said from the doorway. "But *you're* not getting out of here until I beat the everlasting shit out of you."

The look on the miserable little worm's face when he whirled around should have been comical, but the red glory of Fitz's rage left no room for humor. He lunged forward and seized the bastard by his lapels and flung him into the hallway. The man almost went to his knees but recovered himself and ran. In no mood to let him escape, Fitz caught the bastard in two strides and hurled him into the living room.

The man fell over the back of the couch before quickly regaining his feet and spinning to face Fitz. He still wore the bug-eyed expression of surprise, but his identity was unmistakable.

"So, Stevens," Fitz growled as he strode into the living room, "not only are you an embezzling thief, you're a rapist, too?"

Stevens quickly scampered to the other side of the room, keeping the couch between them. "No! I wasn't going to rape her. I wouldn't."

"You lying bastard."

"No, I swear! I was just trying to scare her. I need her to help me. She has to get her father to drop the charges. I can't go to jail!"

Fitz snorted. "Oh, you're going to jail, all right. And I hope you wind up getting passed around every night." The man's face blanched bone white with terror, but Fitz felt no compunction about raising the cretin's discomfort. "What's the matter? It's all right for you to rape someone, but it's not okay to happen to you?"

He shoved the couch out of the way, leaving nowhere for Stevens to hide. "Don't worry. By the time I get through with you, what's left probably won't attract any takers."

The door to the suite opened just as he planted his fist in the man's jaw. Stevens fell to the floor and let out a pathetic whine as Fitz reached for him again.

"Fitz, stop," Tobie ordered as Ian and Maddie moved to grab Stevens.

Fitz faced his boss, his need for vengeance nowhere near

satisfied. "He just tried to rape Erienne. I'm not even close to done with him."

Erienne touched his arm. "Please, Fitz," she said softly. "I'm all right, and he's just not worth it." Her calming tone, her look of both vulnerability and concern reached through his furious haze. She wrapped her arms around his waist, and his anger slowly dissolved as he returned her embrace. Erienne was still safe, and that was all that mattered.

"What's going on here?" Marcus entered the suite, followed closely by Tanner. "Erienne, are you okay?"

"I'm fine, Dad. Fitz took care of me." She stepped away from Fitz to hug her father.

Tanner looked at Stevens and then did a double-take. "How the hell did he get in here?"

"That's what I'd like to know," Tobie snapped. "Your team was in charge of hotel security!"

"Is that true, Tanner?" Marcus asked.

"Yes, sir. And believe me, I will find the one responsible for this inexcusable breach."

"It was Carol DiMarco," Erienne said. "She's been letting him stay in her suite for weeks. And she has a master key to every room in the hotel."

"That does it," Marcus erupted. "It's one thing for Bruno to have a blind spot regarding his daughter's snobbery, but this is criminal. I'm going to make him see sense about her and rein her in right now." He hugged Erienne again before he and Tanner left to find Bruno DiMarco.

Fitz pulled her close again. "You'll be pressing charges, of course."

"Absolutely."

"No, Erienne! Wait, you can't! I love you and I want you back!"

"Are you kidding me?" Erienne scoffed. "You are a

worthless human being who has never loved anyone but himself. I ought to have my head examined for ever going out with you to begin with." She spotted Carol now standing in the doorway of the suite. "He's all yours."

"No thanks." She turned her gaze to Fitz. "I'm in suite 2016. When you're ready for a woman with experience, feel free to drop by." She sauntered away, ignoring Kevin's pleas for her to help him.

The police arrived shortly thereafter, and Fitz was proud of how well Erienne handled herself with them. She gave her statement clearly and articulately, unmoved by Kevin's howls of protestations as they hauled him away in handcuffs.

Ian shut the door behind them. "Never a dull moment," he quipped.

After everyone left, and with two of Tanner's men standing guard outside the door and Maddie assigned to the suite's second bedroom, Erienne retired to her room. Fitz started making up the couch, and Maddie rolled her eyes and asked him who he thought he was fooling.

"Everyone guessed the two of you had a thing for each other. After tonight, everyone is positive. Don't be a fool. Go be with your woman."

He sputtered a denial, but Maddie raised a palm and shook her head. "Don't even bother. But if you want to sleep out here instead of with her, that's your idiotic decision. I've got to get out of this stupid dress. Good night, loser."

Fitz stared after her departing form, and then looked toward Erienne's room. He could hear the soft sounds of her moving around. He looked back to the couch, which seemed to shrink before his very eyes as he thought about the queen-sized bed in Erienne's room.

"Screw it," he muttered as he dropped the sheets and went to Erienne's bedroom and opened the door.

Across the room, Erienne stood at the entrance to the bathroom wearing nothing but a towel and a vixenish smile to match the gleam in her eye. "What took you so long?"

His groin asked him the same question. "I'm not sure. But I'm here now."

He closed the door, and she dropped the towel. "Get naked and meet me in the shower."

Undressing in record time, he rolled on a condom and entered the steamy bathroom. Erienne had left the lights off, opting for several candles placed strategically throughout the room. He joined her in the large shower, the candlelight and water giving her skin a luminous glow. She pulled him under the spray and rubbed her soapy hands over his shoulders and down his arms. Stepping closer, she pressed against him as she lathered up his back. The feel of her slick breasts against his chest was heaven, and he swooped down to capture her mouth with his own.

Her tongue met his, thrust for thrust, and blood raced to his loins as he slid his hands up and down her satiny back before cupping his hands under her butt and lifting her onto his pulsing shaft. She wrapped her legs around his waist as he pressed her against the shower wall and sheathed himself inside her, losing himself in her very essence. He fought to keep control, but the events of the evening had awoken in him a primal feeling he could no longer deny. The mere thought of anyone else's hands on her was intolerable, and he claimed her now with an almost brutal force.

Her eyes met his, her look of desire deepening with each piercing stroke. She flexed her legs around him, as if trying to press him inside her even deeper. He seized her lips for another soul-shattering kiss, reveling in the feel of her nails digging into his back. She broke the kiss, pressing her face against his neck as she cried out her release. Her orgasm pulsed around him, sending him to new heights of ecstasy, and as he poured himself into her, he was overwhelmed by a feeling of utter contentment he'd never experienced before.

Her legs unlocked and slid slowly over his hips and down the sides of his legs. He held her as she unsteadily regained her feet, arms draped around his neck, head nestled against his shoulder. "Are you okay?" he whispered.

"I'm great," she whispered back. "But I'm so tired. Let's go to bed."

They toweled off and blew out the candles. Fitz scooped her up in his arms and carried her to the bed, gently laying her down amid the downy pillows. He slid in beside her and she snuggled up against him, falling asleep instantly.

Unfortunately, the memory of Kevin Stevens's assault on Erienne tortured Fitz, keeping sleep at bay and ruining what should have been blissful post-coital contentment. He couldn't remember ever wanting to hurt someone so badly. Not even that prick Graham back during that SEAL special operation in Mexico. If Erienne and the team hadn't intervened tonight, Fitz very well might have killed Stevens and not lost one wink of sleep over it.

That realization burned like acid because it brought home a painful truth. He loved this woman, but he couldn't be with her. Not forever. Not the way she deserved. He was too far gone to be in a civilized relationship.

His thoughts drifted to the time after his mother died. At first, his father spent a lot of time away from home, the memories of his wife too much to bear at the house. But as Fitz got older, his father started bringing women home. One-night stands mostly, but occasionally some of them would make repeat appearances. In a couple of rare cases, they thought they would be moving in. There had been some ugly scenes when Fitz's dad set them straight on that score.

Is that why I always bring women to the Oak? So they won't get the wrong idea? Yeah, that was one reason, maybe even the main reason. He'd never met anyone he'd been even remotely interested in bringing to his apartment, let alone pursuing a relationship with. But what kind of idea were his hookups getting about him when he brought them to the Oak? His pride stung at the thought, and he had to admit he was ashamed of himself.

While it was true he'd had no romantic interest in any woman he'd been with, he had nothing against any of them either and meant them no disrespect. In the brief conversations they would have during the pre-"let's go get naked somewhere" phase, he'd learned they held jobs in all sorts of fields — nurses, teachers, lawyers, sales reps, bartenders. They had parents and siblings, nieces and nephews. None of these topics had been discussed in great detail, but enough for him to know the women he hooked up with weren't barfly deadbeats looking to latch on to someone. They only sought to satisfy a base desire, just as he did.

He'd met plenty of women with no job and no ambitions, and as soon as he learned that fact about them, his eye wandered elsewhere. And maybe that meant something. Had he been looking for someone special all along? Someone to smooth out his edges like his mom had done for his dad?

Fitz thought about his small apartment on the outskirts of Candlewood. He had a crystal-clear vision of him and Erienne sitting on his tiny balcony, sharing a beer as the sun set and the bubbling sound of the creek that ran along the back of his apartment complex serenaded them. And that vision looked right. It felt right. He'd never had that kind of feeling with anyone else.

Erienne shifted slightly and her breath tickled his ear. "What's the matter? Can't sleep?"

He longed to tell her what was on his mind, but an abnormal sense of fear kept his mouth shut. She'd been very clear about not wanting a relationship beyond the physical, and he couldn't deal with her rejecting the idea of taking this thing between them to the next level. Not tonight. "I'm still a little keyed up from dealing with Stevens," he said.

"Mmm, I was too. Until the shower. Want to go back in there?" Her voice was a sleepy mumble.

"No, babe, I'm all right. Go back to sleep."

Her breathing grew deep and even as he held her close. He pushed his morose thoughts aside. Maybe this wouldn't be forever, but he'd enjoy it while he could.

MITCHELL COCHRAN POUNDED his fist on the desk, his blood boiling as he read the news articles reporting on the Stuart charity event held last evening, as well as the announcement about CS180. It would be commercially known as "Cassoline" in honor of the late Mrs. Stuart. Could that family be any more fucking sappy?

Marcus Stuart had never invited Mitchell to the yearly charity event, and Stuart also rebuffed every business offer Mitchell had ever made to Stuart Enterprises. And now the sanctimonious bastard and his perfect daughter were going to beat Mitchell in cornering another lucrative market.

No.

Mitchell would not let that happen. Time to change tactics and wreak some havoc. He grabbed his phone.

Pruitt answered on the first ring. "Yeah?"

"It's me."

"Where the hell have you been? I've been trying to reach you. I —"

"Shut up. I've got information for you."

"Fuck that. I need you to get the charges against me dropped."

"I will. But you need to take care of something for me. Something that will benefit you, too."

There was a pause and Mitchell could practically hear the little wheels turning in Pruitt's greedy little head.

"What are you talking about?" the worm finally asked.

"I have more information on your friend Fitzpatrick. His real name is Mordecai Fitzjames, and he's not a cop. He's a private investigator. I can give you everything you'll need to find him and the people he works for. The people who are protecting him." He relayed the pertinent information. "Get rid of Mordecai Fitzjames and any of his fellow operatives you can, and I will call the right people to make those charges go away."

"What about the Stuart bitch?"

"Leave her to me. She has access to something I want. Something that can make us both a great deal of money." As if Mitchell was really going to let a piece of street-slime like Pruitt in on any partnership. But he needed to dangle the temptation. "Have you ever heard of CS180?"

"No. What is it?"

Mitchell gave him a bare-bones summary of the project and the problems that had been holding it back. "But I can see uses for both the unmodified version and the clean version. There's money to be made from both CS180 and Cassoline."

"What did you have in mind?"

"We need to get our hands on it first. Then we'll figure out how best to use it. In the meantime, just be sure to get rid of Fitzjames." He disconnected and immediately made another call.

"Yes, boss?"

"Do it now," Mitchell ordered. "Keep her alive and out of sight until you hear from me."

CHAPTER SIXTEEN

THE DAY after the carnival found Erienne enjoying a late lunch with her father at a chic French restaurant not far from the hotel. Fitz, Ian, and Maddie, as well as two of Tanner's men assigned to Marcus, were scattered about the dining room. More of Tanner's men were stationed at the exits.

Erienne had wanted Fitz to join them for lunch, and she'd been very disappointed when he declined, pointing out he was still part of her bodyguard detail. She'd barely refrained from snapping at him that being her bodyguard hadn't stopped him from sleeping with her, so why should it stop him from having lunch with her? She sighed deeply, pushing her food around on her plate.

"What's wrong, Goldilocks?" Marcus asked.

She smiled at her father. "You haven't called me that in years."

Marcus chuckled. "But today you remind me of my little girl on those rare days when she pouted about something and played with her food instead of eating it. What's bothering you?"

She put her fork down and pushed her plate away. "Oh, it's nothing, really. I'm just tired of the disruption to our lives, and the need for constant protection and secrecy of our movements."

"I know, sweetheart, I feel the same way. But we can't stop. Not until that criminal is caught and sent to prison."

"But we're the ones being imprisoned in a way."

"Yes, in a way, but it's temporary and hopefully not for long." He took her hand in his. "No matter what, I will not risk losing you. We're just going to have to deal with it for the duration."

"I know. You're right. I'm just feeling sorry for myself, I guess."

"Happens to us all sometimes." Marcus rose from his seat. "I have a meeting in twenty minutes, so I have to go. Why don't you order a big gooey dessert to cheer yourself up? That always worked on that pouty little girl."

"Maybe I will," she laughed as he bent to kiss her cheek. "Bye, Dad."

Fitz approached the table as Marcus left through the kitchen with his bodyguard detail. "Are you ready to go?"

"I'm debating whether or not to have dessert. Care to join me?"

He shook his head. "Get it to go. You shouldn't linger in public places." His tone reminded her he had not wanted her to come to this lunch at all and had only relented at her firm insistence.

"No, I don't really need it. Let's go." She released yet another sigh as she stood, a wave of disappointment sweeping through her.

They exited the restaurant as her father had and climbed into a black SUV with tinted windows. Maddie drove, while Ian sat in the front passenger seat, Erienne and

Fitz in the back. She hated being so close to him yet not being able to touch him, but she'd agreed they should behave in a strictly businesslike manner in public. He'd told her what Maddie had said. Everyone suspected there was something between the two of them, but it wouldn't be fair to any of the other operatives if Fitz acted less than professional.

Was that his only reason, though? Her own feelings for him grew stronger every day, but his were a mystery. He definitely liked her, and when he made love to her he made her feel so special and cared for. But what did any of that mean long-term? What did she want it to mean?

As they left the city behind, she stared out the window. The autumn leaves had advanced to their full glory, but she hardly noticed the vibrant reds, golds, and oranges. Visions of Fitz with his honey-brown eyes, his warm and tender grin all but consumed her thoughts.

When she'd met him she'd thought him attractive, of course, but she'd never thought about how he would look when they were intimate. She'd never pictured him smiling down at her as they shared tender, sleepy passion with dawn's rays spilling gently across the room, never pictured the wicked gleam in his eyes as he pressed her against the shower wall, nor his devilish grin as he served her pancakes in bed after an ardent night — and ultimately introduced her to all sorts of alternative uses for maple syrup.

No, her thoughts of what their joining would have been like had been vague, her knowledge of the basics of how it was done limiting her imagination. She'd thought of kisses and some touching followed by the standard missionary position, all conducted in some dark motel room.

Like the Oak Motor Inn.

Well, not exactly. The reality of the Oak was nothing like

she'd pictured in her head. While she hadn't been expecting four-star amenities, she hadn't been expecting a sleazy dump, either. A sleazy dump with which Fitz was very well acquainted.

Was she crazy to want more with him? Their lives were so different. The fact that he was so familiar with the Oak meant that one-night stands were clearly his norm. Gorgeous as he was, sensational lover that he was, he could have his pick of women. If he wanted to settle down, surely he could have done it by now.

But, crazy or not, she did want more. And she wanted him to want more, too.

She glanced in his direction. His imposing profile revealed nothing of his thoughts. The mirrored aviator sunglasses he wore added an aura of mystery and intensity, making him look every bit the imposing bodyguard. He'd die to protect her, and not just because she was a client. She knew that deep in her soul. That had to mean something, right?

"Shit!" Maddie swore as a dark sedan shot out of a side road not far from the Stuart estate. She swung the wheel to avoid a collision and hit the gas. The sedan sped up and raced alongside them.

"Get down!" Fitz yelled as the passenger window of the sedan lowered. He pushed Erienne to the floor. She crouched as low as she could, covering her head with her arms.

"Hang on!" Maddie shouted. She floored it for a minute before hitting the brakes and swinging the vehicle around on screeching tires. Erienne was flung against the back of the front seat.

"Maddie, what are you doing?" Ian's voice held a potent blend of admiration, panic and exasperation.

"Let's get these bastards."

The SUV accelerated and Fitz tensed. Leave it to Maddie to take on the bad guys with a game of chicken. Ian looked at Maddie, opened his mouth but shut it without speaking. He glanced back, and Fitz nodded a mutual understanding. Now was not the time to distract the woman at the wheel.

The sedan loomed closer before swerving to avoid the collision. The driver lost control, and the car skated across and off the shoulder before coming to a jarring stop in a ditch, narrowly missing a large maple tree. Maddie skid to a stop, bolting out of the SUV and racing toward the sedan with gun drawn, Ian right behind her.

"Stay here, hit the door locks, and stay down," Fitz said, opening his door.

"Okay," Erienne squeaked out.

Another sedan, similar to the first, sped toward him, slowing down as it approached the SUV. Fitz drew his Glock and pointed it at the driver. The man's eyes widened and he hunched down behind the steering wheel and quickly went around the opposite side of the SUV. Fitz ran after it for a few seconds, just long enough to get part of the plate number before it sped down the road and out of sight.

Spying no other immediate threat from either direction, he hurried to join his colleagues. A man and a woman, both in their early twenties, stood beside the disabled sedan, a camera with a large zoom lens hanging from a strap around the young woman's neck. Both of them kept their hands raised as Maddie pointed her weapon at them. "They say they're freelance journalists," she said, her tone dripping with disbelief.

"We'll know soon enough," Ian remarked. He had their wallets and used his phone to take pictures of their credentials and license plate, and forwarded them to OASIS headquarters, while Fitz texted the partial plate number of the other sedan to Jake as well.

"You can't hold us like this," the woman with the camera said. "We're just doing our jobs. Haven't you heard of freedom of the press?"

"When James Madison wrote that amendment, I doubt he meant you have the freedom to cause an accident just to get a picture," Fitz said.

"We didn't cause an accident," the woman snapped before nodding her chin toward Maddie. "She did."

"Who's James Madison?" the young man asked.

Fitz shook his head, ignoring the question as he patted both of them down, and then checked the sedan for weapons. Nothing.

As he closed the trunk, Ian's phone buzzed with an incoming message. "Their ID checks out," he said. "They work for an online gossip rag. Hollywood divorces, politicians having affairs, who's going into rehab, that sort of thing."

Maddie snorted at the couple. "You call that journalism?" The woman's face turned pink as she glared at Maddie.

The young man just shrugged. "It pays the bills."

"Who was in the other car?" Fitz asked. "More of your pals?"

"They weren't with us. I don't know who they were."

"The partial wasn't enough to identify them," Ian read from his phone, sending a frisson of unease up Fitz's spine.

He approached the woman and extended his hand. "Camera please."

"No way."

"You can give it to me, or I can just take it. Can't guarantee it won't get broken in the scuffle."

Biting a trembling lip, she handed it over. "I saved up for eight months to buy that."

Fitz deleted the several pictures she'd managed to snap before Maddie ran them off the road. Ian returned their wallets but took their phones and car keys. "We'll leave these and the camera on the side of the road about a half a mile up."

"No! What if someone steals it?" Tears came to the woman's eyes.

"Sorry, but we can't have you taking any more pictures."

They climbed into the SUV and took off. The couple immediately started jogging after them, the woman out in front.

"She's determined to get that camera back," Maddie chuckled as Fitz helped Erienne back onto the seat.

"Are you okay?" he asked.

"Yes." She took a deep breath and gave him a rueful smile. "Ian was right. Never a dull moment."

"Yeah, well, don't expect boredom any time soon," Ian said as he looked at his phone. "We've got another text from Jake. He's got a lead on the Pruitt kid. Tobie wants us back at the office right away to figure out the next step."

Fitz heard the command, but he didn't like it. He'd grown confident in Tanner and his team, but after what just happened and the near-miss with Kevin Stevens last night, Fitz didn't want to leave Erienne. But he'd have to get over that because the best way to keep her safe would be to end the threat of Pruitt in her life. In *both* their lives. "Okay. We'll go as soon as another protection detail gets here," he said as they arrived at the estate.

"I don't think so," Erienne said, folding her arms in front of her.

"We have to go. This is important. It may be a way to get our hands on Pruitt."

"I understand that. But you are not leaving me out of this. If there's new information, I want to know what it is."

"You need to get some rest. You've got a busy day tomorrow. I'll call you as soon as I know anything."

"No, you won't, because I'm coming with you." Her eyes held a steely determination. "I'm not going to be able to sleep a wink tonight. I'll just go crazy wondering what's going on, so I might as well go with you and get the information firsthand. If you leave without me, I'm just going to get there on my own."

Fitz bit his lip in frustration, knowing full well she would do exactly as she'd said if they left her behind. Ian and Maddie looked at him with raised eyebrows, and he shrugged his shoulders. "We're supposed to be her detail for tonight anyway. We might as well bring her."

"I already texted Tobie that Erienne was coming with us," Maddie said. "I knew you were going to lose that argument."

Erienne giggled, and Fitz felt his cheeks grow warm. Maddie was never going to let him live that down, but he didn't really care. Because the truth of it was he wanted to keep Erienne as close to him as possible.

Always.

THE SUN SET as they drove back into Manhattan, the sky growing dark with night. They arrived at the OASIS offices and went straight to the conference room, where Jake and Tobie waited for them.

"Let's get started," Tobie said, as they took their seats. "Jake? What have you got?"

"Okay, I checked for all of Pruitt's residential holdings. Aside from the Manhattan penthouse, he's got a modest mansion in Florida he visits two or three times a year. He's also got a suite at Caesar's Palace Casino in Las Vegas that he rents year-round. He's got a townhouse in Chicago and another penthouse in Los Angeles. The police and the FBI have checked them all. According to their reports, the staff at all the residences say the same thing. No one's seen Pruitt at any of them for months, and they say he's never brought a child to any of them. And that's it. I can't find any other residential holdings."

"Which means he lied to Anita," Fitz said. "There's no country house, and her daughter could be anywhere."

"I'm afraid so," Jake said. "I'm still looking into his business holdings. He's a slick bastard, though, and there isn't enough of anything to get a warrant to search those properties. We've been conducting our own searches under the guise of delivery people as much as we can, but there's no sign of a little girl."

"So why are we here now?" Maddie asked. "Tobie said there was a lead."

"There is. I went back through all his records for the past several months since Anita's daughter was taken away. For the most part, his movements are pretty predictable. But right around the time Maisy was taken away, Pruitt's EZ Pass shows him going over the Tappan Zee Bridge at odd hours several times a week. He never did that before."

"Where did he go?" Erienne asked.

"Well, there's no way to tell for sure. He doesn't go far enough north on the thruway to where the tolls kick in. And I haven't found him on any of the traffic cameras so far. But I also found that he makes a payment to a woman named Myra Leydon every month. She lives just over the Tappan Zee Bridge. In Nyack, NY."

"Who is she?" Tobie asked. "A girlfriend?"

"I doubt it," Fitz said. "Tommy Pruitt told me once that it was a point of pride for Dave that he would never go to a woman. They would come to him whenever he snapped his fingers. And that's exactly how the sick twist operates. If he wants to get laid, the women come to him."

"I'm surprised he wasn't on any of the Iceman Tapes," Maddie muttered.

"I'm not. Paying a woman for sex, even if it was presented in the idea of owning her like a slave, wouldn't appeal to him. He thinks women should do whatever he wants them to, and do it for free. In his warped mind, he believes it's because they want to. The fact that he's hiding Anita's child from her and essentially blackmailing her into doing what he wants doesn't even figure into his thinking. As long as she stays, he thinks it's because she wants to."

"So how do you explain the payment to this Leydon woman?"

"Paying a woman for a non-sexual service is different. His accountant is a woman. Whatever he's paying Leydon for, it isn't sex."

"She could be the child's nanny," Tobie said thoughtfully. "It's as good a place as any to start. Ian, Maddie, you two drive up there and look into it. Check in with me as soon as you arrive. If Maisy is there, get her out. And try to do it without scaring her. Bring the nanny along if it makes Maisy feel better."

"What if she's not there?" Erienne asked.

"We'll keep digging into Pruitt's life and see what we can find. Worst-case scenario is we've ruled out this possibility."

Erienne sighed deeply. "So we still don't know where Pruitt is, do we?"

"I'm afraid not. But don't give up hope," Tobie said. "I know we're close."

Fitz's phone rang. "You're not gonna believe this," he said as he looked at the readout. "It's Pruitt."

Shocked silence filled the room as everyone stared at Fitz. Then Tobie took control. "Jake, start a trace. Fitz, put it on speaker," she said.

Fitz pressed the speaker button. "Pruitt. Can't say this is a pleasant surprise."

Pruitt's oily voice filled the room. "Ah, Fitz, always the joker, aren't you? Tell me, how do they like your comedy act up there at the headquarters of an elite detective agency? Still want to try and tell me you didn't set my brother up to get arrested?" He chuckled comfortably. "Whatever. It doesn't matter right now. What matters is that we have this chance to talk. You see, I know all about you and your friends. And I'm here to tell you that you shouldn't be so confident in your abilities to protect Ms. Stuart. I will get to her. And not only will I see to it that she happily sucks my cock, one way or another she's going to put some serious money in my pocket."

Erienne shuddered, Fitz gently squeezed her hand in his. "Let me be clear, you arrogant dick. If you lay one hand on her, I will tear off your precious cock and feed it to you."

Pruitt snorted. "I'm *so* scared. Tell me, is everyone who works for Ms. Armstrong there with you now? Ian Westlake? Jake Hooper? I'm given to understand that Reeve Buchanan and his lovely new bride, Jessie, are on their honeymoon at the moment?"

Fitz whipped his gaze around the room. He met Tobie's eyes, seeing shock mingled with fury there. Whether the fury was at him or the situation in general, he didn't know. He'd never let his cover slip in Pruitt's presence, and Jake's firewalls had never been penetrated. The rest of the team looked just as stunned. How the hell did the bastard know all this?

No one said anything. Fitz placed the phone in the center of the table.

Pruitt's sleazy chuckle filled the room once more. "I see I have your attention. Good. Now listen carefully. If Ms. Barnes is there, maybe she could take notes for you like a good little secretary."

Fitz hadn't thought it was possible for a person to really turn the shade of a tomato, but Maddie just proved him wrong. If his own desire to beat Pruitt to a bloody pulp wasn't so strong, it might have been fun to let Maddie get her hands on him.

"So here's the deal, Fitz*james*," Pruitt went on calmly, as if he were ordering a sandwich. "I'm fully prepared to give up my alone time with the luscious Miss Stuart. And much as I would prefer otherwise, I'm willing to let you live, even though you're the reason my baby brother is dead. In exchange for my generosity of spirit, I want two things. First, I want the two of you to withdraw the kidnapping complaint. Next, I want CS180. I want the specs and all documentation related to it, as well as all of the working samples in original form."

"What? No!" Erienne cried. "You can't be serious!"

"Oh, I'm quite serious, bitch. Giving up my time with you is one thing. I've got plenty of women to choose from. But letting my brother's murderer walk away requires a large favor in return. And I haven't forgotten the false promise you and Fitz made to me. Since you're obviously not going to put me on the board of directors, this will fulfill your obligation to me.

"Now, I want everything delivered to me in twenty-four hours. I'll be in touch again to let you know where. Oh, and one more thing. Once you've collected all the data and the sample, I want you to destroy the lab where the work is being done, and erase all the data from the databases."

Jake looked up from his laptop. "Humor him," he mouthed.

"How the hell do you expect us to pull off something like that in twenty-four hours?" Fitz snarled.

"That's not my problem, shithead, it's yours. Hooper's a computer hacker. One of the best in the world, from what I understand. He should be able to take care of the databases. And, Ms. Barnes, aside from your winning secretarial skills, I understand you're very good with explosives. I'm sure you can handle the demolition aspect."

He paused a moment before continuing. "Well, assholes, you all have your assignments, and I'm sure I don't need to warn you about keeping all of this quiet. No need for the authorities to be involved."

"What if we say no?" Erienne asked.

"You won't, because if you don't do as I say then I will make it my mission in life to see you both dead. Neither the law nor you will ever catch me. I have powerful friends willing to help me. You'll be looking over your shoulders for the rest of your lives. As will your father, your cousin, and everyone you've ever cared about."

Fitz glanced at Jake. The frown on his forehead indicated he still hadn't gotten the trace.

"Prove it," Fitz said. "You're on the run from the law right now. Where and who are these powerful friends of yours? Why should we believe anything you say?"

Pruitt chuckled once again, and Fitz's hatred of the man tripled.

"You shouldn't believe me, really. I knew this was a long shot," Pruitt said. "This call was largely for my own amusement. So the only thing I'm going to prove to you, Fitzjames, is that there is always more than one way to get what you want."

The line went dead and Jake looked up from his laptop. "He's in Manhattan, not far from here. But I couldn't pinpoint the exact location."

Before anyone could respond, the lights went out, and a split second later an explosion rocked the building.

CHAPTER SEVENTEEN

"WHAT THE HELL?"

Fitz raced to the window. "There are flames and smoke down by the street. We need to go," he said, his words rising to a shout as the building's fire alarm started shrieking. The emergency lights flickered on, casting an eerie red glow to the room.

"Everyone out. Now." Tobie headed toward the door. "If we get separated for any reason, we'll rendezvous on the steps of the New York Public Library. We won't use any of the safe houses until we find out how Pruitt knows so much. Activate your personal trackers immediately. And be careful. Pruitt could be right outside the building for all we know. Arrogant bastard."

Erienne nearly jumped out of her skin when Fitz grabbed her arm. "Let's go," he said, towing her along and into the hallway behind Tobie.

"The elevators will have shut down. We'll have to take the stairs." Tobie held a hand up for them to stop when she got to the door to the stair well. She placed a palm on the door to test it for heat and then opened it a crack and sniffed. "I smell smoke, but it's faint. Have you all got your master key codes to the other floors?"

All the OASIS operatives nodded or voiced their assent, and Erienne wondered just how the other tenants of the building would feel if they knew about those master codes. She had a feeling they were unaware OASIS had full access to their premises.

"Good," Tobie continued. "If it starts to get too smoky in the stairwell, duck into another floor and we'll figure out what to do next. If at all possible, I want to get out of here before the police arrive. We don't have time to help them with their questions and reports right now."

She pushed open the door and they all filed into the stairwell and started down. They made it to the garage level, and while the smoke in the stairway was heavier, it wasn't overpowering. Tobie touched the door to the garage. "It's hot. Dammit! We'll have to exit through the lobby. Go, now!"

They hurried back up one flight, and this time Fitz checked the door. He looked back at them all and nodded. He opened the door a crack and peered into the lobby. "It looks clear as far as I can see, but there's only the emergency lights, so there are a lot of shadows."

"We have no choice," Tobie said. "The stairwell is getting smokier. Everyone stay low and keep your eyes peeled."

Fitz stepped into the lobby. Erienne followed him out and took two steps toward the main doors when a shot rang out. Fitz threw himself at her and tumbled them both toward the floor as the lobby erupted in a barrage of gunfire.

Erienne regained her breath but was too terrified to scream. Fitz lay full-length on top of her and was somehow crab-walking them toward the doorman's desk. Seeing his goal, she propelled herself forward rather than being dragged along.

They reached the desk, and Fitz shoved her behind it before whirling around and pulling his gun out of his shoulder holster. He fired a shot, and Erienne's blood ran cold when she heard someone scream in agony.

Tobie and Jake laid down covering fire from the stairwell door, allowing Maddie and Ian to make it behind the desk. As they joined Fitz in taking shots over the top of the desk, Erienne ducked down as low as she could and clapped her shaking hands to her ears. The noise was deafening, and she didn't know how much more she could take. She looked around and spotted a door slightly ajar behind her. She tapped Fitz on the shoulder and pointed to the door.

He fired another shot over the desk. "Cover me," he hissed quietly to Ian and Maddie. They obliged, and he scooted over to the door and stuck his head in. "It's clear," he said, and motioned for Erienne to enter. "Stay down and we'll be right behind you."

Keeping low, she scrambled through the door and found herself inside a small office, barely bigger than a walk-in closet. She kicked the door shut. The noise level diminished slightly, and she tried to calm herself with a few deep breaths. On the opposite wall, an exit sign illuminated a gray steel door.

A bullet pierced the door behind her, sending her crawling across the room. There wasn't even a proper desk to hide behind, just a folding table with some delivery boxes piled on top of it. She crouched into a corner, making herself as small as possible and crossing her arms over her head. The battle continued in the lobby, and she whimpered as another bullet came through the door and knocked one of the smaller boxes from the table. Two more bullets came through, one of them passing so close to her she felt the wind of it on her ear.

Her terror consumed her as she realized the room was almost as lethal as the lobby. She crawled to the exit door, swallowing a cry of pain as something sharp scraped her palm. Snatching her hand to her chest, she spied an open box cutter lying next to the package that had fallen. Confirming her wound was not deep, she grabbed the box cutter and hurried to the door.

Cringing at the loud squeaking of the door's hinges, she scanned the alley the exit led to. It was frustratingly shadowy, but as another bullet pierced the office door, she knew she had to risk it. The door gave another loud rusty squawk as it swung shut. She debated which direction to go until sirens sounded from the street, and she hurried in that direction. As long as the gunfire persisted, she knew Fitz and his team were still fighting, and she was going to do whatever she could to help the police identify the good guys from the bad guys.

A man stepped out of the shadows and grabbed her, spinning her around to face him. Erienne opened her mouth to scream, but he clapped a meaty hand over her mouth.

"Well, well, well. Look who we have here." Cooney's evil little eyes bored into her with undisguised malice. "Just the lady I was hoping to run into."

Terror ripped through her as Erienne struggled to get away.

"Oh, no you don't," Cooney snarled. "You and I have got some unfinished business. Nobody gets away with macing me. You could have blinded me, you bitch!"

She raised her arm with every intention of slashing his face with the box cutter.

"Oh, you really want to owe me, don't you?" he snarled as he spied the weapon in her hand. He seized her arm as she brought it down, twisting it up sharply behind her back and pulling her flush up against his chest, trapping her other arm between them. She whimpered against his palm, the smell of his sweat making her gag.

"That's nothing," he hissed. "By the time I'm through with you, you'll wish you'd never even heard of mace or box cutters. Or me." He squeezed her wrist until she dropped the box cutter and then manhandled her toward the back of the building, away from the police and fire activity up front. Away from Fitz.

They passed the door she'd come out of. Erienne screamed against his palm, but muffled gunshots still sounded from inside, making it unlikely Fitz or the rest of the OASIS team would hear her cries. Panic clutched her soul, and Erienne struggled against Cooney with all her might. But fear and stress were taking their toll and draining her strength.

"C'mon!" Cooney barked. "I need to take you back to the boss, but you and I are gonna have a little dance first."

Shards of terror swept through her as the beefy man pushed her along in front of him. She managed to pull her trapped arm free from between them and clawed at his hand over her mouth, but his vise-like grip didn't budge. A loud, rusty squeaking sound reached her ears as tears came to her tired eyes, blurring her vision.

"Aww, isn't that sweet," Cooney mocked. "Crying like a little girl. Ha. Just wait till we get going."

"I don't think so, asshole." Fitz's voice was deadly calm, but he yanked Cooney away from her with a fury. Cooney released her to defend himself, but it made no difference. Fitz delivered three quick punches directly to the man's face. Cooney went down, his body motionless, eyes glazed and nose bleeding.

Erienne would have thrown herself into his arms, but Fitz grabbed her hand and pulled her in the same direction Cooney had been heading, away from the police and fire trucks. When they reached the end of the alley, he carefully looked up and down the street. Satisfied there were no more of Pruitt's goons lurking about, he hurried to the street, hailed a cab, and pressed her into it.

"Wait! What about the team?" she asked as she tumbled into the cab ahead of him.

"We can't wait." He slammed the door shut. "Forty-third Street, between Fifth and Sixth," he ordered the driver before sitting back and pulling her to him. "Are you all right?"

She nodded her head against his chest, not even attempting to speak in the loud cab. The radio was blaring "Better Now" by Post Malone, and the driver was singing along loudly. He raced through the streets like a maniac, blaring the horn as he approached each intersection. Much as she wanted to ask him to turn the music down, she wondered if it would be wise to draw his attention away from the road.

Horns clamored as the driver flew through another intersection a split second after the light against him had turned red. "Well, I'm safe from Cooney and Pruitt for now. But I think I'll be a lot safer when I get out of this cab," she quipped into Fitz's ear.

A hint of a smile touched his lips, the first one she'd seen since they'd left the restaurant. Amazing how just a slight raising of his lips and softening of his jaw changed him from gorgeous to heart-stoppingly devastating.

"Where are we going anyway? That's not the intersection for the library."

"We'll be out of the cab soon enough. Then we'll talk."

They reached their destination and Fitz handed the lunatic behind the wheel a few twenties as Erienne eagerly got out of the cab.

"Now what?" she asked.

"This way." He led her down the street to a parking garage, where Fitz nodded to the attendant before leading Erienne to yet another black SUV. He punched the code on the door's keypad and, once inside, retrieved the keys from the glove box.

"How many of these do you own?" she asked, as they pulled out into traffic.

"I don't own any, actually. These all belong to the company. Tobie keeps a few of them in different lots around the city, just in case."

"In case of what? Are all of your assignments so cloak-and-dagger?"

"No, not usually. Not until we got involved with the Iceman Tapes. Before that, most of our cases were fairly low-key. Well, low-key in the violence department, anyway. We tracked down runaways, followed and photographed philandering spouses, investigated employees who might be skimming from their bosses, ran background checks. Things like that."

"Uh-uh, I'm not buying it. Doesn't really sound like the sort of thing you'd need to have all this 'just in case' stuff for. All these secretly located cars. Safe houses."

"We do most of our work for the rich and famous, and even more for the rich and not-so-famous. They expect results and they expect them quickly. That means being prepared. Tobie takes that very seriously. And some body-guarding cases require last-minute changes of plan and avoiding the press. Believe me, these extra wheels come in handy."

"Are we going to pick everyone else up at the library?"

"No. Change of plans. Maddie was hit during the fight back there."

"Oh my god!"

"She's okay, just a graze. But Tobie insisted the EMTs check her out and take her to the hospital. Which means Tobie has to deal with the police after all. Ian and Jake, too."

"How come you don't have to talk to the police?"

"Once we'd neutralized Pruitt's men, I slipped out after you. The police don't know I was there."

"Did you get Pruitt?"

"No, he either ran when he heard the sirens or he wasn't there to begin with. He wasn't among the dead or wounded."

Her heart sank. "So what does that mean? I have to go back into hiding?"

"Maybe. But right now, we have to go to Nyack and get Maisy."

"We're not even sure she's there."

"It's as good a place as any to start."

"I suppose," she sighed. "Don't get me wrong. I really hope she's there. But I don't know if I can take anymore setbacks."

"It's been a hell of a night. For all of us. But we have to keep pushing through. It's the only way to put an end to it. And if Maisy *is* there, I know I'll feel a lot better getting her out." He took her hand and made to press a kiss to her palm, spying the dried blood. "I thought you said you were okay. Did Cooney do this to you?"

"No, it's nothing. I scraped it on a box cutter in that office by accident. It's not deep."

"There's a first aid kit in the console."

She cleaned up and bandaged her wound, hoping they would find the little girl in Nyack. Fitz was right, she would feel better knowing Maisy could soon be reunited with her mother. As they reached the highway. Erienne felt a small sense of relief at leaving Manhattan and Dave Pruitt behind. But she'd rest a whole lot easier when he was caught and behind bars.

Until then, she would never be safe.

***

"This is it," Fitz said, peering up at the street sign. He turned onto the tree-lined road. At this hour, most of the houses were dark, and the branches dancing in the light breeze threw eerie shadows in the dull moonlight. It reminded him of something right out of a horror movie.

"This place gives me the chills," Erienne said, echoing his thoughts. They continued down the street and rounded a curve. The road dead-ended with a large Victorian house centered at the end of the street. Like the other homes on either side, it was dark — except for one lone, dull light coming from a small window up on the third floor, further cementing the horror movie feel.

"What do you want to bet that's our target?" Fitz muttered. He turned off his headlights and slowed the vehicle. They cruised slowly past the mailbox, the dim moonlight just bright enough to read the number by. "Yep. That's it."

"It figures."

He drove the vehicle back the way they'd come about fifty feet and pulled to the curb under the shade of a large elm tree.

"Wait here," Fitz said. "Keep the doors locked. I'm going

to slip around to the back and see if I can get a look in any of the windows."

"I'm coming with you." Erienne reached for the door handle.

"No, I need you to stay here." He handed her a spare OASIS phone. "I need you to text me if anyone goes in or out that front door."

She looked as if she was ready to argue, but he cut her off. "Listen, that's the best way you can help. Until the others can finish up with the police, you're all the backup I've got. I need your eyes up here."

"All right, but hurry."

"I will. Keep the doors locked. If I'm not back in five minutes or if something goes wrong, take the car, get out of here and call Tobie. She's the first name in the Contacts list."

Erienne shuddered a bit but nodded her agreement. He got out of the car, waiting until she locked the doors before walking away. Keeping to the shadows, he hurried along the sidewalk, and then vaulted himself over the waist-high picket fence surrounding the house, landing in a weed-infested flower garden.

The front and side windows were dark, and quick peeks inside showed nothing but shadowy furniture. He moved quietly toward the back of the house.

Rounding the back corner, he saw light spilling from a ground-floor window. He crept closer and positioned himself under it. At first, all he heard was water running and the clinking of cutlery.

"I can't believe the damn dishwasher broke again," a woman's voice cut through the darkness. "I thought you were going to tell him we needed some extra cash so we could get a new one."

"Well, with his little brother getting shanked in jail, plus a bunch of kidnapping charges leveled at him and all, it never seemed like the right time to ask," came a man's sarcastic response.

A ripple of excitement ruffled through him. Fitz didn't recognize the man's voice, but at least now it was certain the Leydon woman knew Dave Pruitt. Hopefully she'd say something that would explain why she was on the bastard's payroll.

"There's always an excuse," she went on angrily, her voice rising and shrill. "This place is falling apart, and you can never get him to pay for the repairs. You'd think he'd want better for his lousy little brat!"

"Keep your voice down!" the man hissed.

"What the hell for? She's all the way upstairs. She can't hear me. The brat sleeps like a log, anyway. You should see the trouble I have getting her out of bed in the morning. I'm telling you, Buzz, she's a royal pain in the ass."

"You need to be nicer to that kid. Pruitt will cut you to pieces if he ever catches you talking about his little girl like that."

Bingo — Maisy was here. But who the hell was this Buzz guy?

"He won't. I'm careful. Stop treating me like an idiot!" the woman screeched.

"Dammit, Myra!" There was a sound like a hand smacking the top of a table. "Keep your damn voice down. It's not the kid I'm worried about hearing you. We've got a special guest, too. Remember?"

"You knocked her out. Remember?" Myra echoed mockingly. "She's not gonna hear, and I'm not saying anything incriminating anyway. Besides, you really think she's gonna be around to spill her guts? She's already seen too much. She'll be dead in a few hours."

"Probably," Buzz said. "But that's not for us to decide. In the meantime, you keep an eye on her."

"What? You're gonna leave her here?" The water turned off and Myra's voice carried loud and clear through the window.

"Sorry, babe, but those are the boss's orders. He told me to deliver the merchandise and leave her here for a while."

"What the hell am I supposed to do with her? What if one of the stupid ass neighbors comes by selling Girl Scout Cookies or something?"

"Keep her the hell out of sight and order me a box of Thin Mints."

The sound of a chair scraping back across the floor drowned out Myra's angry response. The light went out in the kitchen, and their voices faded. Fitz risked a quick glance through the window but all he saw was their shadowy shapes as they moved down a hallway.

He pulled out his phone and quickly texted Erienne. *A man is coming out. Will drive past you. Get down so he doesn't see you.*

Okay.

Fitz crept back to the front of the house and hid in the shadows by the corner of the porch. The door opened and a tall, dark-haired man walked out. His dark silhouette revealed nothing of his features, yet Fitz thought there was something familiar about him. A motion sensor light came on as the man approached the driveway on the other side of the porch. He pulled a phone from his pocket as he turned and leaned against the gray van parked in the driveway. Even without seeing the tattoo on his neck, Fitz recognized Buzz instantly. He'd been at the Steel Horse the night Fitz and Erienne met.

Dammit! He'd known there was something off about

that guy and should have followed his instincts. It didn't matter that he'd never seen the guy in Pruitt's presence. He should have had Jake looking into him. With that hornet tattoo, Buzz probably would have been easy to find.

Mentally kicking himself and calling himself ten kinds of fool, Fitz knew why he hadn't acted. He had allowed the vision of Erienne in that stunning, body-hugging dress to distract him. The wrong head had been making the decisions.

"It's me," Buzz said. "Everything is taken care of just like you asked. The woman is stashed and I'm on my way to make the drop off. I'll meet you as soon as it's done." He disconnected and got into the van. Like the house, it was old, tired-looking, and a bit run down. It started easily enough, though, and Buzz drove out of the cracked driveway and down the street.

Once Fitz was certain Erienne remained undetected, he called Tobie, quietly relating the gist of the kitchen conversation, as well as Buzz's brief phone call.

"Who's the hostage?" Tobie asked.

"I don't know. They didn't mention a name. All I know is it's a woman."

"All right. See if you can find out. But your first priority is to get that child. As quickly as possible."

"Yeah, I got it."

"We've mostly finished with the police here, so I've sent Ian up there to back you up. If he gets there in time, he can help you with the hostage if it's necessary."

"Okay." Fitz disconnected and returned to the back of the house. His phone buzzed and there was a text from Erienne. *It's been five minutes.*

I'm fine. he texted back. *Going inside. Five more minutes and I'll be back. Stay put.* Pocketing the phone, he examined the back door. There was no alarm, and the locks looked to be as old as the house. "You'd think criminals would know better," he muttered as he went to work on the locks.

Fifteen seconds later, he was standing in the kitchen. Glock in hand, he slowly stepped toward the hall. He froze as the sound of footsteps walking across a creaky floor came from above his head. Good, she'd gone upstairs.

Fitz moved down the hall and reached the wide entry to the living room. A short-haired blonde woman sat on the couch. She was gagged, and her arms were pulled behind her back as if bound. Her head lolled back at an uncomfortable-looking angle.

He approached and lifted her eyelids. Her pupils were pinpointed but responsive, and she groaned softly through the gag as her head rolled to the other side. He checked her pulse before taking a picture of her with his phone, forwarding it to the team. *Found the hostage. Drugged, probably Fentanyl. Not in immediate danger but need to get her to the hospital as soon as we recover Maisy. See if Jake can ID her.* Fitz wanted to know if she was friend or foe before cutting her loose.

He crept back to the hall. As he put his foot on the first step, a quiet scurry of footsteps sounded from the back of the house. He whirled, raising his Glock and then quickly pointed it toward the floor. Erienne, her eyes wide with panic, hurried toward him, just barely keeping her approach quiet. He raised his finger to his lips but she ignored this as she waved her phone at him.

"Where's the woman in the picture?" she whispered. "It's Kylie!"

CHAPTER EIGHTEEN

"THAT'S KYLIE?" Fitz whispered back as Erienne spotted her cousin and hurried over to remove the gag. "Sorry. I only met her at the carnival and never saw her without her mask." He pulled out his knife and cut the bonds from Kylie's wrists, and together they laid her down on the couch.

A door slammed above, and a rattle of footsteps fading from the stairs could be heard.

"Shit!" Fitz swore. He vaulted up the stairs and crouched low as he rounded the newel post on the second-floor landing. A blonde woman with a petite frame ran along the landing toward the stairs to the third floor.

"Freeze!" Fitz shouted.

The woman whirled and took a shot that went wild. Fitz aimed carefully, firing a shot and hitting her in the thigh. The woman howled as she fell to her knees but she still held on to her gun, firing another wild shot before falling over to her side.

"You bastard!" she screamed as she finally dropped her weapon and clutched both hands to her bleeding thigh.

Keeping his Glock trained on her, Fitz hurried down the hall and kicked her gun away.

"Where's the little girl?"

"Drop dead," Myra snarled. "You shot me, you prick!"

"Hey, you shot first. What did you expect? You should be glad I need information from you. Otherwise I would have aimed for your heart."

Hatred flared from her eyes. "Get me a doctor!"

Fitz used his knife to open Myra's pant leg. The wound was bleeding, but not copiously. Good. If he had hit an artery, there wouldn't be time to interrogate the woman.

"I said get me a doctor, dammit!"

"Shut up." Fitz cut the rest of her pant leg off and used it to bandage the wound.

Myra hissed in pain. "You're a real bastard, you know that?"

"Yeah, so I've been told once or twice. Now, stop trying to piss me off. Where's Maisy?"

"Screw you."

"Sorry, I'm not in the mood for skank." Fitz pulled her to a sitting position. He produced a zip tie from his pocket and bound the angry woman's wrists behind her back. A bandana pulled from another pocket served as a gag. "Be right back," he smirked at her, dismissing her muffled outrage as he headed back down the stairs.

Erienne held Kylie close. "She's still unconscious. We need to get her to a hospital."

His phone vibrated in his pocket. "It's Ian." He pressed the answer icon. "Where are you?"

"I've just parked behind your SUV. Jake is with me and he swears that's Kylie Stuart in the picture. Looks like her to me, too. What's the situation?"

"Yes, it's Kylie. Get in here. It's clear, but Myra Leydon's been shot."

"Dead?"

"Not if the running of her mouth is any indication. Come around the back. The kitchen door's open." Pocketing his phone, he knelt beside Erienne. "We need to look for Maisy."

"You go. I can't leave Kylie." She rubbed her cousin's brow and clutched one of Kylie's hands close to her chest.

"Maisy's terrified of men, remember? I need you."

Erienne looked up as Ian and Jake hurried in, then looked back at Kylie. She was so still and so pale. "We should get her to a doctor."

"Jake will take care of her. But we have to find Maisy. From the conversation I overheard, Myra wasn't taking the best care of the girl. Maisy may need medical attention, too."

Erienne looked into his eyes, his worry for the young child evident. He was right. She wasn't going to be able to do anything for Kylie right now, but she could help that little girl. She rose to her feet and faced Jake. "You won't leave her?"

"Not for a second." he said. There was something in his voice that made Erienne believe he'd die before leaving Kylie alone.

She turned to Fitz. "Okay, let's go."

Fitz nodded and headed back for the stairs, Erienne and Ian right behind him. "Myra's tied up on the landing. I've gagged her but she still may manage to make a racket. Just ignore her."

"Is she badly injured?" Erienne asked.

"We'll get her to a doctor, too, but no, her injury isn't that bad."

They reached the second floor. At the far end of the landing a small blonde woman lay bound and gagged. As soon as she saw them, her eyes blazed with fury and she began a screeching tirade that was barely muffled by the gag. Though garbled, there was no mistaking the slew of foul epithets the woman spewed at them as she demanded a doctor.

"Knock it off," Fitz snapped.

Considering his line of work, Erienne supposed it was understandable he could be so blasé about just having shot someone, but she felt a twinge of sympathy for the woman's pain. Although when Myra made threatening remarks regarding Kylie and the child they were searching for, Erienne's compassion for the woman slipped a few notches. Maybe it wasn't so hard to become desensitized after all.

Pushing the thought aside and ignoring the furious woman as Fitz had suggested, Erienne followed him to the first door along the hallway.

He entered first and took a quick look around. "I don't think Maisy's in this one," he said, stepping aside for Erienne to enter. The room was virtually barren, holding only a rickety-looking chair and a few sealed boxes. Erienne walked across the room and looked in the small closet. Empty.

Ian stood at the door of the next room, a look of disgust on his face. Erienne peered around him into a large, spectacularly messy bedroom. Plates with half-eaten meals congealed on them littered the nightstand and bureau surfaces as well as the floor. The bed was unmade, and there was an explosion of clothes and underwear strewn about the whole room. Apparently, Myra was partial to hot pink, black lace, and thongs.

Gamely, Erienne waded in among the mess, but Fitz

grabbed her arm. "Let's not waste time. This isn't the girl's room."

"But she could still be in here. Maybe she's hiding. She's bound to be scared out of her wits with all the strangers in the house, not to mention the gunfire."

She continued into the room, bracing herself to kneel on the disgusting floor so she could look under the bed. She took a deep breath, but a muffled thump above her head stopped her from going to her knees. Her eyes met Fitz's and he nodded. Maisy was upstairs.

They stepped over Myra like she wasn't even there, adding to the woman's already impressive fury, and headed briskly up the stairs to the third floor. There was no hall up here, only a small landing and a single door with a padlock on it. Erienne had barely blinked before Ian picked the lock and removed it from the loop and flipped back the hasp. Fitz looked in first and then stood aside, motioning for Erienne to enter.

This room took up all of the third floor, and was sparsely furnished with a single bed, a child-size dresser, a desk and matching chair, and a small flat-screen TV bolted to one wall.

Crouched in a corner with her arms wrapped tightly around a doll clutched to her chest was a small girl, her resemblance to Anita unmistakable. Erienne walked slowly across the room.

"Hi Maisy," she said softly. "My name is Erienne. Your mommy sent me to come and get you."

The child's obvious terror wrenched at Erienne's heart. For the first time, her fear of Dave Pruitt vanished, replaced by an all-consuming rage. Any man that could put a child, his *own* child, into this kind of a situation was beyond scum. She knew if the bastard were here in front of her right now, she would cheerfully rip his heart right out of his chest. Hell, right now she was ready to go downstairs and kick that awful woman right in her bullet wound.

Yeah, under the right circumstances, it was easy to become desensitized.

Fitz put a hand on her shoulder. "I know what you're thinking," he whispered. "I feel the same way, but you've got to forget that for now. It won't help Maisy."

Erienne nodded. More rage would only further terrify the little girl. She took a step closer to Maisy, and the poor creature tried to shrink even deeper into the corner. Erienne forced calmness into her voice. "Your mommy sent me to help you. She misses you very much."

A mixture of hope and distrust flared in the girl's eyes. "Where's Mommy?" she whispered.

"We're going to take you to her." She hated not being clear that it might be a little while before that reunion could happen. When Dave Pruitt disappeared, so had Anita.

"At Daddy's?"

"No. Somewhere else."

"Will Daddy be there, too?" Her little voice shook. Anita had said that Pruitt hadn't paid any attention to Maisy since she was born, but Erienne wondered if that were really true. The child was clearly terrified of her father.

"No, sweetie. Your daddy won't be there. Just your mommy."

The child brightened a bit, a brighter glimmer of hope growing in her eyes. "Just like Mommy promised? We'll go away? Just the two of us?"

Erienne nodded. "Yes. Just like your mommy promised." And Erienne swore to herself right then and there that she would do whatever she could to keep Maisy away from her sorry excuse for a father. She'd give Anita the money to get started somewhere else, and set up a trust fund for Maisy to go to college. But first things first.

She reached out a hand. "We have to go now. Will you come with me?"

Maisy looked at Erienne's outstretched hand and then flashed her eyes quickly up at Fitz and Ian. "Are they coming with us?"

Erienne gave her a small smile. "Yes. These are my friends, Fitz and Ian. They are very nice, and are here to help you."

Maisy shook her head and stood stubbornly in the corner. "Make them go away. I don't like them."

"We'll wait downstairs." Fitz said. They left the room, their footsteps fading on the stairs.

Erienne smiled and took a step closer. "It's going to be all right, Maisy. I promise. No one is going to hurt you."

"Myra wants to hurt me. She says so all the time."

"Well she can't. Fitz is going to send her to jail."

Surprise and a ghost of a smile swept across the child's thin face. "Really? *He's* going to do that?"

Erienne nodded and smiled as a small lump grew in her throat. How sad that Maisy had no idea there were good men in the world, too. Erienne hoped the child was young enough to forget the horror of her early years and grow up without an irrational fear or hatred of men.

"Yes, he is. And I'm going to help him. We won't let her say those things to you anymore." She extended her hand again. "It's time to go, sweetie."

"Can I bring my doll? Mommy gave her to me."

"Of course you can. Is there anything else you want to bring with you?"

Maisy shook her head and took Erienne's hand.

Erienne led her to the first floor, relieved to see that Fitz and Ian had taken Myra with them on their way down. She paused before entering the living room. Fitz caught her eye and mouthed *Myra* as he jerked his head toward the kitchen. Erienne brought the little girl into the living room, noting with a sad pang how when Maisy caught sight of the men she tightened her grip on Erienne's hand and moved closer to her leg. Sensing the child's fear, both men smiled warmly at Maisy and then looked back toward Kylie.

"Who's that?" Maisy asked. "Is she sleeping?"

"Her name is Kylie. She's not sleeping, really, she's... she's..."

"Did Myra give her something to make her sleep forever? Like the wicked queen in Snow White?"

"Something like that."

Maisy smiled up at her. "Then don't worry. We just have to find her prince to kiss her." Maisy looked at Jake. "Are you a prince? If you are, you have to kiss her to wake her up."

"Um, no, I shouldn't kiss her. I'm not a prince." This earned a snort from Fitz. Jake tossed him a glare bubbling with the promise of vengeance.

Fitz's mirth died on his face as Maisy turned to him, clearly ready to demand if he should be the one to do his princely duty. He was spared by a muffled outburst of indignation from Myra in the kitchen.

"Oh, bite me," came Maddie's response as she emerged from the kitchen and walked down the hall. Her rainbow hair seemed to glow in the dimness of the living room. "Hey guys. What's going on?"

"What are you doing here?" Ian asked. "Did Tobie send you?"

Maddie lifted her chin and said nothing.

"Dammit, Maddie!" Ian exploded. "She told you to go to the hospital and get that wound checked."

"It's fine." Maddie flexed her arm indicating the makeshift, bloodstained bandage wrapped around her bicep. "Besides, Tobie's my boss, not my mother."

"She's not going to be your boss much longer if you keep on pissing her off like you do. She's going to fire your ass."

Maddie glared at him, but a moan from Kylie prevented her delivering any sort of retort.

"Kylie!" Erienne rushed to her cousin, pulling Maisy with her. "Are you all right? It's me. It's Erienne."

Kylie's eyes fluttered open. "Erienne? You're safe?"

"Yes, I'm fine. Are you okay? What happened?"

"I…I'm not sure. I came home from seeing a movie with some friends. There was a man with huge bee tattoo on his neck waiting in my kitchen. He had a gun and he told me you'd been kidnapped."

"What?"

"That's what he said. He had a picture of you gagged and blindfolded."

"It must have been photoshopped," Jake said.

Kylie looked around at the sound of his voice, just now realizing there were other people in the room. "Well, it looked real enough," she said. "And it scared the hell out of me. He said if I didn't do exactly what he told me to do, they would kill you."

"What did he want you to do?" Fitz asked.

Kylie's eyes widened and what little color she had in her face drained away. "Oh! Oh my god!" She shot up straight on the couch and then quickly placed hands on her stomach. "Oh, jeez, I feel sick."

Erienne dropped Maisy's hand as she reached for Kylie's shoulders and tried to gently nudge her back. "Shhh. Sit back and relax. I haven't been kidnapped. We'll get you to a hospital right away. Everything's all right."

"No, Erienne, that's just it. Everything's *not* all right. They've stolen CS180."

"What?" Terror iced Erienne's soul.

Kylie clutched Erienne's hand. "That's what he wanted me to do! He told me if I ever wanted to see you alive again, I had to help him get CS180. He had a Stuart Enterprises employee ID so he was able to get past building security, but he needed me to get into the secure lab. He took a dozen canisters."

"That's everything we had!"

"I know." Kylie's eyes were ripe with fury and anguish. "He killed Marty."

Erienne clapped a hand to her mouth as tears filled her eyes.

"Marty Wagner?" Fitz said. "The security guard?"

"I couldn't stop him," Kylie wept. "Other than Marty and a few other security people, there was no one at the lab today. Uncle Marcus gave everyone the day off as a thank-you. No one questioned Tattoo Man's presence because apparently he started working there recently. Plus he was with me. Then Marty came into the storage area while we were there. Tattoo Man didn't even hesitate. He shot Marty right in the head."

Tears rolled down Erienne's face. Marty had twin six-year-old girls, and she remembered how proud he'd been when they were born. Over the years he must have shown her a thousand pictures of his adorable daughters. And now the poor man was dead.

"Erienne, what are we going to do? We've got to get those canisters back. If they use it without isolating the toxins—"

"I know." Erienne's mind raced with the horror of what could happen. A few vehicles or a small plane going through strategic areas could wipe out the wheat belt, destroy the Everglades. She rose to her feet, Maisy clutching her leg. "We have to get it back. Now."

"I'm coming, too." Kylie struggled to sit up.

"Oh no, you're not. The only place you're going is a hospital." Erienne picked up Maisy and marched across the room to Maddie. "Maisy, I need you to do me a favor. This is Maddie. She's very nice and she needs someone to tell her the story of Sleeping Beauty. Do you think you can do that?"

Maisy nodded solemnly.

Maddie's eyes grew wide as saucers. "I can't take care of a kid!"

"There's no other option. Maisy is afraid of men." Erienne passed the little girl over to Maddie.

"I like your hair," Maisy said simply as she fingered Maddie's bangs.

Maddie looked as if she'd just been handed a paper bag filled with rattlesnakes. "Uh-uh, no way." She tried to give the child back, but Erienne ignored her as she turned to face Fitz.

"Let's go talk to Myra. Maybe she can tell us where the canisters are."

They walked into the kitchen. Myra lay facedown on the floor, her ankles bound as well as her wrists. Fitz picked her up and sat her in a chair at the table. He removed her gag and took a seat opposite her.

"You realize you are in a whole heap of trouble, don't you? Kidnapping, endangering a child—"

"That kid's father paid me to watch her. That's not kidnapping," Myra said with a smug smirk.

"What about the woman in the living room? I'm pretty sure she's more than willing to press kidnapping charges."

"That wasn't me. It was Buzz."

"Seeing as how you've done nothing to help her, I doubt

the court will have any other choice but to see you as Buzz's accomplice."

Ian strode into the room. "Not to mention this." He tossed a bag of heroin on the table. "We found that only searching one room. I'm guessing we'll find plenty more if we keep looking."

Fitz folded his arms. "Things just went from bad to worse for you, Myra. Endangering a minor with all those drugs around? I figure you're looking at a nice long stay at the gray-bar hotel."

"I'll say you planted it," Myra sneered.

Fitz nodded toward her bare arm. "With track marks like that, who do you think they're going to believe? Besides, I'm guessing your fingerprints are all over the works you've got hidden around here someplace."

"No, really. It's Buzz's junk. I don't touch smack. I swear."

Fitz shook his head. "We're not stupid, Myra. And I'm guessing you're gonna need a fix pretty soon. The longer you hold out on telling us what we want to know, the longer it's gonna be before you can get one."

A mixture of desperation and hate filled Myra's eyes. "You bastard."

"So you've said." Fitz folded his arms and leaned back. "What's it gonna be?"

Myra glared her hatred. "Buzz said he was meeting Pruitt at Einstein's house."

"Who's Einstein?"

"I don't know his real name. They call him Einstein because he used to work at a research laboratory, but he got fired a few years ago because of his drug habit. Now he's got his own lab at his house and he cooks up meth for Pruitt."

"Where's he live?"

Myra bit her lip and looked down at the floor.

"Hey!" Fitz straightened up and pounded a fist on the table. "Now, Myra! Where is this lab?"

"They'll kill me if I tell!"

Fitz reached across the table, grabbed her jaw, and forced her to look at him. "Face it, Myra. You're screwed either way. We're not going to let you go, and that in itself makes you a liability to Pruitt, so you might as well tell us. If you cooperate, we can get you into witness protection. After you go through rehab."

Myra glared a moment more. "Fine!" she snapped, jerking her head out of his fingers. "Einstein lives with some crazy hippie chick who makes soap from plants when she's not high as a kite. They've got a place on Clements Road. I've only been there once. I don't know the house number, but it's gray with black shutters. And there's a Confederate flag for a curtain in the front window."

Fitz raised an eyebrow. "A Confederate flag?"

Myra shrugged. "Buzz said Einstein grew up down south. Mississippi, I think."

Fitz nodded at Ian and Erienne. "Let's go."

"Hey, wait a minute. Gimme my fix!" Myra jerked against her bonds.

"The police and EMTs will be here soon. They'll take care of you and start getting you detoxed — after you've been booked."

Ignoring Myra's angry outburst, they headed to the living room just as Jake opened the front door to admit Tobie.

"New York's Bravest were able to get the fire under control pretty fast," she said. "They've declared the building off-limits while they inspect the damage. Catch me up here."

Fitz filled her in as he looked up Clements Road on his

phone. "It's not too far, and not a very long road, so we'll find the place easy enough. How do you want to handle it?"

"Quick and quiet," Tobie said. "You, me, and Ian will go."

"I'm coming, too," Maddie said, standing in the middle of the living room with a hand on one hip, trying for all the world to look like she didn't have a small child wrapped around her other hip.

Tobie leveled a cool, cold stare at her. "You will take Maisy to Sully's cabin and stay there until we can get her reunited with her mother."

"But—"

"One more word and you can start looking for another job right now."

Maddie's mouth snapped shut with an audible click. Maisy leaned her head back and tapped Maddie on the shoulder.

"Will you take me to my mommy now?"

Maddie's shoulders slumped and she looked down at the little girl. "Yeah, okay, I'm gonna take you someplace where we can meet your mommy." She hoisted the child a little higher on her hip and stomped out of the house.

"I saw a car booster seat on the front porch," Ian called after her, barely suppressing a smile at the muttered snarl Maddie hurled back at him.

Tobie turned to Jake. "I want you to take Kylie and Myra to the hospital. Stay there with Erienne until we've got Pruitt."

"I'm coming with you," Erienne said.

Tobie shook her head. "I really think you should stay with your cousin."

Kylie struggled again to sit up. "She will be with me because I'm going, too."

Erienne whirled back. "You are going to the hospital. You aren't in any condition to go anywhere else."

"Erienne, I have to go. This is my fault—"

"No, it most certainly is not your fault. It's mine. If I had listened to you in the beginning, none of this ever would have happened."

Fitz stepped forward. "We're wasting time."

Erienne turned back to Tobie. "He's right. Let's go."

"It's too dangerous."

"CS180 is my responsibility. So unless you are planning to physically restrain me, I'm going." Tobie scowled at her, and Erienne scowled right back.

"All right," Tobie said finally. "You can come. But your own safety and for that of the team, you need to follow our instructions. Agreed?"

"Agreed."

"This is a bad idea," Fitz said, folding his arms as he looked at Erienne. "But I know there's no point in asking you to reconsider, is there?"

"None," Erienne said. She gave Kylie a quick hug. "Try not to worry. We'll get it back. I'll come see you as soon as I can."

"Stay safe," Kylie said. "Listen and do what they tell you."

Erienne nodded and followed the OASIS team out the door.

CHAPTER NINETEEN

Buzz drove away from Myra's house and spotted the shiny black SUV parked half a block down. It didn't belong there. He drove around the block, parked the van, and crept through the neighboring backyards, arriving at Myra's back window just in time to hear her give up Einstein's location. Stupid bitch.

Hurrying back to the van, he called his boss and filled him in. "Should we call this off?"

"Hell no. Everything is working out fine. Take whatever shortcuts you can and get to Einstein's before they do. They won't know what hit them."

"There it is," Fitz said as they drove slowly down Clements Road, another tree-lined street with ripply shadows.

Erienne looked at her surroundings with some confusion. The area was definitely not a wealthy one, but the homes were all nicely kept. She imagined in the daytime, without all the shadows, it looked like your average, middle-class neighbor-hood. Even Einstein's house looked normal, the Confederate flag hanging in the window nothing more than a poor and insensitive decorating choice. Certainly nothing to indicate the house concealed a dangerous, illegal laboratory behind its doors. She shuddered to think just how many such labs existed in neighborhoods like this one all across the country.

A lone car sat in the driveway, and the garage doors were closed. A few vehicles were parked along the street, but there was no way to tell if those cars belonged to other neighborhood residents or if they were indicative of who might be in the meth house.

Tobie and Ian parked behind them and then approached Fitz's driver's-side window. "You two wait here while Ian and I check it out," Tobie said.

"I should go with you," Fitz said.

"No. I want you here with her until we have more information."

"But the real danger is in there." He made to open the door.

"Hold it." Tobie put a hand on his shoulder. "I'm running this operation, Fitz. And I'm getting a little bit tired of my subordinates defying me. I meant what I said. You stay here." She turned to Ian. "Let's go."

They walked quickly toward the house. The mature trees provided plenty of shadows, and with their dark clothes they blended in seamlessly. Once they reached the side of the house, Erienne could no longer make them out.

Fitz remained silent, an unmistakable tenseness to his shoulder and jaw. Erienne knew how he felt. The events of the last few hours had her in knots. How could he stand doing this for a living?

"Does that sort of thing happen a lot?" she asked, unable to stand the waiting anymore.

"What sort of thing?"

"Threatening to withhold a fix from a junkie."

"No. I told you earlier what kind of cases we handle." There was an edge to his voice she didn't like.

"Are you lying to me, Fitz?"

He released a heavy breath. "No."

"Fitz?"

He took her hand. "Okay, yeah, maybe I'm lying a little. Most of us worked side by side when we were SEALs. We went through a lot of shit together, and did a lot of things we had to do that the average citizen might not understand. It's the same since we joined OASIS. We do what we have to do to get the job done. I'm not proud of how I treated Myra, but it was necessary."

The tortured look on his face broke her heart. "Of course it was necessary. She tried to shoot you, she was holding critical information about where to find CS180, and with the horrible way she treated Maisy, I was ready to smack her myself." She tugged on his hand and pulled him closer for a kiss.

There was a soft tap on the roof of the SUV, and they jumped apart.

"Way to have our backs, bro," Ian smirked at Fitz. "Let's go," he continued. "There's no activity on the main level. If this Einstein character is at home, he's probably asleep."

"What if he's not?" Fitz asked. "Erienne should stay here."

"Save it," Erienne said. She opened her door and got out. Fitz swore under his breath and followed suit.

"There was a cheap-ass alarm system," Ian said quietly. "I've already disabled it. Tobie picked the locks on both the front and back doors. She and I will go in the front and head straight up the stairs. You and Erienne will go in the back and cover that exit."

Silently, they made their way across the street. Tobie stood in the shadow of the porch. "Are we all clear on the plan?" She stared meaningfully at Fitz.

He glanced quickly at Erienne before nodding at Tobie. Waiting meekly in the kitchen while Tobie and Ian went into the unknown upstairs didn't sit well with him. But Erienne's lack of training left him with no choice.

"All right," Tobie whispered. "Let's go."

Tobie and Ian moved silently toward the porch steps. Fitz pulled out his Glock and headed to the side of the house, Erienne right behind him. Dim moonlight filtered through the trees, providing just enough light for them to avoid bumping into the trashcans lined along this side of the porch. A dog barked a house or two away, but otherwise all was silent.

They reached the end of the alley and entered the back-yard. Another porch, half the size of the front one, clung soggily to the rear of the house. They climbed the two steps up to the back door. Thanks to Tobie, the knob turned easily in his hand. He slid inside the kitchen, tugging Erienne's hand and keeping her close behind him.

Myra hadn't been kidding about the plants. They were everywhere: on the floor, hanging from the ceiling — where ever Einstein and his hippie girlfriend ate, it wasn't at the kitchen table, which was covered with plants, plant food, watering cans, and an array of spray bottles.

Fitz scanned the room, not liking the shadows all these plants made. But a double check of the area showed them to be alone. They moved farther into the kitchen toward the door leading to the hallway. Ian and Tobie were there, just inside the front door. They quickly checked the front room before slowly ascending the staircase.

Fitz stepped around a large banana plant standing right by the kitchen door, stumbling a little against it as his foot caught on some peeling linoleum. Regaining his balance, he leaned against the door frame and motioned for Erienne to stay close to him.

She ignored him and walked to a cluster of tall plants in the opposite corner of the room. Quietly pushing them aside, she revealed a dozen canisters tucked up against the wall, all bearing the Stuart Enterprises logo. She faced him with a smile. "They're all here," she whispered.

Tobie and Ian returned from their sweep of the upstairs. "All clear," Tobie said, holstering her gun. "Myra must have lied. We found soap-making supplies stored in one of the bedrooms, but there's no evidence of a meth lab, and nobody's here."

"Buzz *was* here, though." Erienne indicated the canisters. "We have to call my father. He'll send our hazmat team to pick up the canisters. They need to be transported properly and safely."

Tobie nodded. "Ian and I will go to the hospital and see if we can get any more info on Buzz from Myra." She and Ian hurried out the front door.

Erienne smiled at Fitz. "I'm so glad we found the canisters. But let's go outside and make that call. These plants are making me claustrophobic."

They started toward the front door, Fitz fishing around in his pocket. "Wait a minute," he said. They stopped in the hallway as he patted the front and back of his jeans. "I must have dropped my phone."

He took one step back the way they came when a panel in the wall under the stairs slid silently open. Buzz stepped out just behind Fitz and put a gun to his head. A second man came out quickly and grabbed Erienne, brutally twisting her arm behind her back.

"Hello, sweetcheeks. Remember me?" Cooney's oily voice slithered in her ear. "We're not done yet."

Dave Pruitt and that mutant Maddox, green and yellow bruising radiating from his nose, stepped out from the panel, followed by a small, wiry man with a long and bushy dark beard. "Knock it off, Cooney," Pruitt spat. "Take her downstairs and come right back."

"Let her go," Fitz said. "It's me you want. She's got nothing to do with this."

"She's got plenty to do with this. The simple fact that she's pissed me off is enough to see her dead."

"Her father will pay a fortune to get her back. If you kill her, you'll get nothing."

Pruitt smirked. "You still think I don't have a clue, don't you? You think I don't know what that chemical is worth? Billions. And I've got a partner who's legit and will make sure Stuart doesn't have any more claim to it. I'll be richer than Stuart ever was."

His smile became feral. "So you see, I really don't need her at all. Except to make you squirm. First, we're going to beat the shit out of you because it's time for you to pay for my baby brother's death. Time for you to feel the pain I feel. And then I'm gonna let Cooney and the boys have their fun with your rich bitch here. I think it's only fair considering all the trouble and pain she's caused. And you, you lying, murdering son of a bitch, will get to watch."

"Pruitt, listen—"

"Shut up!" Pruitt backhanded him across the face. Blood spilled from Fitz's mouth, and Erienne's heart leapt to her throat.

"How much longer y'all gonna take?" the bearded man asked. "My old lady will be home soon, and she don't like no strangers near her plants."

"Shut up, Einstein," Pruitt snapped. "Cooney, take her downstairs."

"No, wait, please!" Erienne tried to reason with Pruitt. "My father—ow!" she cried as Cooney twisted her arm high up behind her back.

"Weren't you listening, sweetcheeks? Your daddy can't help you now." He shoved her toward the opening in the wall, but she tripped over her own feet and stumbled sideways toward the kitchen before crashing into the banana tree and falling to the floor in mess of soil and leaves.

"Get up!" Cooney snapped, aiming a foot at her.

She just barely dodged the kick, crawling quickly over the fallen plant. Her hand brushed something hard in the scattered soil and she spotted Fitz's cell phone. She dropped herself on top of it and managed to slip it down the front of her blouse before Cooney grabbed her arm and hauled her to her feet. She crossed her other arm in front of herself and cringed away from him, praying he wouldn't see the outline of the phone.

"C'mon, sweetcheeks," Cooney sneered. "The sooner we get finished with your boyfriend, the sooner I can get started on you." He grabbed at one of her breasts, just missing the phone. Terror and revulsion gripped her, tremors ripping through her body.

Cooney smirked, forced her back to the opening and pushed her through it. Inside the space was a door. He pressed a code, and the door clicked open to reveal a set of stairs disappearing down into inky blackness. "Go on, get down there," he commanded.

Erienne didn't hesitate. The sooner he locked her in, the

sooner she could call for help. She clung to the banister and hurried down the stairs, gagging a little at the rotten-egg, sulfurous stink that grew stronger as she descended, and trying very hard not to think about what kind of spiders, bugs, or rodents might be waiting below.

"See you soon, sweetcheeks," Cooney sneered, and slammed the door.

She reached the bottom, startled by the sound of quiet weeping.

"Who's there?" Anita's tear-choked voice came from the darkness a few feet away.

"It's Erienne. Where's the light?"

"Erienne! Help me, I'm dying!" Anita sobbed. "Dave sprayed me with that stuff in the canisters. I'll never see Maisy again!"

Fumbling the phone out of her blouse, Erienne accessed the flashlight. She scanned it around the room, revealing Einstein's meth operation before the beam found Anita curled in a fetal position in the corner, wrists and ankles bound. Her yellow tee shirt and blue jeans were soaking wet, and her hair was dripping, clinging to her tearstained face in stringy clumps. The bastard must have thrown a bucketful of the stuff on her.

Erienne hurried forward but stopped short as she drew nearer the prone woman. Drenched as she was, Anita should have been screaming in agony from the skin burns, not merely sobbing in despair. Looking closer, Erienne detected no redness or blisters on Anita's exposed skin. Nor could she detect the strong and distinct burnt-paper odor associated with CS180. Just the rotten-egg stench of the meth lab, underlined with the musty reek of a dank basement.

"Anita, listen to me. Did your skin burn when he splashed you?"

Anita didn't answer, her sobs growing more piteous by the minute.

Erienne closed the distance between her and the sobbing woman. She hesitated only one more brief second before stooping down and grabbing Anita by the arm. "Anita! Did it burn?"

"N-no." Her tear-washed eyes widened in horror. "Is that what's going to happen? Is it going to burn me to death?"

"No. It attacks the respiratory system. But it burns when it first touches the skin." Erienne felt cautious relief seeping through her veins. She leaned in closer and smelled Anita's wet shirt. No doubt about it. CS180's distinct odor was definitely missing.

"What are you doing?" Anita sniffled.

"You're going to be okay," Erienne said with a happy sigh as she untied Anita's bonds. "It wasn't CS180. Whatever they splashed you with was fake."

"What? How can it be fake? Buzz brought it in those canisters with that fancy company logo on them. I saw him pour it into a spray bottle. Then they brought me down here. At first Dave sprayed it on me. Sprayed it and laughed. They all laughed, the bastards. Then he got tired of that. He opened the bottle and dumped it all over me. A couple of drops splashed on his shoe and he freaked out. But Buzz said it wouldn't go through leather."

Erienne's mind raced as she undid the final knots around Anita's wrists. If Pruitt freaked out, he didn't know it was fake. Why would Buzz trick Pruitt? And more importantly, what was Buzz planning to do with the real CS180?

Anita's voice broke into her thoughts. "Are you sure it's fake? Am I really going to be all right?"

"Yes, I'm positive. It would have burned you on contact and it has a very distinct smell."

"I don't smell anything other than the meth stink."

"Exactly."

Anita wiped the last of the tears away from her face and smirked. "So Buzz is double-crossing Dave then. Good. It's what the rat bastard deserves."

Erienne pressed Tobie's name on the phone. *No network coverage* blinked on the screen. A muffled thump sounded from above. Erienne pulled Anita to her feet and towed her toward the stairs. "We've got to find a way out of here. Pruitt's got Fitz and is going to kill him."

"Wait." Anita dug in her feet.

"There's no time! Fitz needs help, and we've got to get the real CS180 back."

"I don't care about any of that." Anita yanked her arm free and fumbled at the wall for a second before finding a light switch and flicking it on. "I only care about Maisy. Did you find her?"

"Yes, we did. She's fine."

"Where is she?"

"At a cabin in the woods."

"What do you mean? Who's got her?" She grabbed Erienne by the upper arms and dug her nails in. "What have you done with my daughter?"

"Ow, stop it! Fitz's friend has her." Erienne wrenched herself free. "I promise, Anita, she's fine. And I promise to help you get to her as soon as possible. But in order to do that, we have to get out of here and help Fitz."

Anita searched her face and must have decided she was telling the truth. "All right. I can get us out of the basement."

"How?"

"I know the code, but there's a slew of armed men up

there. How are the two of us going to stop them? We need help."

Erienne held up the phone, and tried the number for Tobie again, receiving the same *No network coverage* message. "Dammit!"

"Dave's probably jamming any signals. He said he didn't want Fitz to be able to call out once he got here, so he told Maddox to take care of it."

"Then we'll have to sneak outside and get the call through. Fitz's friends can't have gotten very far. But we have to hurry."

"Okay, but I'd feel better if we had a gun."

Erienne glanced around the basement, looking for a weapon, her eyes falling on a shelf lined with large plastic spray bottles. Grabbing one, she instructed Anita to stand behind her before squeezing the trigger. A stream of clear liquid shot several feet out before dropping to the floor. She sniffed the nozzle and nodded.

"What's that stuff?"

"Plant fertilizer." Erienne took a second bottle and thrust it into Anita's hands. "If we run into any of those goons, we'll use it like mace and tell them it's the real CS180. Aim for their eyes. It will burn and sting a bit, so hopefully that will be enough to panic them. Are you ready?"

They crept up the stairs, and Anita punched some numbers into the keypad.

"How do you know Einstein's code?" Erienne asked.

"He doesn't know I know it. Just like Dave doesn't know I have all the codes at his penthouse. None of those goons Dave has working for him are very careful. I always watched whenever they punched in the numbers. They never noticed."

The red light turned green, accompanied by a quiet

click. They slipped into the hallway. Erienne froze when a hoarse male cry erupted from upstairs, followed by a chorus of male laughter. Ice ran down her spine at the thought of what they were doing to Fitz. She gave Anita the phone. "Get out of here and make the call."

"Are you crazy?" Anita hissed. "You can't take all of them on by yourself. Come with me. Let's go call for help."

Another anguished cry tore through the house, making them both wince. "There's no time. He'll be dead before they get here." Erienne pushed Anita toward the door. "Press speed dial one. Go! Now!"

Anita nodded and bolted out of the house.

CHAPTER TWENTY

On shaking legs, Erienne walked toward the stairs, remembering all too well Pruitt's promise of using her to further torment Fitz as well as Cooney's plot for personal revenge. But much as she would like to wait for reinforcements, it was a luxury she couldn't afford. She couldn't bear to hear Fitz in pain for one more minute.

Butterflies the size of vultures danced the cha-cha in her stomach. She took a deep breath and tried to stop shaking. If those bastards sensed her fear, the game would be over before it began. For her plan to succeed, she needed *them* to be afraid of *her*.

Panicked laughter threatened to bubble forth but she bit her lip. Lil' ole Erienne was going to frighten a roomful of street-hardened criminals. Yeah, right. She fired another test shot from the spray bottle. The stream reached about eight feet. Not bad. She would be able to stay out of arm's reach of the bastards. But they still outnumbered her, so the element of surprise was vital, and she would have to act fast before they could overpower her.

Slowly, with her heart pounding so loudly she was sure

it would give her away, Erienne inched toward the stairs and started to climb. The fifth step creaked, and she froze. No one appeared, and she released her breath.

Holding the spray bottle in front of her, ready to blast anything that moved, she continued her ascent. The second-floor landing was empty. A dull light and more thumps and groans emanated from a room at the end of the hall. She crept in that direction, praying no one came to the door.

She neared the room and could see a mirror hanging above a dresser, partially hidden by yet more plants. Standing stock-still, Erienne peered through the plant leaves into the mirror. Einstein and Maddox held Fitz by the arms while Cooney and Buzz took turns delivering blows.

Pruitt stood off to one side with a sick sneer on his face. "Glad to see you can take a punch, Fitz, because we're just getting started." He smacked his fist into his other hand. "I haven't done any hands-on beatdowns in years, but I still spend time with the punching bag every day. Working out on you tonight will be a nice change of pace." He took a step forward. "Step aside, you two, it's my turn. This asshole is going to regret what he did to Tommy."

Erienne's heart pounded like a train barreling down the tracks as she stepped into the room. "Get away from him!" Her hand shook as she squeezed the trigger but she managed to spray Cooney right in the face. He shrieked and threw his hands to his eyes. Erienne swung and managed to blast Pruitt as well before he had time to react.

Eyes wide with shock, Einstein dropped Fitz's arm, and Erienne knew a brief moment of relief when Fitz immediately used his freed hand to punch Maddox right in the flower of bruises blooming from his nose. Maddox howled in pain and dropped Fitz's other arm. Fitz delivered a second punch to the same spot. Maddox crumpled to the floor and lay still.

Einstein ran for the window, threw up the sash, launched himself onto a tree and shimmied down the trunk. Buzz threw his arms over his face and charged toward Erienne. She sprayed him, causing him to veer away from her at the last minute. He bumped into her with his shoulder, spinning her around and knocking her to the floor. The spray bottle spun away from her as Buzz kept running and raced out of the room.

Grunts and thumps reached her ears and she looked across the room to see Fitz fighting with Pruitt. Although his face was reddened and his eyes streamed tears from the blast she'd given him, Pruitt seemed oblivious to the pain as he threw punch after punch at Fitz. Frantically, she looked for the spray bottle, spying it just as it rolled under the dresser. She got to her knees but was tackled from behind before she could move further. Her forehead smacked painfully against the dresser.

"You bitch!" Cooney hissed. "I'll fucking kill you!"

She bucked up but could barely move his weight. "Go ahead!" she snarled. "Kill me. But that's not going to change anything. I hit you with a full dose of CS180. I'd say you've got about one minute before your lungs close up."

"But at least I'll die knowing I killed you first!" He slipped his fingers around her throat and squeezed.

She tried to pry Cooney's hands away, but his grip was like iron. She dug her nails into his hands and scratched as hard as she could. He grunted in pain but didn't release his hold. With her strength waning, she reached for the spray bottle, but her fingers only brushed the sides of it before it spun out from under the side of the dresser and out of her reach.

Just as her lungs hit the bursting point, a pair of denim-clad legs came into her dimming peripheral vision and a hand picked up the spray bottle. Two seconds later, Cooney roared with pain and released her throat. His roar was cut short by the sound of a fist hitting his face, and he toppled off of her. She struggled to draw air, and for a panicked moment she didn't think it would be possible. But then sweet oxygen finally rushed in, and a feeling of relief swept over her even as she coughed and gasped and tried to regain her breath.

Strong hands pulled her to her feet and she nearly wept at the sight of Fitz's bruised and bloodied face.

"Are you all right?" he asked softly.

She nodded, coughing and wheezing as she looked around the room. Pruitt sat in the corner, a dazed expression on his face as he cradled what looked to be a broken arm. Maddox still lay motionless, as did Cooney.

"Are you sure?" he asked, wincing as he pulled her close.

She coughed once more before finding her voice. "Yes, I'm all right. What about you?" She could see his lips tighten in pain as they walked into the hallway.

"They might have cracked a rib."

"We need to get you to a doctor." A creak on the stairs reminded her they weren't safe yet. "Buzz and Einstein got away," she whispered.

Fitz raised the spray bottle as Erienne stooped down and checked Cooney's pockets for a gun, her eyes glued to the stairs. She let out a breath she hadn't realized she'd been holding when Tobie's head came into view.

"What's going on?" Tobie hissed.

"It's all clear," Fitz ground out. "Pruitt and his goons were hiding out in the wall—"

"In the wall?"

"Yes. There's a hidden entry under the stairs leading to Einstein's meth lab," Erienne explained as Ian used zip ties to bind Pruitt, Maddox, and Cooney. "But Buzz got away. And he still has CS180."

"What? No, the canisters were in the kitchen," Fitz said.

"Those canisters are either empty or fake." Erienne started moving them back toward the stairs. "Anita was in the basement with me. She told me Pruitt sprayed her with CS180, but he couldn't have. Her clothes were soaked but she was fine. If she'd really been doused with it, she would have been in agony from the burns."

"Wait a minute," Fitz said, holding up the spray bottle. "Wasn't that CS180 you sprayed them with just now? They all screamed like they were on fire."

"Plant fertilizer. I found it in the basement." They reached the first floor. Erienne hurried to the kitchen, flipped on the light and took a good look at the canisters. "These are fake. That's not the real Stuart Enterprises stamp."

"So, Buzz switched the canisters. And he lied to Pruitt. Why would he do that?"

"Some sort of double-cross. Anita said as much." Erienne reached into Fitz's pants pocket and pulled out the car keys. "Fitz needs a doctor," she said to Tobie. "I'm going after Buzz. I have to know where he's taking those canisters. I'll call you with a location. " She'd gone two steps before Fitz caught her arm. She arched an eyebrow. "Doing a Cooney impersonation?"

"Of course not." He dropped her arm. "But you're not going after him alone. I'm coming with you."

"No, your ribs—"

"Save your breath," Tobie cut in. "He's as stubborn as you are. As long as he can move, he'll come with us. *All* of us. But that's not the issue as I see it. The problem is we've lost the trail. None of us know who Buzz is really working for or which way he went."

"I do."

All eyes swung to the back door. Anita stood in the frame, holding Fitz's phone aloft. "I had to go several houses away in order to get coverage. I saw Buzz drive past. He was headed for the thruway. But I don't know who he's working for."

"Did you see which way he went? North or south?"

"No."

"Let's split up," Fitz said. "Erienne and I will go south, you and Ian go north. He can't have gotten that far ahead." They hurried for the door.

"Wait!" Anita cried. "What about me? Where's Maisy?"

Tobie whipped out a business card and thrust it at Anita. "Call that number and ask for Tanner Montgomery. Tell him Tobie said for him to meet you here with the police. Once the cretins upstairs are in custody, Tanner will take you to your daughter. You can trust him."

Anita nodded and took the card.

"We're looking for a gray van," Fitz said as they headed for their vehicles. "Old and beat up."

"Got it." With a screech of tires, they headed for the thruway, and in a few moments Fitz and Erienne reached the Tappan Zee Bridge. At this late hour, there were only a few other cars and a handful of trucks making the crossing. No sign of a van.

"We're never going to find him." Erienne shuddered at the thought of CS180 out in the open.

"Yes we will."

Crossing the bridge in record time, they hurtled along the highway. They rounded a curve just in time to see a set of taillights right before they disappeared down an exit ramp. "Do you think it's him?" she asked.

"Yeah. That looked like a van to me."

Erienne dug her phone out of her purse and updated Tobie, putting the woman on speaker.

"We're turning around," Tobie responded. "We haven't seen any vans going in this direction."

"Hang on!" Fitz reached the bottom of the exit ramp and barely slowed down as he took the turn. Erienne's heart stuttered as the vehicle lifted slightly onto two wheels before slamming on the road and roaring forward. Several blocks ahead, the taillights flared brighter for a moment as the vehicle, which she could now see definitely was a van, made a left turn.

Fitz floored the pedal as Erienne relayed the street names to Tobie. They took the left turn at lightning speed. Buzz's vehicle was much closer now, stopped at a red light just a block ahead. As Fitz straightened their vehicle and raced forward, Buzz all of a sudden shot through the intersection, not waiting for the light to change.

"He's spotted us, Tobie." Fitz's words were tinged with a tense energy. "And I can't try bumping him. Not if he's got CS180 in that van."

"Don't lose him. We'll be there asap."

Erienne's mouth went dry as the SUV roared forth. They approached the intersection, and the light turned green as they reached it. Their luck held even further that at this late hour there was no one else on the roads.

Buzz took a turn ahead at high speed and Fitz did the same, closing the gap between the two vehicles. They reached a fairly open stretch of road, with nothing but large fields dotted with the shadows of a few trees and bushes on either side. A lone motorcyclist approached from the other direction, but there was no other traffic. Buzz shot ahead, but Fitz once again closed the gap. They passed the motor-cyclist in a blur.

A deer shot out from one of the shadows, running directly in front of the van. Buzz swerved and lost control. Fitz swore, slamming on the brakes as he swung around Buzz on the other side, narrowly missing the deer himself before the animal raced off into the darkness on the other side of the road.

With a keening little cry, Erienne braced one hand on the dashboard and the other on the ceiling of the SUV as it spun around a full 180 degrees. It came to a jerky halt just in time for them to see Buzz's van roll over twice before coming to a stop on its side in the field. The back door of the van had come open, and the bright yellow canisters bearing the name of Stuart Enterprises were strewn all over the road and field.

They bolted from the car and hurried toward the van, giving the canisters as wide a berth as possible, and looked into the driver's-side window. Buzz lay crumpled against the opposite door, blood streaming from his head. A canister lay against his leg, liquid falling in small drips on his thigh. He did not appear conscious, but he was moaning.

"We have get him out of there," Erienne said. "If he's exposed for too long, he won't be able to breathe."

"There's a first aid kit and a blanket in the back of the SUV. Go get them while I try and get the door open." She raced away while he climbed onto the side of the van. He tried to pull the door open, but the frame was bent and he couldn't do it. He clambered down to the ground, and walked to the front of the vehicle.

The windshield was cracked, and one end of it had come loose from the frame. Fitz pulled the loose end. Erienne returned, dropping the blanket and first aid kit on the ground before squeezing beside him and helping to pull. Though his injured rib screamed in protest, he kept at it until they'd made a big enough gap. He reached into the cab of the vehicle, caught Buzz under the arms, and pulled him gently from the wreckage.

"Be careful of that canister," Erienne whispered.

As if he could forget it. The smell of burnt paper was so strong, Fitz nearly gagged. Plus, Buzz's moans, though increasing in volume, were beginning to sound more strangled. *Damn, that's fast!*

He dragged Buzz away from the van and set him down. The burnt-paper smell wouldn't clear his nostrils, and Fitz backed away for a second, afraid he might wretch. Erienne folded the blanket and placed it under Buzz's head. The man's eyes fluttered open. "Am I on fire?" he wheezed. "I'm burning alive!"

"No, you were splashed from one of the canisters. But it was just a little on your leg," Erienne said. "It might not even scar."

"No," he rasped, "not my leg. My stomach."

Fitz pulled a flashlight from his belt and aimed it at Buzz's torso. A large wet spot soaked the man's tee shirt from the hem up to just below his chest. Erienne looked from the stain to Fitz, her eyes filled with horror. She shook her head. Buzz wouldn't make it.

"Hang in there, man," Fitz said quietly. "An ambulance will be here soon."

"Oh, man, it fucking burns!"

Fitz lifted the neck of his shirt above his nose and dropped to his knees, ignoring the smell and careful not to touch Buzz. "Listen, you're going to be all right," he lied, "but I need you to tell me who you were working for. We know it was someone besides Pruitt. Who wanted you to steal CS180?"

Buzz wheezed pitifully. "The man on the phone."

"Who is it? Who's the man on the phone?"

"My boss. He's...he..." Buzz's breathing grew more labored and desperate. His eyes widened and he reached for Erienne's hand. She took it, holding it away from his body, away from the wet shirt. "Help me!" he rasped. She stroked the back of his hand and kept her gaze on his. Buzz gave a final shudder and lay still.

Erienne laid his hand on the ground and quickly got to her feet. "Let's get away from these fumes. We have to call for the hazmat team."

He wrapped an arm around her waist, and they walked back to the road, Fitz hissing a bit as they climbed the small embankment up to the pavement.

"We need to get you to the hospital."

"I'll be fine."

"No arguments. You're going."

They reached the SUV just as Tobie and Ian arrived. "Are you two all right?" Tobie asked.

"Yeah." Fitz quickly explained what happened while Erienne called her father.

"We still don't know what the hell Buzz was planning to do with those canisters. Or who he was working with." Ian shook his head. "I don't like it."

"We'll talk to Myra again," Tobie added. "She might know something more."

Fitz winced inwardly. He'd been pretty rough on Myra, and he hated that Erienne had seen that side of him. Why would she ever want to be with a man whose job had him strong-arming a woman half his size? Never mind the woman in question was a strung-out junkie holding vital information. He could only imagine what Erienne thought of him now that she had seen firsthand what his life was really like, no matter what she'd said about it earlier.

Erienne's worried voice reached him as she spoke to her father, and Fitz blamed himself for dragging her and her family into his sordid, thuggy life. If it hadn't been for him, none of this would have happened. Erienne never would have come onto Pruitt's radar, Kylie never would have been kidnapped, and CS180 would have remained safely in the lab where it belonged. But at least it was over now. Pruitt was in custody, and Erienne's life was no longer in danger.

Which meant it was time for them to go their separate ways.

CHAPTER TWENTY-ONE

Erienne sat with her father in the back of his limousine. The throbbing lights of the first responders' vehicles cast an eerie, uneven glow to the limo's interior. Even so, Erienne could see the worry etched on her father's face.

"I'm sorry, Dad. This is all my fault."

Marcus looked at her with an astounded expression. "What? Don't be silly. I don't want you or Kylie blaming yourselves for any of this. The thieves who stole CS180 are the ones responsible. I just thank the stars above that both of you are okay."

He gave her a fierce hug, and she hugged him back with the same fervor. Her father was a good man and, of course, he wouldn't place any of the blame with her. But she knew the truth. The events of tonight were a direct domino result of her having gone to the Steel Horse with the stupid idea of losing her virginity to some random guy. If she'd stayed home that night, none of this would have happened.

But if she'd stayed home that night, she never would have met Fitz, a man she most likely wouldn't have spared a second thought had they met under different circumstances.

She'd never thought of herself as a snob, but maybe she'd been a closet one. Fitz was so far removed from the type of man she'd always imagined herself winding up with. Any time she'd thought about it, she'd always pictured herself with someone with a similar background to her own, another scientist, perhaps, or an executive type. Someone like...Kevin.

Well there was an eye-opener. Kevin was exactly the type of man she'd envisioned herself with, and he'd turned out to be a thief and a possible rapist. Fitz, a man who hung around criminals and got his hands dirty, was the one with a good moral character.

Erienne couldn't lie to herself any more, and the truth was she'd been judging books by their covers her whole life. Even her own mother. Sure, all the other mothers had worn the stylish clothes and lunched at all the trendy restaurants, but what had they accomplished? Heck, now that she thought about it, most of her friends' moms were on their second or third husbands. Lucrative marriages were their chosen career paths. Yet right up until it was too late, Erienne had let her teenaged insecurities blind her to just how exceptional her mother had been.

And now she was doing the same thing to Fitz. She'd pictured a man like him as someone to maybe have some fun with, yet never considered he could be her life's mate.

But he was.

Beneath his rough exterior was a tender, thoughtful lover with a heart of gold. She couldn't even entertain the idea of sharing her body or her heart with anyone else.

Her father cleared his throat, interrupting her thoughts. "There's nothing more you or I can do here. Let's go home and leave this to the professionals."

She looked out the window. The OASIS team stood at

the edge of the road, watching the clean-up proceedings. Fitz turned at that moment, as if he'd sensed her eyes on him. His smile to her was weary but heartwarming. She could only imagine how exhausted he was, and wondered how he managed to stay on his feet after the beating he'd taken at the hands of Pruitt and his degenerates.

"You go ahead home, Dad. I'm going to get Fitz to the hospital. I'll check on Kylie while I'm there."

"You're in love with him, aren't you?" She turned back in surprise, and her father chuckled. "Don't look so shocked. It was written all over your face at the carnival."

"Are you angry?"

"Angry? About what? He's a good man. And he obviously thinks the world of you, so I know he has good sense. I'll let you in on a little secret. I wasn't fond of the idea of you dating Kevin."

"What? How come you never said anything?"

"Because you are a grown woman, and I trust your judgment. And the truth of it is, Kevin was a very good con man who fooled us both. I didn't really like him, it's true, but I did respect his so-called business sense and work ethic. Not many people can fool me, but he did for a while. In fact, it was your dating him that led me to uncover his thievery. Once he started keeping company with my little girl, I started keeping a much closer eye on him. And I told Tanner to take another look at him. He did, and he found a new offshore account that Kevin opened after he'd been hired."

"I just wish I had seen Kevin for what he was sooner."

"We all make mistakes. But I know you're smart enough to learn from them." Marcus smiled at her fondly. "Now, go take care of your young man. I spoke to Kylie's doctor already, but still, call me after you've seen her."

"I will." She kissed his cheek and got out of the car. Reaching Fitz's side, she took his hand. "Let's go. I'm taking you to the hospital."

"I'm all right."

"No, you're not."

"She's right," Tobie said. "Go get checked out. That's an order."

Erienne pulled him to the SUV. She more or less pushed him into the passenger seat and drove to the emergency room. While the doctor looked him over, Erienne inquired after Kylie and was directed to her private room. She opened the door to find her cousin asleep and Jake Hooper sitting in a chair in the corner. He stood up when she entered.

"She's going to be fine. The doctors want her here for observation tonight, but she can go home in the morning."

"Thank goodness. Thank you for looking after her."

"I promised you I would."

"Yes, you did. Fitz is getting looked over down in the ER if you want to talk to him."

"You'll stay with her in case she wakes up?" Jake asked, and Erienne was touched by his concern.

"Of course."

Jake left the room as she walked to the bed and took her cousin's hand. Kylie looked a little pale but otherwise normal. Erienne breathed a sigh of relief. If Kylie suffered any permanent damage from all this, Erienne would never forgive herself.

Kylie's eyes fluttered open. "Hey. Stop looking at me like that. I'm fine."

"I know. But I can't help worrying."

"Did you get the samples back? Did you find Tattoo Man?"

"Yes. His name was Buzz Kruger."

"Was?"

"He's dead. There was an accident and one of the canisters leaked onto his chest."

"An accident? Oh my god! What about the other canisters?" Kylie's eyes were wide with panic.

"Shhh," Erienne soothed. "The hazmat team is there and the situation is contained. Buzz was the only fatality. It's going to be all right."

"Thank goodness."

"Go back to sleep. The doctor says you can go home in the morning."

"Yeah," Kylie said sleepily, her eyes drifting shut again. "That's what Jake said."

A ghost of a smile flitted on Kylie's lips when she mentioned Jake, arousing Erienne's curiosity. As far as she knew, they'd only met twice — at the Steel Horse, and then at the carnival. Had those brief encounters been enough for some sparks to fly? She'd have to ask Kylie about it when she was home and feeling better.

Jake returned a few minutes later. "How is she doing?"

"She woke up for a little bit, but she's gone back to sleep. She sounded all right."

Relief flooded his face. "Good. Fitz just told me about Buzz working for someone else. I'll crawl all over his phone records. If there's a pattern that leads to his mystery boss, I'll find it."

"I'm sure you will."

"Listen, they want Fitz to stay for a while, but he's hellbent on leaving. Maybe you can talk some sense into him."

She nodded. "I'll go down now." As she left the room, Jake settled into the chair again. Yes, she was definitely going to have a nice long Jake chat with Kylie.

CHAPTER TWENTY-TWO

THE ELEVATOR DOORS OPENED, and Fitz's voice reached Erienne loud and clear. "I am *not* staying. I'm fine."

"Sir, the doctor wants to make sure you don't have a concussion."

"I don't, darlin', trust me."

Erienne rounded the curtain to see Fitz struggling to put his shirt back on. A nurse with short salt-and-pepper hair stood next to his bed, her arms folded and not offering him one iota of assistance. She had a scowl on her face lethal enough to scare a rabid grizzly back into his den.

"Now you listen up, young man. I'm not about to let some beefcake sweet-talk me. I've been here too long and seen it all before." She caught sight of Erienne. "Is this your wife? Maybe she can make you see reason," the nurse huffed as she rolled her mobile workstation toward the hall. "The doctor wants him to stay a while."

"I'll see what I can do."

"Don't even bother," Fitz said when they were alone. "It's a cracked rib, just like I thought. All I need is some rest, and I can do that at home. I'm outta here."

"Oh no you're not." Erienne walked over and pulled off his shirt.

"Ow! Hey, it just took me ten minutes to get into that!"

"Which is exactly why you're staying."

He lay back on the bed, closing his eyes. "Hospitals are hell. Why are you doing this to me?"

"Because I love you."

His eyes flew open. "No, you don't. You can't."

"Why not?"

"I can't be the man you need."

"That's ridiculous. Says who?"

"Me, that's who. I'm not good enough for you."

"I can decide that for myself, thank you."

"Look, tonight you saw what I do. What I really do. The time at the cabin was something else. A fairy tale. That's not who I am in real life."

She folded her arms. "Stop it. I know who you are in real life. You are a man who, in an effort to save victims of an atrocious crime, spends almost every waking hour of every day looking at videos that would crush anyone else. You could walk away from all that any time, but you don't."

"I spend too much time with criminals."

"To stop them! Don't tell me you want to beat yourself up about that. Look, Fitz, I'll admit I've seen things these past few weeks that I would rather I hadn't. I've always known there were bad things in the world — hunger, crime, child abuse, and heaven knows what else — but I'd be lying if I said I hadn't led a fortunate life, sheltered from the worst the world has to offer. Sure, I've volunteered and made donations to help combat some of those awful things. But with you, I've seen what it's like to really get down and dirty and *fight* those things. It's easy to throw money around, but not easy at all to do what you do. It takes a special kind of man to do that."

"I'm not special, Erienne."

"Yes, you are."

"No. I've spent too much time with criminals. I've become a thug. It's who I am now."

"Stop it! I will not let you talk about the man I love like that."

He smiled sadly at her. "Erienne—"

"No! Not one more derogatory word. I know you said the time at the cabin wasn't the norm for you, but you're wrong. Look how easily you slipped into it. Think about it. I want you to remember how happy you were. You *were* happy, right? You weren't just acting?"

"I was over the moon happy."

"And was it hard for you to feel that way?"

"No. It's easy to feel happy around you."

"So I think you're worrying about that thug thing for nothing."

"Erienne, have you forgotten where we met? Do you know what I was doing that night? Just waiting for a willing woman to show up. *Any* willing woman. *That's* the kind of guy I am. What's more, I would have taken you to cheap motel. *For your first time!*"

"You didn't know it was my first time. And it wasn't like you were forcing me to go. I wanted it. I wanted you. I still do."

The look on his face betrayed a glimmer of hope, and her heart soared. She had to get through to him. He was her world now, and the thought of him not in it cast a shroud of darkness on her future. "Fitz, if you had to choose right now — and you do, by the way — which of these would you want? To come home with me, now and forever, or go to the Steel Horse and pick up a stranger?"

His eyes glowed with longing. "Princess, you know I'd choose you."

She smiled. "So? Do I really need to say more?"

He smiled back, a glimmer of tears in his eyes. "No," he said hoarsely, "I guess you don't."

She leaned over and kissed him, long and deep. "I love you, Fitz."

"I love you, too."

"Good. Now, let me go find your doctor and see about springing you out of here."

"I thought you wanted me to stay."

"Only if it's really necessary, of course. Otherwise, I want you home and all to myself."

"Works for me."

With a happy heart and humming "I Will Always Love You" to herself, Erienne headed for the nurses' station. After lengthy conversations with both his nurse and doctor, in which she assured them Fitz would get the best of care at her home, she retraced her steps down the hall, release papers in hand.

"Okay, let's get you out of here." She swept the curtain aside and her smile disappeared. His bed was empty and his clothes were gone. A red-and-white trifold brochure titled *Heart Health and You* lay propped against the pillow. With a sinking heart and shaking hands, she picked up the brochure to read the words scribbled across the top.

Dear Erienne, I do love you, and that's why I can't be with you. You deserve better. Be well. Love, F

CHAPTER TWENTY-THREE

MITCHELL COCHRAN PULLED into his immaculate garage and lined his motorcycle up with the several others he owned. He'd been on his way to meet Buzz at their pre-arranged rendezvous point when the fool tore past him with Fitzjames hot on his heels. When Buzz's van flipped over, Mitchell thought that was the end of his plan to acquire CS180. But while Fitzjames and the Stuart woman were involved in rescuing Buzz — do-gooders did have their uses — Mitchell had been able to jog back to the accident area without being seen and grab one of the canisters that had been thrown to the other side of the road.

Unlike Buzz, Mitchell fully understood the danger of what they were dealing with and had made sure to wear protective clothing underneath his motorcycle garb. The canister he'd found looked intact, but Mitchell took no chances. Handling it with protective gloves on and placing it very gingerly in his backpack, he'd driven home slowly, carefully avoiding both the oncoming first responders and any potholes in the road.

Now, he headed down to his palatial estate's lower level.

He had, among other things, a secure storage facility that would safely house CS180 until Mitchell could get his own team of scientists to analyze and duplicate it.

There would be no way for him to bring it to market now that Stuart Enterprises had already announced it. Marcus Stuart would have Mitchell in court faster than the speed of light, and it wasn't worth that hassle.

But CS180 in its uncorrected state could be a powerful weapon. And Mitchell loved nothing more than wielding power. A day might come when he could use the substance to his advantage.

For the most part, his evening had been a success. He'd gotten CS180, and according to the police band he'd monitored on the ride home, Buzz was dead, tying up that particular loose end very nicely. Fitzjames was still alive, though. A minor yet very annoying setback that Mitchell would rectify later on. His determination to destroy OASIS was still firmly intact, and it would be fun to watch Fitzjames and the rest of them squirm and bungle around a bit more.

With that happy thought in mind, Mitchell changed out of his biker and protective gear before heading down the hall to his private playroom. He unlocked the door and flipped on the lights. A large pool table dominated the center of the room, while an elegant bar lined one wall. On the opposite wall, two lovely young girls — one fully clothed, the other stark naked — blinked their eyes and ducked their heads down from the light. They'd been chained to the wall here in the dark all day.

Mitchell went to the bar and poured a scotch, tossing it back quickly before heading toward the girls. Their whimpers as he approached sent a surge of delight to his groin. He'd bought them last night and had them delivered here this morning. Now it was time to begin their training.

He unlocked the chains of the clothed one and pushed her back flat against the wall, refastening her bonds so she stood spread-eagle against the wall, her toes barely brushing the floor. He released the nude girl and quickly tied her hands behind her back. He pulled her over to a straight-backed chair, sat, and threw her over his lap. Her sweet bare ass looked up at him prettily. Locking one leg over both of hers, he picked up a leather paddle that hung looped on the chair.

When he was finished, the girl in his lap had lost consciousness. He carelessly tossed her to the floor. Walking slowly and deliberately toward the wall, he unzipped his fly, releasing his throbbing erection. "Would you like to avoid the same treatment?" he whispered to the terrified girl, her silent tears an additional aphrodisiac to his soul. She nodded her head frantically.

"Then you will do whatever I tell you to do, won't you?"

Another nod, and he released her from the wall. "Remove your clothes and get on all fours."

She unbuttoned her blouse with shaky hands, and he admired her large, creamy breasts spilling over a lacy bra. Indeed, she was exquisite.

And she was his.

"You're an idiot. You know that, right?" Maddie tilted her beer glass in Fitz's direction before taking a sip. "She's the best thing that ever happened to your sorry ass, and you walked away."

"Leave him alone, Maddie," Ian said. "We're here to relax, not point out Fitz's flaws."

"Gee, thanks for the backup," Fitz muttered.

"Any time." Ian smirked at him as he lifted his own beer mug.

Fitz wished he was back in his apartment. But Ian and Maddie had shown up at his door an hour ago and insisted he join them at the Steel Horse. Maddie had marched into his living room, sat down on the couch, and picked up the remote. "Tobie and Jake are meeting us there. You can either come with us willingly, or we can stay here while I make you watch all seven seasons of *Gilmore Girls*," she'd threatened.

"She means it, bro," Ian said, "and my sisters watch that all the time. Take it from me, you want to suck it up right now and come out with us."

So here he was. His friends meant well; he knew that. But being here now was like a punch in the gut. Fitz hadn't been to the Steel Horse since the night he'd met Erienne. He hadn't seen or heard from her in the two weeks since he'd left the hospital to go hide out at his place and nurse his wounds. He missed her so much it was a physical pain, worse than any of the injuries he'd sustained from the beating by Pruitt and his men.

Jake and Tobie returned to the table with another pitcher of beer. "What did we miss?" Tobie asked.

"Nothing much," Maddie said. "Fitz and Ian are just sharing that Navy SEAL brotherly love."

"Hooyah," Jake said.

"Pruitt still not talking?" Fitz asked, hoping to steer the conversation in another direction before Maddie said anything about Erienne again.

"Not a peep. Maddox or Cooney, either. But that doesn't surprise me. They've all been through the system enough times. They have good lawyers and will keep their mouths shut."

"And we still don't know what they did with the missing

canister?" Fitz knew Erienne had to be beside herself with worry about CS180 being in the wrong hands.

"No, and there's been no trace of it found anywhere. Not at any of Pruitt's holdings, not at Buzz's apartment, nor at Myra's house or Einstein's."

"And we still don't have any idea who else Buzz could have been working for," Jake added. "That burner phone found in his van was used to communicate with only one phone number. It belonged to another burner phone that was used in and around the tri-state area, but never the same place twice. I'm still looking for a pattern, but no luck yet."

"Myra still swears the only person Buzz ever worked for was Pruitt," Tobie added. "But considering we found an itinerary in Buzz's apartment that showed he was planning to head off to the Caribbean with another woman, I'm sure there's a whole lot of stuff he was keeping from Myra. I really don't think there's anything more she can give us."

"At least Maisy is back with her mom and away from that psycho bitch," Maddie said.

"Amen to that," Fitz said. "I'm glad Anita and Maisy can make a new start." Anita was currently in witness protection with her daughter. She was sharing everything and anything she knew about Pruitt's illegal activities, more than happy to help put him away after the way he'd treated her and threatened the welfare of their child.

"Me, too," Tobie said. "Tanner told me that Erienne has set up a trust fund for Maisy and is giving Anita a generous amount of start-up cash. Anita will be able to take good care of her daughter with enough left over to go back to school and start fresh."

"I knew there was something I liked about that princess," Maddie said, giving Fitz the side-eye.

Fitz squirmed in his seat a moment, trying to think of a way to divert the conversation, when Tobie glanced at her watch and pushed back from the table. "Sorry, guys. I have to go. I'm meeting an old friend for a late dinner. Enjoy yourselves. Put the drinks on the company credit card. Good night."

Jake drained the last of his beer. "I'm going to take off, too. I want to take another crack at those phone records and see if I can come up with anything." He stood and squeezed Fitz's shoulder as he passed him. "Glad to see you looking better, bro."

Maddie reached for the pitcher and topped off their beers. "So, Fitz, are you going to be a complete dork and mope around for six months before you realize you should call Erienne?"

Anger spiked at her needling. "Mind your own business, Maddie."

She rolled her eyes. "Don't be an—"

"Ready for me to kick your ass at a game of pool, Maddie?" Ian asked.

She swung her head toward Ian so fast, Fitz swore he felt a breeze.

"In your dreams, Westlake. I'll beat you so bad you might as well not even pick up a cue."

Ian waved a twenty at her. "Put your money where your mouth is."

"You're on, loser." She headed over to the pool tables and began racking up the balls.

"Thanks, man," Fitz said.

"Any time. But just for the record, I think Maddie's right. You're crazy about Erienne and she's crazy about you."

"I'd only bring her down."

"That's bullshit. I just hope you come to your senses

before it's too late." Ian picked up his mug and the half full pitcher of beer. "Want to come and play the winner?"

"Nah, I can always play Maddie another night."

"Wiseass."

"I only speak the truth, dude. You suck at pool."

"Geez, nice to know you have my back," Ian chuckled.

"Get over here, Westlake!" Maddie hollered.

Fitz watched them play for a while as he nursed his beer. He looked around the room, noting the crowd to be thinner than usual for a Saturday night. Several regulars were at the bar, and a few couples were shaking it up on the dance floor. There was no sign of any of the college kids that usually showed up on the weekends, but considering one of them got shot in the parking lot a few weeks ago, that wasn't surprising. They'd probably return in a semester or two when the memory of the violence faded.

Several attractive women caught his eye, but he didn't let his gaze linger long on any of them. He had no interest in hooking up with anyone. Truth of it was, if his friends hadn't dragged him out, he'd have been perfectly content to sit home alone, although *content* wasn't exactly the right word. Hell, he hadn't been content since the last time he saw Erienne. But finding a random partner and heading for the Oak wasn't going to help.

With a sigh and a stifled groan, he eased himself off the tall chair and walked over to the bar. He'd have one more beer while Ian and Maddie duked it out at pool. If they wanted to stay longer than that, he'd call for a car and head home on his own.

Terri the bartender was at the other end, accommodating a waitress's large drink order. His phone buzzed and he pulled it out of his pocket, finding a text from his dad. *Hey kid. Hope your rib feels better. Sully and me and a couple other guys going to the cabin next weekend for poker and fishing. You coming?*

Fitz's brain immediately filled with images of Erienne at the cabin: in her slouchy sweats and hunched over her laptop; in her sexy, silky bathrobe and sitting across from him at the breakfast table with a mischievous look in her eye after a steamy, passionate night; in the shower, pressed up against the wall, her skin sleek with water and her baby-blue eyes steeped with desire. He wasn't sure he was ready to go back to the cabin, or if he could ever go back there. Not when he would see Erienne in every corner.

Blaming his rib and work commitments, he replied to the text saying he wouldn't make it this time, and then tapped over to his photos. The day before they'd left the cabin, he and Erienne had taken a short hike to the nearby lake. The weather had been a perfect combination of unseasonable warmth blended with the riotous colors of autumn. He'd been unable to resist capturing Erienne's beauty amid Mother Nature's gorgeous display. When they'd reached the lake, he'd suggested skinny dipping, promising to keep her warm in the cool water, but her bear phobia was too strong to allow her to relax enough to shed her clothes.

She did, however, remove her shoes, roll up her jeans, and wade about knee-high into the lake. The last picture he'd snapped was a candid shot. She was sideways toward the lens, head back, eyes closed, a soft and sultry smile on her lips as she enjoyed the feel of the sun on her face. The lake stretched out behind her, casting her against a backdrop of deep crystal blue topped with the reds, oranges, and golds of the trees on the opposite shoreline. He'd never seen anything so breathtaking.

His heart throbbed with the sharp pain of loneliness and loss. He'd never in his life missed anyone like he missed

Erienne. Because he'd never been as happy with anyone else. He'd never *let* himself be that happy. And he shouldn't have done it this time. Especially this time. By letting himself feel the joy that was Erienne, he'd set himself up for a lifetime of despair.

But he'd made the right choice. He could never be the one to make her happy.

He put his phone away and closed his eyes, but it made no difference. He could envision her with a stinging clarity brighter than the sharpest digital pictures. He took a deep breath in and could have sworn he detected the scent of her subtle perfume, that's how powerful and clear her image was in his mind.

"What'll you have, Fitz?"

Terri's voice intruded on his vision of Erienne. A vision he needed to make go away. "Gimme a boilermaker," he muttered without opening his eyes.

"I'll have the same."

Fitz whipped his eyes open to find Erienne standing next to him. She wore a dress in the same coral shade as the night they'd met, and although it wasn't as tight, it still managed to hug her curves in all the right places. But he knew in his soul that she could be wearing rags and still be the most beautiful woman he'd ever seen. The urge to pull her close and kiss her senseless obliterated every other thought in his brain. He stared at her, drinking her in until he finally found his voice. "What are you doing here?"

"Slumming. As I recall, you don't have a problem with that."

"Erienne—"

She pressed her fingers against his lips, and it was all he could do not to kiss each delicate digit.

"I need you to listen to me, Fitz. The truth is, I'm not

slumming. You are the most honorable man I have ever had the privilege to know. I'm lucky to have you in my life. I've spent the last two weeks trying to respect your wishes and feelings, but I came to the conclusion that your wishes and feelings on this are dead wrong."

He took her hand from his mouth. "Erienne, the life I lead is no life for you."

"Is it the life for you?"

"What do you mean?"

"I mean since you are so confident it's not a good way to live, why are you doing it? It sounds to me like you're ready to move on."

"I can't walk away from OASIS. We've all made a commitment to help as many of those girls and their families as we can."

"I'm not saying you have to walk away from that commitment. But there are plenty of ways to help without having to live a life you no longer want."

Her words gave him pause. Tobie had told him often enough that he didn't have to do deep undercover if he didn't want to. He had to admit that he didn't enjoy it as much as he used to. So why did he continue to volunteer for it?

"In your face, Ian!" Maddie's voice carried clear across the room, heralding the victory Fitz had known to be a foregone conclusion.

"Rematch!" Ian yelled.

And there was the answer to why Fitz always volunteered for the gritty assignments. Maddie, Ian, Reeve, Jake. All of them had lives and family outside of OASIS. Good ones. Fitz loved his old man, but their relationship wasn't close-knit. They barely spoke, and whenever they got together, it was mostly for weekends like the one Fitz had just turned down. He knew he had the least to lose, so that's why he was always willing to go undercover.

Until now. Just having Erienne standing here next to him gave Fitz the most peace of mind he'd felt in the last two weeks. That he'd felt *ever*. Now that he'd known his life both with and without her in it, he knew he would never be happy alone.

And he wanted to be happy.

Terri brought their drinks. Erienne lifted her shot glass, raising an eyebrow at him until he did the same. "To new opportunities?"

He nodded and they tossed back their whiskey. Erienne shuddered and reached for her beer. "I don't know how you stand that stuff."

"Practice."

The jukebox changed songs and played the familiar guitar riff of a rock ballad. She smiled at him. "I played our song on my way in. Dance with me?"

She tugged his hand and he followed her onto the dance floor. In that moment, he knew he would follow her anywhere. She draped her arms around his neck as he placed his hands on her hips.

"Tell me you meant what you said at the hospital before you left," she whispered. "Tell me you love me as much as I love you."

"I'm so sorry I left. It was the biggest mistake of my life. Because I do love you. More than I ever thought I could love someone. And if you'll let me, I'll spend the rest of my life making you as happy as you make me."

Her radiant smile warmed him from head to toe. He dipped his head for a kiss, and the touch of her lips was like coming home. Pulling her close, he took what she gave, his sense of peace growing and wrapping around him like a warm blanket.

Breaking the kiss, Erienne tucked her head into his shoulder as they swirled slowly around the dance floor.

"I love you so much," he breathed into her ear as the song drew to a close.

"And I love you." She lowered her arms and hugged him around the waist. He winced as the embrace pinched his battered rib. She pulled back. "Sorry. Let's get you home. You shouldn't be on your feet."

They headed for the exit, and Fitz nodded at Ian and Maddie as they passed the pool tables. Maddie gave him her trademark smirk. "I told you she's the best thing that ever happened to you."

Erienne snuggled close to him on his non-injured side as they approached her Mercedes. "Maddie's wrong, you know," she said. "I think *we're* the best thing to happen to *us*."

Fitz smiled as he held the car door open for her. "Darlin', I couldn't agree more."

THANK you for reading Taming The Bodyguard. I hope you enjoyed Fitz and Erienne's story. Would you like to read about their wedding day? It's full of all sorts of surprises. Sign up to join The Troy Inner Circle for this special bonus scene. Join The Troy Inner Circle Today (If you are already a member, you will have access to the bonus. No need to join again.)

If you enjoyed Taming the Bodyguard, you would make this author very happy by leaving a review on your **favorite storefront** and/or **Goodreads**. Reviews are crucial to authors, and a brief line or two goes a long way to helping other readers find my books. Thank you.

THE ADVENTURES of the OASIS Team continue with Maddie and Ian's story in NEEDING THE BODYGUARD Book 3 in the OASIS Series. Here's a sneak (unedited) peek:

"Damn, Maddie, Doug is so hot!" Angie Carson was practically drooling as she watched Doug Barnes, shirt off and sweat gleaming on his chest, unload the explosives from the back of the van.

"Um, Angie, that's a little gross. He is my brother, you know." Maddie sipped from the cup of iced tea Angie handed her. She knew the iced tea had been an excuse for Angie to leave her serving station at the food tent in order to watch Doug as he unloaded his van and prepared for the fireworks show that would officially kick off the Candlewood, CT's annual summer festival. For the last year and a half, the poor girl had had such an obvious crush on Maddie's older brother. But at fifteen years old, Angie wasn't anywhere on twenty-seven-year-old Doug's radar.

"I'm glad he's not *my* brother," Angie sighed. "Do you think he'll dance with me tonight when the band starts?"

"I think you better ask Maureen that question."

Angie twisted her lips into a pouty scowl. "Is he still so serious about her?"

"I'm afraid so."

"Maybe if I can get him to dance with me, he might change his mind."

Maddie didn't know whether to laugh or be shocked at the girl's chutzpah. "Angie, you really ought to think about dating someone closer to your own age. I've noticed Blake Gerard watching you lately."

Angie tore her gaze away from Doug. "Blake Gerard? Really?"

"Yep. Haven't you noticed him hanging around the food tent all day?"

"Well, yeah, but I figured he was just hungry. He's the school's best linebacker. Big guys like him always eat a lot, don't they?"

"I suppose. But it looked to me like he was talking to you more than he was eating anything." Maddie was surprised that Angie hadn't noticed this herself. The girl wasn't dull by any means. Had her crush on Doug blinded her to the attentions of anyone else? "I don't think it was the food he was really interested in."

Angie looked back toward the food tent where Blake was still hovering. He'd been joined by a few of his fellow football players. They were laughing and jostling each other, but Blake's eyes never spent more than a few minutes not looking for Angie. He blushed when he saw Maddie and Angie watching him, but gamely gave Angie a big smile.

Angie smiled back before returning her attention to Doug. "Blake's okay I guess," she allowed, but the pink tinge to her skin told Maddie she was pleased with the young man's attention. "He's probably not much of a dancer, though."

"I don't know," Maddie said casually. "I bet he can manage the slow dances pretty well."

Angie cast another sidelong glance at Blake. "Maybe. I guess he'd do all right. If Blake asks me to dance with him tonight, I'll give him a chance."

Maddie bit her lip to keep from smiling. She'd make sure to let Blake know he should ask Angie for a dance.

"Hey, Angie!" Doug's cheerful voice cut across the grass. "Am I gonna get one of those iced teas or what?"

Angie's face lit up like a sunbeam. "You bet!" She hurried over to Doug and handed him the other cup she held. Doug took the cup and downed the contents in one long gulp. "Ah, just what I needed. Would you be an angel and get me another one?" He brushed his index finger under her chin.

Maddie thought the girl might melt into the ground. "Of course, Doug," Angie all but moaned at the attention. She took the empty cup and hurried back to the food tent, not even glancing at Blake, and thereby completely missing the scowl the young man threw in Doug's direction.

Maddie walked over to help her brother unload the van. "You need to watch it with Angie, Doug," she said.

"What are you talking about? She's a sweet kid."

"Who's got a ginormous crush on you."

"Really?"

"Oh, don't pretend you haven't noticed."

Doug gave her a look of genuine perplexity. "What? I mean it. She's a nice kid. I know she likes me but I didn't think it was anything big."

"Well, it is. She's besotted. And because of it she's ignoring boys her own age. Blake Gerard's got it bad for her and she barely notices him."

"Huh. Okay, I'll start talking up Maureen whenever Angie's around. She'll lose interest pretty quick. Especially when she hears that Maureen and I are engaged."

"You're that confident Maureen will say yes tonight?" Maddie teased. She really didn't doubt it. Anyone who saw Maureen and Doug together knew how deeply in love they were.

"Yes I am. Maureen's no dummy. She know's what a

catch I am. And when I tell her that Angie is waiting to snatch me up, it'll really be a no-brainer. She'll be all to eager to stake her claim for the Douggie-love." He waggled his eyebrows up and down.

Maddie laughed. "You're such a dork. It would serve you right if Maureen said no."

"Maybe, but she won't."

"Arrogant loser."

"Jealous brat."

A woman's soft laugh had them both turning around from the back of the van. Mrs. Hunnicutt, their long-time housekeeper and family friend stood there with her hands on her hips. "Are you two ever going to outgrow the name-calling stage?"

"Probably not," Doug teased. He hoisted a box on his shoulder and headed toward the staging area for the fireworks display, sneaking a quick kiss on Mrs. Hunnicutt's cheek as he passed her.

Mrs. Hunnicutt shook her head as he sauntered off. "That brother of yours. Always the a charmer."

"Yeah. Too bad the big doofus knows it. If his head swells anymore, he'll never be able to wear a hat."

"He wouldn't want to cover up all those gorgeous blond curls anyway. It's one of his main attractions."

"Et tu, Mrs. H? Don't tell me he's got you under his spell."

"I'm not too old to notice these things," she said primly. "But never mind your brother. What's going on with you and Ian? You haven't said a word since he went back overseas last week. I thought you two had worked everything out."

"We have. More or less."

"What does that mean?"

"It means we had some fun while he was here on leave, but I still don't think he's really forgiven me for not accepting his marriage proposal."

"I'm sure he has. Although I don't understand why you turned him down in the first place."

"He was proposing for the wrong reasons. He just wanted to get me out of my father's house."

"And that would have been a bad thing?"

Maddie nodded absently as she watched Angie hurry down to the barge after Doug with another cup of iced tea. "Yes. I want what any other woman wants. To be proposed to because the man wants to spend the rest of his life with me and have lots and lots of babies."

"You don't think Ian wants all that?"

"He says he does, and I don't think he's lying. But that's not why he proposed. Besides, he was about to leave for boot camp. It wasn't the right time. He was proposing out of desperation. There's no way I could accept. He was only looking to protect me, which is not what I need. I can take care of myself."

"Anyone who knows you knows that. I don't know why you feel you have to prove it all the time."

Maddie shrugged. Mrs. Hunnicutt had come to work for her family after Maddie and Doug's father had gone to prison. She hadn't been there through the years when Fletcher Barnes had indicated his daughter could never do things his son could do. Fletcher had never embraced equality between the sexes, but he'd been the only parent Maddie had. She'd spent so much of her childhood trying to prove to her father she was just as capable of anything as Doug. It was a hard habit to break.

Mrs. Hunnicutt pulled her into a quick hug. "Cheer up, sweetie. You and Ian are going to be fine. I know it." She stepped back. "How about you let me buy you some lunch?"

"I really should finish helping Doug. One of his crew called in sick so he's short-handed."

"You can help him after you eat. I know you skipped breakfast this morning. C'mon, and we'll order some food for him, too."

Used to Mrs. Hunnicutt's gentle bullying, Maddie allowed the woman to lead her to the food tent. Her stomach was growling and there was a lot of work left to do this afternoon. Mrs. Hunnicutt was right. She should eat first.

Halfway to the tent, the deafening sound of an explosion ripped through the air. Maddie whirled around to see flames leaping up from the fireworks barge. Black smoke poured into the sky. "Doug!" she screamed and ran toward the flames. Others joined her but the heat soon drove them all back. "Doug!" she screamed again.

"Angie!" Blake yelled.

Maddie's stomach dropped as she remembered the young girl heading after Doug. *Dear God let them both be okay.*

Sirens sounded in the distance. Maddie screamed their names until she was hoarse, but neither Doug or Angie appeared or answered. Desperate and near hysteria, Maddie lunged toward the barge, only to be pulled back by other onlookers. "It's too late," one of them said quietly.

"No, let me go. They need our help. Let me go, dammit!"

The firefighters arrived and battled the blaze. It seemed the whole town had gathered to watch. Angie's parents clung to each other, Blake sunk to his knees next to them.

It took what seemed like forever for the firefighters to bring the blaze under control, and at least another eternity before the fire chief approached Angie's parents. Angie's mother let out a keening wail as he sadly shook his head. Her husband hugged her, sobbing his own grief against her shoulder.

The fire chief turned to look at Maddie. "No, no, no," she whispered, shaking her head and backing away as he approached. "Please, no."

A gentle hand touched her shoulder and Maddie whirled into the arms of Mrs. Hunnicutt. The woman's own sobs mixed with Maddie's as the crush of reality hit them both.

Maddie pulled away and Mrs. Hunnicutt stuffed a paper napkin into her hand. She mopped her eyes looked around, not knowing what she should do next. A large crowd surrounded Angie's parents. Taking a deep breath Maddie took a step in their direction. Blake blocked her way.

"Stay away from them," he hissed.

"Blake! What are you doing?" Mrs. Hunnicutt said. "Get out of her way."

"No," he snarled, his tear-streaked face a mask of hate. "Hasn't she and her family done enough? Don't they get tired of killing people with their bombs?"

Mrs. Hunnicutt gasped, and a slice of pain ripped through Maddie so fast and so harsh she thought for sure she would fall to the ground in two pieces.

"Oh, yeah, I know all about it," Blake went on. "I was just a kid but I remember what your old man did. and I remember how your brother always said his father was a hero. Well he wasn't. He was a crazy murderer and your brother is too! I'm glad Doug blew himself up. But Angie didn't deserve this. I hope your crazy brother rots in hell!"

Rage replaced the pain in her gut, and Maddie pushed at his chest. It barely phased the six-foot-three linebacker. He raised his hands to push her back but bystanders intervened, seizing both of them around their waists and pulling them away from each other.

"It's not true," Maddie yelled. "Doug didn't do this!"

Mrs. Hunnicutt put a comforting arm around her, and convinced the others to let Maddie go. "C'mon, sweetheart, let's get you home. You can talk to Angie's parents later."

"No! You stay away from them!" Blake shouted as they walked away.

The crowd parted as she and Mrs. Hunnicutt headed for the parking lot, and Maddie felt as much as saw how they looked at her. A few people appeared genuinely shocked and sorry, offering her their condolences as she passed. But mostly, people were looking at her in anger. A low muttering began at the back of the crowd and grew steadily as she walked.

She knew it was coming, but when a lone voice finally spoke out, the virulence of it shocked her to the core anyway.

"That fucking Barnes family. They're all a bunch of murderous lunatics."

GET NEEDING **The Bodyguard** today and see what happens next!

JOIN MY FACEBOOK READERS GROUP, Maura's Mavens. We'll talk about the OASIS team and their adventures in a non-spoilery way. There may be the odd giveaway now and then. And most likely lots of man-candy.

· · ·

Books by Maura Troy
    The OASIS Series:
    Book 1: Safe with a SEAL: Trusting the Bodyguard
    Book 2: Safe with a SEAL: Taming the Bodyguard
    Book 3: Safe with a SEAL: Needing the Bodyguard

Join Maura's Facebook Group: https://www.facebook.com/groups/204642791675234

Follow Maura on Goodreads: https://www.goodreads.com/author/show/21985241.Maura_Troy

Follow Maura on Twitter: https://twitter.com/MauraTroy

Follow Maura on Instagram: https://www.instagram.com/mauratroy1/

Visit Maura's website at MauraTroy.com

ACKNOWLEDGMENTS

A huge thank you to L.D. Rose, doctor and author extraordinaire, for answering my medical questions. Please note, dear readers, that any screw-ups in that area are mine.

My beta readers - Kylie Gilmore, Wendy LaCapra, Barbara Bettis, LM Pampuro, Gwen Hernandez, Linda Avellar, Denise Alicea, Sailaja Ledalla, Mary Evans, Maureen Raftery, Caryn Brittain, and Beth Falk. Once again, your thoughts and insights were invaluable. Thank you so much.

Thank you to my family and friends for continuing to cheer me on. It helps. A lot.

And, of course, to Larry Troy and our best pal, Spike. Thank you for keeping me company and making me laugh. Love you!

www.ingramcontent.com/pod-product-compliance
Lightning Source LLC
Chambersburg PA
CBHW061101190726
48286CB00006B/1836